Anthony Gilbert and The Murder Room

〉〉〉 This title is part of The Murder Room, our series dedicated to making available out-of-print or hard-to-find titles by classic crime writers.

Crime fiction has always held up a mirror to society. The Victorians were fascinated by sensational murder and the emerging science of detection; now we are obsessed with the forensic detail of violent death. And no other genre has so captivated and enthralled readers.

Vast troves of classic crime writing have for a long time been unavailable to all but the most dedicated frequenters of second-hand bookshops. The advent of digital publishing means that we are now able to bring you the backlists of a huge range of titles by classic and contemporary crime writers, some of which have been out of print for decades.

From the genteel amateur private eyes of the Golden Age and the femmes fatales of pulp fiction, to the morally ambiguous hard-boiled detectives of mid twentieth-century America and their descendants who walk our twenty-first century streets, The Murder Room has it all. **〉〉〉**

The Murder Room
Where Criminal Minds Meet

themurderroom.com

Anthony Gilbert (1899–1973)

Anthony Gilbert was the pen name of Lucy Beatrice Malleson. Born in London, she spent all her life there, and her affection for the city is clear from the strong sense of character and place in evidence in her work. She published 69 crime novels, 51 of which featured her best known character, Arthur Crook, a vulgar London lawyer totally (and deliberately) unlike the aristocratic detectives, such as Lord Peter Wimsey, who dominated the mystery field at the time. She also wrote more than 25 radio plays, which were broadcast in Great Britain and overseas. Her thriller *The Woman in Red* (1941) was broadcast in the United States by CBS and made into a film in 1945 under the title *My Name is Julia Ross*. She was an early member of the British Detection Club, which, along with Dorothy L. Sayers, she prevented from disintegrating during World War II. Malleson published her autobiography, *Three-a-Penny,* in 1940, and wrote numerous short stories, which were published in several anthologies and in such periodicals as *Ellery Queen's Mystery Magazine* and *The Saint*. The short story 'You Can't Hang Twice' received a Queens award in 1946. She never married, and evidence of her feminism is elegantly expressed in much of her work.

By Anthony Gilbert

Scott Egerton series

Tragedy at Freyne (1927)

The Murder of Mrs
   Davenport (1928)

Death at Four Corners
   (1929)

The Mystery of the Open
   Window (1929)

The Night of the Fog (1930)

The Body on the Beam
   (1932)

The Long Shadow (1932)

The Musical Comedy
   Crime (1933)

An Old Lady Dies (1934)

The Man Who Was Too
   Clever (1935)

**Mr Crook Murder
   Mystery series**

Murder by Experts (1936)

The Man Who Wasn't
   There (1937)

Murder Has No Tongue
   (1937)

Treason in My Breast (1938)

The Bell of Death (1939)

Dear Dead Woman (1940)
   aka *Death Takes a
   Redhead*

The Vanishing Corpse (1941)
   aka *She Vanished in the
   Dawn*

The Woman in Red (1941)
   aka *The Mystery of the
   Woman in Red*

Death in the Blackout (1942)
   aka *The Case of the Tea-
   Cosy's Aunt*

Something Nasty in the
   Woodshed (1942)
   aka *Mystery in the
   Woodshed*

The Mouse Who Wouldn't
   Play Ball (1943)
   aka *30 Days to Live*

He Came by Night (1944)
   aka *Death at the Door*

The Scarlet Button (1944)
   aka *Murder Is Cheap*

A Spy for Mr Crook (1944)

The Black Stage (1945)
   aka *Murder Cheats the
   Bride*

Don't Open the Door (1945)
  aka *Death Lifts the Latch*
Lift Up the Lid (1945)
  aka *The Innocent Bottle*
The Spinster's Secret (1946)
  aka *By Hook or by Crook*
Death in the Wrong Room
  (1947)
Die in the Dark (1947)
  aka *The Missing Widow*
Death Knocks Three Times
  (1949)
Murder Comes Home (1950)
A Nice Cup of Tea (1950)
  aka *The Wrong Body*
Lady-Killer (1951)
Miss Pinnegar Disappears
  (1952)
  aka *A Case for Mr Crook*
Footsteps Behind Me (1953)
  aka *Black Death*
Snake in the Grass (1954)
  aka *Death Won't Wait*
Is She Dead Too? (1955)
  aka *A Question of Murder*
And Death Came Too (1956)
Riddle of a Lady (1956)
Give Death a Name (1957)

Death Against the Clock
  (1958)
Death Takes a Wife (1959)
  aka *Death Casts a Long
  Shadow*
Third Crime Lucky (1959)
  aka *Prelude to Murder*
Out for the Kill (1960)
She Shall Die (1961)
  aka *After the Verdict*
Uncertain Death (1961)
No Dust in the Attic (1962)
Ring for a Noose (1963)
The Fingerprint (1964)
Knock, Knock! Who's
  There? (1964)
  aka *The Voice*
Passenger to Nowhere (1965)
The Looking Glass Murder
  (1966)
The Visitor (1967)
Night Encounter (1968)
  aka *Murder Anonymous*
Missing from Her Home
  (1969)
Death Wears a Mask (1970)
  aka *Mr Crook Lifts the
  Mask*

He Came by Night

Anthony Gilbert

An Orion book

Copyright © Lucy Beatrice Malleson 1944

The right of Lucy Beatrice Malleson to be identified as the author of this
work has been asserted in accordance with the Copyright, Designs and
Patents Act 1988.

This edition published by
The Orion Publishing Group Ltd
Orion House
5 Upper St Martin's Lane
London WC2H 9EA

An Hachette UK company

A CIP catalogue record for this book is available from the British Library

ISBN 978 1 4719 0976 4

www.orionbooks.co.uk

Dedicated with affection
To Eileen
In memory of that Haunted Village

CHAPTER ONE

I shall come back at last
To this dark house to die.
E. DAVISON.

1

WHEN DUSK had fallen the hunted man came out of the wood where he had been hiding and began to make his way across country. Though it was almost a generation since he had been here, he remembered the paths, for in this quiet slow-thinking county of England life changes slowly and the curse of ribbon-development and so-called progress that had devastated so much of England had left Mereshire practically untouched. He had seen many parts of the world and penetrated into places the respectable prefer to know nothing about even on paper; in the past thirty years he had roamed the Seven Seas, making big money when the risks were considerable, squandering it as he'd squandered his life, a rootless man, desperate and happy-go-lucky with no eye for the quiet beauty of the countryside, the long lines of marshland, where the lakes lay like precious stones in a magical chain, and the trees all about him had seen his grandfather and his great-grandfather and his forebears three hundred years back moving in their shadow and perhaps taking refuge as he took refuge now.

His destination was one of those villages so small it has neither post office nor station; the woman he had come to see would have no welcome for him. He had no friends anywhere. A man has to be rich to afford the luxury of friends, and he had let his wealth go like air escaping from a leaking pump. As he made his steadfast way through fields, automatically closing gates, because even after thirty years the old habits stuck, his only preoccupation was how much the old girl

1

was good for. Of what lay behind him he did not think. So many incidents, disreputable and violent, strewed his past life, like flotsam and jetsam washed up by the tide, or a path blasted by fire through what could have been a flourishing countryside. He didn't appreciate his danger as a less experienced man would have done. He'd never known security in more than thirty years. And it certainly never occurred to him that he had left all the noise and ruthlessness of the great world behind him in order to run into the arms of an ignoble death in the minute village where, more than half a century ago, he had been born.

Men survive battles and die of wasp stings; they win great reputations and are wrecked by silly women not fit to black their shoes; they acquire a name for wisdom and forfeit the earnings of a life-time in a moment of hot-headed passion. So, after a hundred encounters with danger in all the coloured countries of the world, he slunk back to die in the dark like a beast in its derelict hole.

2

The old woman beamed as she set about the task of preparing the evening meal. This was one of the red-letter days of the year. In a long frugal life she hadn't had many high lights, though she had known what tragedy was like and surmounted it and discovered riches millionaires' wives don't always know. Her life had died thirty years ago with the daughter she loved but never understood and begun again in the new life that survived the mother's death.

During the long period of solitude that had made up her days she had feasted on memories and anticipated the future; and now and again the future merged with the present, as it did to-night, when Ted was coming home on forty-eight hours leave. She'd saved all her points, all her rations, she'd shamelessly told people in the shop that she hadn't any of this commodity or that; she'd hoarded her chocolate coupons and put by week by week her minute portions of dried fruit; she'd gone as far as Horsfall—she who hated a town—searching for suet and even candied peel—because Ted liked her cakes. She shut her eyes to the fact that the men in the Forces were on the whole a good deal better fed than civilians. If Ted, reliable, cheerful Ted, had been the Prodigal Son she couldn't more ruthlessly have rounded up the fatted calf. And now in an hour he'd be here. She looked at the chicken she'd procured—never mind how—and the stuffing she'd made from a shell egg and a lemon that she'd wheedled out of some-one who had a friend in Canada—and soon he and she would be together again. Because he was always like that the first night. To-morrow there'd be Edna—naturally. A man on leave wants to see his girl. But to-night she'd have him to herself. He was so big, so strong. You wouldn't think Elsie, who'd been a slip of a girl, though wiry, could have had such a son, till you remembered his father. But she put that thought quickly out of mind. She never thought along these lines if it could be helped. Everybody had bad luck sometimes, every-one had to climb the obstacles in his path, but it was no good brood-ing over what you couldn't change.

She put the chicken in the pan, decided, in spite of what the Min-ister of Fuel and Power said, to put a match to the fire—these early October evenings were chilly in this eastern county—and excitement began to beat in her old blood. At about the same moment the returned exile closed a gate behind him and came into the lane that led to the village.

She couldn't believe it when the knock fell on the door. Ted early, Ted an hour before he was expected. It was like a present you hadn't dreamed of getting. She thought there was nothing she wouldn't do for Ted. Dying for people was easy, she'd do more than that—suffer for him, sin for him—all her life centred on him. She used to think sometimes that if Edna didn't make him happy, she could even strangle Edna. But you couldn't imagine anyone not being happy with a fellow like Ted.

Rubbing the flour off her hands on to her white apron, she untied the strings and went to the door. She was wearing her best dress, the sort of silk you couldn't buy now, not if you had a hundred coupons and a thousand pounds in the bank. She'd put on the brooch Ted gave her for her last birthday. She'd scolded him for that—he shouldn't have spent so much. Keep your money for Edna, she'd said. I reckon I can buy my wife all the brooches she needs and still have a few coppers left for my grandma, he'd said, and he'd laughed.

3

Not in the police for nothing, he'd said. The Air Force police, of course. She hadn't wanted him to be a civil policeman, a snoopy kind of trade she called that, always poking your nose into some other chap's business.

The knocking on the door came again—quicker now, more violent and somehow furtive.

"I'm coming," she called. And opened the door, a spare neat little figure, hair drawn back, face wrinkled, back erect for all her seventy-odd years. . . .

There was a moment's silence. Then she stood back with a cry that hardly reached her lips. For it wasn't Ted after all. It was a much older man, a man she hadn't seen for a generation, but whom she knew at once, because the heart and the blood don't lie, though eyes dim and ears grow dull.

"Tom!" she whispered, and fell back a step. "Tom, it's never you."

She'd thought of all sorts of things that might happen, even made herself now and again realize that in a war even the police aren't safe. That enemy bombs and shells, like the Lord God, are no respecter of persons; she'd forced herself to realize what it would be like to be an old woman with nothing to look forward to any more but the grave. Terrible things happen to women and they might happen to her; in the past they had happened. She'd lived always with a sense of danger. But danger from this source she hadn't apprehended.

"What a welcome!" said the new-comer, moving closer.

With her thin fierce little body she barred the way. "What do you want?"

"Just to see you, auntie, p'raps. How's the young lord?"

"You leave Ted alone. He's nowt to do wi' you."

"Doesn't know I'm born, I dare say."

"Why should he?"

"Why not? Maybe he'd like to know he had a man in the family."

She said again, "What do you want?" and he, his voice suddenly rough and angry, replied, "First of all to come inside the house. I want a roof. And then I want food. And drink. And money."

She said bitterly, "You've not changed in thirty years. You always wanted those things."

"Show me any man who doesn't. Is your precious Ted so different? Why Ted? Oh, I see. After his father."

"And you can keep your tongue off Ted's father."

"If you don't let me in," said the man, whose name was Tom Grigg, "I'll let the whole neighbourhood know I'm back."

"What's to stop you?" demanded the woman. "They might be more pleased of the news than I am."

He thrust past by a sudden feint and found himself inside the little hall. It was no more than a passage really, with a narrow staircase running up to the next floor.

"Who's got my room?" he asked. "The room I had when me and Elsie were young?"

"If you've any memory you know how many rooms there are. Not enough for a visitor."

"Who sleeps there now then? Ted? Why isn't he at the war? Or has he got a weak heart?"

"Ted's doing his duty in a war just as he did it in the peace and will again," she told him fiercely. "And that's more than you could ever say, you with your wild ways, that couldn't keep a steady job. . . ."

"That's all they ever think of down here. How much do you bring back on Friday night?"

"Women have to think of things like that. It's women have to manage. What have you been doing all these years?"

"I wondered when you were going to ask that. I'm working, if you want to know, just the same as your precious Elsie's precious boy. Merchant seaman, that's what I am. Better than being a gamekeeper up at the House with people that count every hair on a rabbit's pelt. What's the new Earl like?"

"New? He's been Earl nigh twenty years."

"How many sons has he got?"

"He's got one—Mr. Simon."

"And how does the old lady take that? Or doesn't she believe in the Curse any more?"

"What they do up at the Hall is no business of ours," she told him. She seemed compounded of bitterness and fear, but she kept the fear under.

5

"It was your business once," he reminded her. "When Elsie was going with the heir. . . ."

"Elsie's been dead almost as long as you've been away," she told him in grim tones. "We saved the boy, but her . . ."

"Trust you to save the boy," he sneered, and there was a new note in his voice that chilled her blood. "Where is he?"

"He's not here."

"But you're expecting him. Elsie's boy—and the heir's. Maybe if *he* hadn't met with an accident . . ."

"We'll not talk of that," she told him sharply. "And you leave Ted alone. I've had trouble enough, with all the talk about Elsie, and then losing her. . . ."

His face was savage. "I lost her, too, didn't I? Think everything's been velvet for me all these years?"

"Who said life was meant to be velvet? What have you been doing anyway?"

"Everything—barman—steward—show business—and now I'm a merchant seaman. I'm on leave this week-end, and I've come all the way from Swansea to see my auntie."

"For what you could get. I know. What happens to your pay?"

"Know what they give us? And I was never the saving kind. I suppose Ted puts all his into War Savings Certificates. What's he doing?"

"Air Force police."

"Living at home?"

"Of course not. It's just—"

He sniffed appreciatively. "Just that you're expecting him. Funny to think of Elsie's son being a policeman, when you remember . . ."

"You don't have to remember anything," she broke in, and now the fear in her voice was stronger than the anger. "What's done's done. You can't turn back the page. Oh well, stay if you want to. Matter of fact, I thought it was Ted when you knocked."

He looked round. "Place isn't changed much," he said. "You've got all the old stuff." He nodded at the familiar furniture. "Cabinet—dresser—remember how I broke the lock of that trying to find what Uncle Will kept in the secret drawer?"

"Found it empty, didn't you?" The old woman's voice was bitter as Marah.

"Yes." He chuckled. "Where did you keep the household bank anyway? In the old blue teapot, I suppose. You always were clever at hiding things. What's Ted like?"

"He doesn't go breaking open other people's property for what isn't his. But you'll see if you wait."

Now it was he who hesitated and demurred. "I don't know that I want to meet him in particular," he said and his gaze shifted. "Me and the police never did get on."

A new and quite different fear changed her face again. "You don't mean that, Tom? They're not—after you?"

He began to bluster. "I didn't say so, did I? You ask too many bloody questions."

But something in her mind that had begun to stir with his arrival now shot up into the light. "You mean . . . ?"

"I mean I don't want to meet any stuck-up young prig that thinks because he's got into a policeman's uniform he owns the world. Look here, you can put me upstairs, can't you? Ted needn't know I'm here."

"Ted's not a child. Ted's a grown man."

"Got a wife and brats, I dare say."

"He's courting. He's to be married next time he gets leave. Tom, what do they want you for?" But she knew. In her bones she'd known he was in a bad way or he'd never have come.

"Bit of trouble," acknowledged her nephew sullenly. "Look here, it's all one to me where I stay, but you've got to hide me for a night, two maybe. I'm played out. I've come a hell of a way."

"Swansea," she said softly, and it wasn't even a question. And then again, "Swansea! Tom, it was you. But—no, even you couldn't do that."

"I don't know what you're talking about," said Tom Grigg furiously.

She was watching his face as he spoke. Now she went to a drawer in the old-fashioned cabinet and took out a slip of paper. It had a poorly-reproduced photograph on it and some newsprint. She came back with it in her hand.

"So it was you. I thought, when I saw the picture, it was like, but—people change in thirty years. And then the name! Tom, it can't be true."

"I keep telling you it's not me."

She bent her head above the picture; then laid the slip down. "It is you," she said, and hope died out of her voice. "It's not your name, but . . ."

"What's a name?" demanded her nephew. "Just a label. And sometimes it suits a fellow to change the label. You can't talk. Women all change their names if they get the chance."

Now she was rigid, motionless; it hadn't seemed that she had any colour to lose, but now she was chalk-white, an ugly colour, the colour of death.

"So you've done it—again," she said.

"Again?" He moved forward threateningly. When he began to shout she knew he was afraid—and in the wrong. He'd always shouted when he was afraid—and guilty. He'd shouted just like that thirty years ago, when they'd found the heir dead in Lost Man's Quarry, and the police had gone round asking questions.

"Nothing to do with me," he'd shouted. "If the fellow was fool enough to set up an easel on the edge of a quarry he was asking for it. Everyone said he was crazy."

She hadn't said any more, but she'd thought a good deal, and so had a lot of other people. Time, motive and opportunity. That was what the police looked for, and Tom had had all three. Time, because he was out poaching as he often was that afternoon, quite near the quarry. He'd even seen the heir, though he said they hadn't spoken. Motive—he'd been after Elsie, but Elsie wouldn't spare a glance for him, though her mother could have told her she was mad to set her cap at the Cleveland heir. Apart from anything else there was the Curse. It was the Curse that saved Tom really, because everyone knew that no eldest son would ever inherit, and he was bound to be killed anyway, no matter how. In these remote districts the old superstitions died hard. And so they'd said accident at the inquest though Tom was known to hate the fellow, and with good reason said the village, seeing what was the upshot of it all. There wasn't any doubt in any one's mind who young Ted's father was, though Mrs. Manners might have taken her daughter away after the tragedy. A double tragedy really, because Elsie had never come back. She'd been buried in the place where she died, and only the grandmother and the baby had returned. Folks reckoned that baby had saved the old lady's reason. She'd always held her head high, had Mary Anne Manners, and when everyone knew what had happened to your girl—still, she never tried to conceal the baby, and now she was reaping her reward. Because Ted was as nice a young chap as you could look for anywhere.

"What are you looking at me like that for?" demanded Tom, angrily.

She put a finger on the pictured face. "You killed him, didn't you?" she said, "like it says in the paper." Under the blurred photograph were some lines of heavy smudged print. Joseph White, it said, an able seaman in connection with whose death during a Swansea brawl Thomas Smith, a merchant seaman, is wanted by the police. Thomas Smith. But she knew who it really was. Tom didn't even try to deny it.

"No peace anywhere," he said, scowling. "Well, if you don't want your precious Ted mixed up in this you'll keep me hid."

"Ted's seen that cutting," she told him quietly. "He'd know you, and he'd know his duty."

"Doesn't seem to have any more sense than his mother had," sneered Tom. "She never knew when to say No."

"And you can keep your tongue off my daughter. What's done's done. And I won't have you upsetting Ted neither. Ted's his own man. And he's happy. You leave well alone."

"It all depends on who leaves me alone. I don't want to upset Ted. Not unless I have to, that is."

"You can't stay here then. Ted wouldn't hide you, not if I begged him on my bended knees. But I'll hide you somewhere safe." She thought desperately. Her heart beat as though it were a runner, now in her breast, now in her throat. There was so little time. If Ted came early—funny to think a day should come when she would be afraid of Ted coming before he was due. "I know where you could go," she said at last, "where they'd never find you. I'd look after you. And it's only for a night—isn't it?"

"Depends," said the man, his hard pitiless gaze on that old face.

"I'll get you money—to-morrow," she promised. "The bank man comes to-morrow. Then you can get away. And no one shall guess—no one."

"They'd better not," he said. "You wouldn't want any harm to come to your precious Ted, would you? And it might—if I was to talk."

"I don't know what you mean," she faltered.

He leaned nearer and whispered. The light seemed to go out of her eyes.

"Who told you?" she whispered. "Oh, it was him himself. Then . . . it was—you, thirty years ago."

"You think too much," he said roughly. "All you've got to do is keep me hidden. Now where's this precious place?"

She began to tell him, but he broke in after a moment, "Christ! It'll be colder than the grave. I suppose that's your idea. Freeze to death, eh?"

"You can have a fire," she said. "There's a brazier there. You'll be warm enough. And—it's only one night." Her old brain worked faster and faster. It was like wheels going round and round in your head; the thoughts came tumbling over each other, like rats across a granary floor. She felt dizzy, having to plan so much, in silence and in danger.

"And if questions are asked you don't know anything?" he insisted. "All right, I'll chance it. After all, it wouldn't suit your book for anything to happen to me."

"You ought to be getting along now," she told him. "You go first. You know the way. I'll come in a minute, but we mustn't go together. It's getting dark now. No one'll see. And I'll bring some food. . . ."

"And a blanket or something. And some beer. Or p'raps I better take the beer myself. You might forget it."

Wordless, she saw him plunder Ted's precious store. Still, she could get some more in the morning, even if it was in short supply. Where Ted was concerned there was no end to her cunning. And what was beer anyway? The rest of the village might go short, but Ted would get his beer. She'd see to that.

"Give me some matches," said Tom Grigg, turning at the door. "May as well get that fire going."

After he had left the old woman stood thinking. This man might prove the ruin of all her hopes. It was no concern of hers, what had happened that summer afternoon thirty years ago. She had always had her own suspicions, but she had had trouble enough. To carry a secret for so many years, with fear behind you because of the consequences if you are found out, takes toll of the strongest spirit. Intensely superstitious, obstinately brave, she defied facts, she defied Providence. But at the back of her mind was a conviction that Providence always wins.

3

The unwelcome visitor made his way up the long narrow village street, his bottles firmly clasped in his big fierce hands. Already his twisting mind was laying plans. He had information of considerable value, information worth far more than his old aunt could afford to pay. It seemed to him that, judiciously handled, it should keep him in clover for the rest of his life.

But at that time he had no notion how short that life would be.

CHAPTER TWO

There is a skeleton in every house.
PROVERB.

1

As SHE came back to the cottage the old woman heard the bombers roaring overhead. They were going out early to-night, a big raid she supposed. They went over like some giant sewing-machine, whirring ceaselessly through the dark. It was odd how quickly the dusk came down once the light began to fade. By the time Ted arrived you'd want a torch to see your way. The village seemed still enough, quiet

11

and dim under the night sky. All the curtains were drawn and people were eating or washing dishes or just listening to the wireless while they knitted or darned. It was so quiet you wouldn't guess there was a war on, if it hadn't been for the bombers like huge birds setting forth on their night flight. That was the way life was, though, everything so changeless and still, and yet danger all round you.

"If no one saw him come," she thought, "it might be all right. They'll never find him there, and to-morrow I'll get the money and he'll go away. That's all he wants from me now."

Once he'd wanted more, he'd wanted Elsie, but Elsie had never had any use for him.

"When I take a husband I'll have one I don't have to go out scrubbing to keep," she'd taunt him.

"If you get a husband he'll beat you if he's any sense," Tom had retorted.

Elsie had never been afraid of him, though she was such a little thing.

"Why d'you keep him, mother?" she'd asked. "If you turned him out of doors he'd have to fend for himself."

But she couldn't. He was her dead brother's son for one thing and blood counts, and for another she'd felt he was safer under her own eye. Born to be hanged people said of him. Well, it hadn't come to that, though it well might. If anyone tracked him down here—but why should they? Thomas Smith hadn't any links with Kings Fossett. Besides, it was only for a night. This time to-morrow she'd be safe again, she and Ted. There was a stitch in her side and her breath hurt her; she pressed her hand to the place and hurried on. It would never do for Ted to come back and find her away.

It had been difficult to persuade Tom to stay put. "I'll catch my death of cold here," he'd said. She'd had to cajole him.

"There's no other place in the village you'll be so safe. In fact, there's no other place at all."

She'd persuaded him at last and had breathed more easily. If he'd stay there for a while, even if they came looking for him they'd never seek there.

There was no sign of Ted as she hurried up the street; the chicken was browning slowly; she set a pan of milk on to boil, crumbled bread. The smell of onions filled the air. Then she began to set the table. It wasn't often she had to set a table for two. Generally she just ate whatever there was at a corner, not making any ceremony of it, because when you're old and your appetite's the size of a bird's, it's ridiculous to make a fuss. But when Ted came everything had to be perfect. Whatever happened he mustn't guess. By seventy-odd you're used to trouble, you know that it's often easier to carry it alone. And even if it's not you can't tell boys like Ted. Her whole life sounded that one note—Ted—Ted—Ted.

The chicken was just ready when he came. As she heard his step on the path she wondered how she could have been deceived before. No one else in the world had quite that step. Why, if she were dead and lying in the churchyard and he went by, even if he hadn't a thought left for her, she'd hear him and her dust would stir to know him so close, to hear his voice coming through the black earth. No music made by angels on celestial harps would be so sweet. This was the worst sort of love she'd ever known. When you were young you loved lustily, carelessly, because you didn't know what loss was like and disappointment and fear. Life taught you all those things, but it didn't weaken your hold. She'd loved her husband, dead these forty years, she'd loved Elsie, that little spirited thing nothing could tame, and she'd lost them both. She'd never loved Tom. You couldn't somehow, for all his looks and his bravado. Still, other women had loved him all right, and he had been mad enough about Elsie. If that long chap from the Hall goes messing our Elsie about I'll break his blasted neck, he'd said. And Elsie had gone with that long chap, and the long chap had been found in a quarry with a broken neck and Elsie had kept her secret. . . . Even an old woman of seventy-odd could put two and two together.

She creamed the potatoes and gave the bread sauce a final stir as the gate clicked. For Ted there wasn't anything she wouldn't do. She wanted him to have all the happiness, all the safety she hadn't had, that Elsie hadn't had. And she couldn't preserve it for him, not for all her love. Happiness was like a pinch of dust in the palm of your hand that a breath can blow away; it was like a flower that fades under your eyes. . . . She poured the gravy into the tureen as the second knock of the evening sounded on the door.

With his arm round her her fears subsided.

"Well, Grandma!" How strong he was, how warm and confident and young. He seemed to bring light into the little house. Mustn't let him guess anything, mustn't give yourself away; just keep going for twenty-four hours, less in fact. There's not much you can do for the one you love but you can do that, carry through the grave foolish deception, not let him see how your nerves and your heart are twisted. Smile back into those laughing eyes—Elsie had never had blue eyes like these. . . . She brought in the chicken and set it for him to carve. Dark meat for me, she'd say, I prefer it, and he'd tell her, Can't always have what you like, you know, and cut her a wing and take the leg himself. No taste in the breast, he'd tell her. And she'd take the wing and eat it and never taste a thing.

"How's the black market?" he asked, pouring out the beer. "No sense telling me the army gets the pick of the food, not while the civilians can get meals like this one."

And she smiled and asked about Edna and listened to his stories and all the time she was thinking, "The bank gentleman comes to-morrow. Got to cash some of those certificates. How much? What's the least he'll take?" Twenty-five pounds? Would he go for that? Had it better be thirty? Thirty was cheap to keep Ted in the dark. Murder's an ugly word, but it was the word one of the papers had used. He mustn't know, she was thinking, he must never know. I'd take any risks to keep it quiet. Though if they got Tom there wasn't much hope of its being kept quiet. They'd know she'd hidden him, too, perhaps. There was a word for that—accessory after the fact. Made her a criminal, too, she who wouldn't have stolen a row of pins. Only this was different. This was for Ted. That changed all the picture.

They'd reached the stage of her famous jam pudding when the knock came on the door.

She started. "Who's that?"

"Well, who generally calls at this hour?" asked Ted amiably.

"None of the neighbours. They know you're here."

"Don't know why that should keep them away unless they've something on their consciences. I'll see who it is."

"No, no." Like some little fierce bird she barred the door to him.

"I'll go. Once they see you there'll be no stopping them. Chitter-chatter—you always could talk the hindleg off a goat."

It wasn't a neighbour at the door. It was two men and she knew one of them at once. That was Guppy, the local policeman. A little place like Kings Fossett didn't do much in the way of police. One man served both Kings Fossett and Bishops Cleveland, the next village. She essayed a bobbishness she didn't feel.

"Why, it's Mr. Guppy. Not come to arrest me, have you?"

Guppy was very solemn. "We'd like to ask you one or two questions, Mrs. Manners."

"What? At this hour?" Her heart raced. It was Tom, of course. It couldn't be anything else. They knew something. . . . "Come into the parlour."

She heard a step behind her, and there was Ted. He stood six foot two, a big dependable fellow, but she thought of him as someone to be protected with every ounce of her birdlike strength, her sharp tense wit.

"Told you your black market activities would get you into trouble," said Ted. "Or is it me the sergeant wants?"

"Nothing to do with you," she said sharply. "Nothing at all. Just something . . ." She looked inquiringly at Guppy.

"This is Inspector Isaacs," said Guppy. He was a squat little fellow like one of those china toys you put on the nursery mantelpiece. He had an odd gnome-like face, but to-night he looked grave enough.

"Sorry to disturb you, Mrs. Manners," said Isaacs, who was an Inspector at Horsfall, the nearest market town.

"What's the trouble?" asked Ted. He sounded cool enough, but then he was used to trouble.

Isaacs said, "I believe you have a nephew, Mrs. Manners, called Tom Grigg."

So it had come. She felt her heart like a stone in her breast. "Tom? Why, he went away thirty years ago. You—you've not brought news of him."

"Could you identify this?" demanded Isaacs and offered a photograph. She took it and laid it on the table. Old hands shake so easily, give you away though your heart's staunch and your courage like a rock. She looked up; her face seemed bewildered.

"Why—I haven't seen him in thirty years. I couldn't tell. . . ."

Ted looked over her shoulder. "Why, that's the chap they want for the knifing affair at Swansea," he exclaimed. "I heard he was seen this way."

"You didn't tell me." The words shot out of her before she could stop them.

He looked at her in surprise. For the first time she saw him not as her grandson, not as a little boy she'd reared from the breast as it were, but as a policeman, someone remote and dispassionate, someone who represented the law she was defying.

"You hate anything to do with murder." She trembled. He'd said it—not the policeman, but Ted, the word she'd been trying to force out of her mind ever since the instant she'd gone to the door and seen Tom standing there. "Why, you won't even read the crime columns in the Sunday papers."

Isaacs said heavily, "I never said murder."

"The papers have, though, and so will the courts," Ted reminded him, grimly. "Do you mean this is Tom Grigg, really?"

"He registered as Smith, but that's nothing. We're pretty certain it's Grigg, and he's coming this way."

"And you've come to warn me." She managed a terrible twisted smile. "It's a good thing I've got my grandson here to protect me if he's—what you say."

"We've good reason to suppose he's making for this house," said one of the men.

"He wouldn't do anything so mad," exclaimed the old woman. "Why, it's the first place any one would come."

"He may not know he was seen coming in this direction," explained Isaacs. "I suppose you've not seen him?"

"He's not here," said the old lady, "and if he was to come I wouldn't take him in. Well, how could I? Accessory after the fact they call it, don't they?"

"Always supposing you recognized him as the man they want for that trouble in Swansea," agreed Isaacs smoothly. Too smoothly she thought, wild with panic.

"Anyway," she repeated in desperation, "he's not here. You can search the house if you don't believe me."

"They believe you all right," said Ted.

And she broke out, "Why couldn't he have stayed away, instead of bringing more shame on us?"

"If he should come," began Isaacs, but she broke in, "He won't, I'm sure he won't. It 'ud be too risky, even for Tom."

"What the inspector means is, he might want money," said Guppy earnestly.

"No use coming to me for that," said Mrs. Manners. "I don't even draw the pension."

"Any idea where else he might go if he didn't come this way?" inquired Isaacs. He'd make a bad enemy, this cool-eyed unflustered man.

She hesitated, but only for an instant. She was like a stone falling downhill. She couldn't stop. "There's the Manor," she said. "At Bishops Cleveland, I mean. He was a gamekeeper there before he went abroad."

And then she could have bitten her tongue out.

Guppy looked unhappy. "That was thirty years ago."

"That's right," she agreed quickly—too quickly, but if Isaacs felt suspicious he had no time to comment before Ted broke in in his slow way, "Besides, they might have seen the papers, too. Either way it 'ud be a risk."

"That's right," agreed Mrs. Manners. "And the Dowager's a skinflint all right. No, not likely he'd chance going there."

The less trouble you stirred the better, she was thinking. All the same, this was a complication she hadn't bargained for. "They'll put a man on to watch the house," she was thinking. "I'll not dare go near Tom. They'll trip me if they can," and in her shrivelled obstinate breast was born a resolve that, come what might, they shouldn't know, shouldn't find out. If she could dodge them just once, cut through the old churchyard as though she were going to tend her husband's grave, slip round the corner . . . they couldn't surely watch the whole village. Her fear was now that Tom might grow impatient, show himself and betray them all.

"Well, we just thought we'd warn you," said Isaacs, stolidly. "He's a desperate man. You see, he hasn't so much to lose."

17

Ted took a hand. "He won't get in here," he assured the officers. "But thanks for the warning."

After they had gone she shook like a leaf; it was like an illness. She couldn't keep still.

"Policemen at this hour," she whispered, trying to rally.

"That's all right, they've gone. Come to that, you've got a policeman on the premises." He put on a kettle and found some teacups. "All right, all right. You've had a shake-up. You want to rest." He made the tea the way she liked it, thick and red, so that you could float a hen on it. When she had drunk her first cup and he was pouring out her second, he said, head downbent, voice deliberately casual, "Take a word of advice from an expert, Gran. Next time you try to mislead the police don't be so eager."

"Next time?" Panic shook her anew. "But . . ."

"You know where he is, don't you, Gran? All right, all right, don't tell me, but—why didn't you want him to go up to the Manor?"

"There was trouble once," she said slowly. "You don't want me to go into all that. But—he was sweet on your mother, you know, and—after your father died—there was talk, and . . ."

He knew. You can't grow up in a village and not know things like that.

"He knew a bit too much? So that's why you think he may go to the Manor."

She was so still you'd have thought she hadn't heard; only those ridiculous little hands, tight-clenched, shook in her lap.

He brought the tea across to her. "All right, Gran, this is off the record. Only—they won't watch me, see? I might be able to help."

She shook her head. "I can't tell you anything, there's nothing to tell."

"You look out. You think you can tackle the world, but remember, this chap's a murderer. His life's forfeit anyway, and he knows it. A man like that's dangerous."

"Don't I know it? I brought him up after his mother died. He was always wild. All the same," she added quickly, "I don't know anything about him now. And nor do you, Ted. If they come asking any more questions, you don't know anything. You've never set eyes on him." And that, she reflected, was true enough.

He thought how absurd it was that she should defy them all, absurd and futile. Because, in spite of what writers of detective stories tell you, the police generally get their man and if they're defeated it isn't by a little old lady who believes that if you keep your mouth shut you're safe. Silence can be so much more eloquent than speech. As though realizing this danger Mrs. Manners said sharply, "I've sometimes wondered what happened to him in thirty years. Thirty years is a long time. He might be dead."

"He's not dead," said her grandson soberly. "You know that."

But she was in command of herself again. "Do I? I don't know anything. Didn't you hear me tell the police that just now?" She wouldn't talk about him any more. It brought back too much of life's despairs. Instead, grim and indomitable she talked of Edna till it was time to go to bed.

2

The next morning seemed endless. She thought Ted would never have done with eating his breakfast, fiddling with his pipe, looking through the paper. Not that it mattered really; the bank man didn't come till ten-thirty, and she couldn't leave the shop for half an hour after that. She left her grandson in the parlour, doing the crossword puzzle, while she put things straight on the counter. Ted went off about ten. Edna had got a day off from her factory, and they were spending it together. Usually Mrs. Manners hungered secretly for him all the time he was away from her, but to-day she was thankful to see him go. Her customers seemed more choosey, more conversational than usual. They all had stories of how their cousins and aunts and married sisters got more for their points wherever they happened to be living than they themselves did at Kings Fossett.

"I'm surprised you don't go and live along of your cousin (or aunt or married sister)," observed Mrs. Manners tartly.

"It's not right everyone shouldn't have the same. There should be one law for everyone," insisted tiresome Mrs. Timmins.

"You should go and see Colonel Llewellin," retorted Mrs. Manners, putting back the tin of golden syrup she had meant to offer this

19

particular customer, and saying instead, "There's plum and there's gooseberry, and if it wasn't for him there wouldn't be that."

The morning wore away slowly. At eleven o'clock she pinned a little notice on the door—*Back at 11.15*—and went down the street to the little red house with creeper over the window-sill where the bank representative paid out money. Most people came early and she hadn't long to wait. She brought out her little blue book of certificates—because, there being no post office, he would redeem those too, if he couldn't persuade you to change your mind.

"Now, now," he said jocosely, pretending to shudder, "not going to sell up the old home, surely," and he pointed to a poster showing an airman menaced by a dagger and inscribed, Would you stab him in the back? "Got to win this war sometime, you know, and the old folks like you and me that can't fight have to send our money to fight for us." He was a new man; she hadn't seen him before. Instantly she stiffened.

"It's needed—for a family matter," she said coldly. "I'll take thirty pounds, please."

His manner changed at once. He recognized her for one of the old kind that no social insurance will spoil, that'll never be dependent and talk of rights, that accepts its own responsibilities and doesn't ask why the Government won't look after relatives. Her self-respect was rooted so deep you'd never kill it with all your good intentions and philanthropic ways.

He gave her the money, in single and half-notes and a little silver. Last night she'd hated the thought of spending thirty pounds of Ted's money, for that was how she regarded it, on Tom. But things looked different in the morning. She was investing this money for Ted in the best possible way. She had told Tom he must be patient till midday. She couldn't risk being seen coming towards his hiding-place at a time when other housewives were out and about. As a rule she didn't leave the shop at all except for the lunch-hour and then she seldom went farther than the back parlour. There was nothing to do in the village except buy your rations or have beer, when The Man with a Gun had any, so there was no temptation to leave the premises. To-day she waited till the clock struck one, pulled down the blue blind over the glass of the door, put on her black straw hat with the black glass grapes, took up her black cotton gloves and her black and white scarf and picked a few chrysanthemums out of her little garden, so that if anyone saw her they'd think she was going to the churchyard, that desolate spot, to put them on her husband's grave. Even so she had to fight down a conviction that everyone was watching her, that the windows were full of curious heads, that people peered at her from behind bushes and fences, that they were whispering to one another, "There goes Mrs. Manners. Wonder what she's doing out at this time of day?" Even the sunflowers that bloomed so late in the garden of Mrs. Benby, mother of the village idiot, seemed to turn their great brown eyes to follow her progress.

"Brought any more beer?" enquired Tom, when he saw her.

She'd remembered that, remembered food and cigarettes, though she wished he wouldn't smoke. One thing, he was warm enough. He must have kept the brazier almost red-hot. She felt for a minute she couldn't breathe. When she gave Tom the money he said a bit scornfully, "That the best you could do? Money doesn't go far these days."

"You seem to think I'm made of it," she replied. "I've others to think of."

"Suppose I was to stay a bit longer?" he suggested slyly. "Think you might be able to find a bit more?"

"No," she said at once. "This is all I could manage. Staying here won't help you."

"Proper loving auntie, aren't you?" he taunted her.

She took her courage in her hands and told him about the men who had been enquiring for him last night. His dismay, in an unguarded moment was so great that if she'd had any doubts, they would have dissolved like morning dew.

"Did you give me away, auntie? Did you? No, of course you didn't. Not nice for darling Ted if his relative swung for murder. All right, I'll go by the back way. When do the trains run to London? That's the best place for a man who's wanted. Or are these fellows still hanging about?"

"I didn't see them this morning," she whispered. "I told them I didn't know anything. Still, it might be best not to wait too long."

"I can't go in daylight," he said roughly. "And if they think of looking for me here I'm like a rat in a trap. There's no other way out."

"They'll not come." She did her terrified courageous best to pacify him. He mustn't go out by day; by night he could slink through fields and lanes, get a train, go to London, hide like a rat among thousands of other rats, bright-eyed, alert to danger, slippery as eels, fierce as wolves. She didn't much care what he did so long as he went away and ceased to menace Ted. But in her bones she knew it was already too late. The wheel was turning again, and she couldn't stop it. It would turn and crush Ted and Ted's happiness. The superstitions of generations moved in her chill blood.

"What did you tell Ted?" His eyes bored into hers.

"Nothing. Nothing at all."

"If you're double-crossing me," he threatened. "But no, you wouldn't do that. Mustn't hurt Ted's feelings, must we, or upset Ted's young lady. Look here." He laid his big predatory hand on her thin shoulder. "If I write for more funds mind you send 'em— quick. Don't forget that you're in this, too. You know they're after me and you know why. And you knew it when those chaps came last night. And who's to know Ted wasn't in it, too? Funny sort of policeman he'd look, wouldn't he?"

At first she hardly took it in; she hadn't looked further than a few hours ahead. Then it came over her she'd put herself—and Ted— utterly in his power. He could write any day. . . .

"Got it?" asked Tom cruelly.

She put back her head. "You always talked a lot of nonsense even as a boy," she told him. "It's a pity your uncle was so silly about you. And you can say what you like, but you've had all you'll get from me. You can write and write, but you'll not come back here, and if I don't answer, what can you do?"

"I might tell the police the truth," he suggested.

"If so, it 'ud be for the first time since you were born," she flashed back at him. "And why should they believe you? And don't think you could ruin Ted. It 'ud take a better man than you to do that. And if you don't want to be caught, don't leave your bottles and paper bags lying about. I shan't be coming here again."

"I might come along to you," he suggested, "later."

22

But she replied quickly, "It's the working-party this afternoon. I won't be back till late."

"How late?" He wouldn't have known pity if you'd given it him on a plate.

"Oh, late enough," she told him in vague tones.

"Ted," he began, but she said sharply, "No use looking for Ted. He'll not be back till evening. He's out with his young lady."

You might have thought he'd feel shame, seeing her battle so fiercely with such poor weapons, but shame was a word he couldn't spell. It's a good thing human senses are so limited, that a frail wall of skin and bone can hide thought from the man standing at your elbow. If he could have seen into her mind then, seen the mad fears racing there, the hurried plans she made and discarded even as she spoke, he might have realized that the race is not always to the swift nor the battle to the strong. But though he knew he was in danger, he didn't even understand how desperate that danger was.

At the working-party they said she couldn't be feeling well. She didn't seem to know when they spoke to her, and she made the most irrelevant answers. She kept dropping stitches, too, she, the best knitter in the place. Well, I dare say no one else will notice, was all she said when Mrs. Willings pointed out her mistake. Sailors aren't so fussy as you look for.

She came back to her cottage at half-past five. It was darkish now, and perhaps Tom had gone for good. She'd have liked to go up to the church and reassure herself, but it might look queer. She was thinking deeply as she opened the little front door, but in the parlour she stopped aghast. The room looked as though a wild beast had raged through it. Drawers stood open, chair covers had been torn off, the lock of the secretary was broken. Someone had been ravaging here, flinging aside the rugs, tearing up the carpet. It was the same in the bedroom. The bedclothes had been torn off the bed, the mattress ripped open, her garments tumbled and dishevelled. She stood there breathing hard. No need to ask whose work this was. Only someone who remembered the cottage of old would have looked in some of the hiding-places. She glanced at the clock. Thank goodness, it was two hours, probably three, before Ted would be back. And now there was only one thing that mattered, and that was—had Tom found what he'd come for? If so . . . she made her way to the secret hiding-place inside the old china figure on the mantelpiece. A stranger wouldn't know that if you took off the broad-rimmed black china hat, the figure was hollow, and you could put something not much bigger than a letter, something infinitely precious, inside. It would be safe there—from strangers. But Tom wasn't a stranger and so—it hadn't been safe after all. Her shaking fingers explored the hollow interior; desperately she tried to make herself believe she'd hidden it somewhere else. But it wasn't true, and it was a waste of time, as lying to yourself always is. The Bible was right with its saying about a man's foes being of his own household; you can fight strangers, but your own kith knows all the joints in your armour.

This altered everything. Now, never mind what chances, she'd got to make sure that Tom Grigg went away for good, went where he couldn't work harm—or she'd got to get her treasure back. Not for her sake—when you're old things don't matter so much. But she'd got to shut Tom's mouth because of the future—not just her future which couldn't be long anyhow, but the future of the people who now owned the world, the inheritors of the world to come. It might, she knew, be her life against Ted's. She couldn't afford to think about that. She got her torch and tied a shawl over her hair and went towards the door. As she reached it the clock began to chime six. Ping—ping—ping—like little silver notes they were. She went back to the wireless Ted had given her and turned a switch. Mustn't do anything out of the ordinary, mustn't let people guess. Suppose to-night of all the nights in the year there was something momentous in the six o'clock news. Suppose the Prime Minister made a special statement. Everyone knew she listened in at six and if she missed it this once they might think it queer. You have to be careful when you're battling for a life.

But there wasn't anything special after all, and a few minutes later she had opened the door and crept out into the dark, and was stealing, a little anonymous figure, through the village street.

She wasn't away long and when she came back she was whispering, "I'll never go there again. Never, never, never."

But in vowing this she had reckoned without Arthur Crook.

CHAPTER THREE

If there were no bad people there would be no good lawyers.
CHARLES DICKENS.

MR. CROOK CAME into the hamlet of Kings Fossett by bicycle from
the infinitely more cheerful hamlet of Bridget St. Mary. Cycling was
as strange to him as taking holidays or spending his time in innocent-
looking villages. Still, if danger is an added thrill to existence, then
he was blessed indeed. Holidays were an adventure to him to begin
with, in the sense that they were practically unknown. A man of
abounding energy, he wouldn't have found it restful in the normal
course of events to go away for a week and do nothing, but his London landlord had belatedly decided to effect some essential repairs
to the large shabby London house where Mr. Crook occupied the
top floor, thus making the place uninhabitable. In vain did Crook
protest that he was wasting his time, that Jerry would doubtless
knock it all down again as soon as it was built up, that he himself
wasn't a fussy man and a few cracks in the ceilings and drips in the
corners weren't important during a world war. He even urged that,
since the place had stood up for a couple of years since the bombing
it could stand for a couple more without interference, and he didn't
imagine it would last longer than that in any case, so why bother to
patch? The landlord, however, was adamant. Crook thanked his stars
that the Government, from whom he so frequently and violently
differed in the course of his activities, had had the sense to prevent
human ghouls like his landlord from doing five pounds worth of
repairs and putting forty pounds on to the rent.

This, then, explained his unusual preoccupation with country
lanes, obscure villages and bicycles.

He went to Bridget St. Mary by the simple expedient of opening
the Bradshaw and sticking a pin, blindfold, into the pages. The pin
indicated the village of which, not unnaturally, he had never heard,

25

and twenty-four hours later, by a series of the slowest and least-enterprising trains he had ever encountered, he found himself in the heart of Mereshire. The heart of Mereshire seemed to have few arteries. There was one car for hire, but you could never be sure of getting it, because it might be summarily ordered out to attend a funeral, a childbirth or an emergency hospital case. The station was two miles away, whence the trains ran four times in twenty-four hours to other equally unheard-of spots. The only bus ran on alternate days and to get into it you had to traipse up to the starting-place and stand in a queue at least half an hour before it was due to leave. There was one village shop that was also the post office, and about a mile out a glaringly new villa served teas and charged accumulators. Crook stayed at the Duck and Dragon; the landlord was also the church-warden and the landlord's wife kept cows and supplied milk over the saloon bar counter. Those were positively all the entertainments the place could boast.

"And I said London was dull and all the best crimes were committed in the country," moaned Crook at the end of the first interminable day. "Well, if they ain't, it only shows how unenterprisin' country folk are. I could commit a couple of murders a week myself just to liven things up."

He had left the Scourge, his famous (and infamous) little red car in London, to be decarbonized, believing, like all true patriots, that even if you run on gas you should use it for business and not for pleasure, and he had spent that first day on his own feet. By evening he decided that the charms of the countryside have been grossly exaggerated by the poets. Grass is all right in its way—it gives officials an opportunity to put a notice—Please Keep Off The Grass—all over the place, but there was altogether too much of it in the country. As for cows, doubtless Providence had the good of mankind in view in creating them, since there were people who liked milk, though he wasn't among them, but for himself he felt uneasy unless there was a good stout fence between him and them. True, you didn't often hear of cows goring people, but surely sooner or later it would occur to one of their number that their horns were provided for some purpose, and then they might start making experiments, and you could never be sure it wouldn't be at the moment when a defenceless Mr. Crook was walking innocently through a shady lane.

He asked what were the alternatives to Shanks Mare, and was told that he could hire a bicycle.

"I hope it's a nice small one," remarked Crook prudently, who held his own view as to the suitability of bicycles for stout gentlemen of fifty-three. His nice solid figure had served him well all those years and he felt it deserved something better than to be flung into a ditch or over a wall because of an obstreperous machine.

"Just your size," said the landlord heartily, who'd have said the same if it had been a fairy cycle.

Crook went to view it with foreboding and found, as he anticipated, that it was a great ugly brute of a thing that had probably killed half a dozen men in its time. Still, he was accustomed to taking chances and next morning he set forth, a striking looking figure in a bright brown golfing suit, a brown cap pulled over one eye and a natty purple silk handkerchief in his pocket.

The landlord asked him chattily where he was going and Mr. Crook, with more wisdom than most men possess, said wherever the Brute chose to take him. He spun out of the yard, down the road, narrowly missed a collision with a lorryful of lime and wobbled equally perilously towards a grass-grown ditch. After that he became reckless and gave the machine its head.

The bicycle, not unnaturally, preferred going downhill and Crook went with it, a little to his own surprise, he having supposed they would part company quite early on the expedition. The downward road led him between low hedges where the last small unripe blackberries clung to their thorny trails, past some bullock sheds, round a corner, into a bumpy lane where he clung to his machine as vehemently as Mrs. Micawber claimed to have clung to her spouse, was almost blown off by a horse putting its head over a gate and snuffling loudly at him—(Don't DO that! said Mr. Crook, reproachfully) and presently felt certain enough of his balance to admire the picturesqueness of the landscape. The bricks and tiles of the farms and buildings hereabouts were a shade of orange-red, delightfully mellowed by years of exposure. Set in fields of golden stubble, offset by the yet more golden ricks, they made a picture that would have pleased a more censorious critic than Mr. Arthur Crook. In one field a red hay cart stood in a blue shed; he slowed down, the bicycle graciously permitting, and watched the effect of sunlight on the golden trees. He was genuinely enchanted by the scene, and admitted that the poets had something on their side.

"It's as good as the ads in Paddington Station," he observed admiringly. It showed it paid you to knock off work now and again. He'd always believed they were spoofing until now.

The bicycle, however, considered they had lingered long enough and shot round a corner. Crook, unimpressionable though he liked to think himself, gave a gasp. For they seemed to have shot into a different world. Whatever this world might be it was inferior. For one thing, there was no sunlight in it. He didn't dare look over his shoulder to see whether the sun was still shining behind him, and the metamorphosis was common to the whole scene or whether he had really in some mysterious way left the normal creation out of sight and got into the underworld instead. Certainly the air was, as he would happily have expressed it, pregnant with doom. He found himself in a long narrow village street. Two or three isolated cottages, obviously coming under the classification of Ancient Monuments, stood sullenly in little overgrown gardens. They had the kind of windows you find in old-fashioned dolls' houses, that are not intended to open. He would have been certain they were only tenanted by spiders but for the fact that they all had comparatively clean curtains and pots of ferns or fresh flowers behind the unyielding glass. But there wasn't a face at any window, no one came into the little front gardens to pick a runner-bean or test the tenderness of a vegetable marrow with a darning-needle. No cat sunned itself on a step—not that it could, of course, since there was no sun—but it might at least have come out and spat in a typical manner. No dog leaped up to protest in formal fashion at the arrival of the foreigner, there was not even the familiar village brat to try to commit suicide under the wheels of a stranger's machine.

All this Crook noticed with what psychologists call the subconscious. His immediate preoccupation was how to stop the bicycle, which seemed to be going faster and faster. Applying the brakes made no difference. It was that sort of bicycle. Being a natural gambler he ran the machine into the hedge and jumped unhandily when disaster seemed imminent. On the whole the bicycle suffered more from the experiment than he did, but he did stand still for a moment, pulling himself together and taking stock of his surroundings. The more he saw of them the less impressed he was. The most striking feature of the landscape was the village church, that seemed to have been built for a much larger place. Its great octagonal tower was too tall for the rest of the structure, and seemed to lower at him. The word that came most readily to his mind was menacing. It wasn't only the darkness of the sky—he was accustomed to the London blackout and that had never managed to intimidate him—or even the bleak aspect of the single street that seemed to stretch from Nothing to Nowhere. It was the incredible silence, the absence of life that bothered him.

"The Village That God Forgot," he reflected, and decided to look for the pub, that sure refuge of the downhearted.

Then it occurred to him that he might for once be the thorough tourist and look at the interior of the church. In preparation for this momentous week he had been studying the daily articles of Timothy Tramp in the *Evening Hope*, and Mr. Tramp advised his readers to get out of the home atmosphere on what he mistakenly called "that manly machine, the pedal cycle" into some of "our priceless lesser-known villages." Mr. Crook imagined that even Timothy Tramp, whose standard appeared to be high, would class Kings Fossett as one of our lesser-known villages, and the first object of interest on Mr. Tramp's list was the village church.

"Other objectives," he said, "may be examined later."

Mr. Tramp's latest disciple, therefore, opened the big iron gates with some difficulty, owing to the fact that the front wheel of the bicycle no longer pointed in quite the same direction as the back, and indeed showed a tendency to sidle round and butt him in the stomach; but he mastered it and stood, monarch of all he surveyed, in a forest of mouldering head-stones and chipped granite crosses. There hadn't, he realized, been a funeral here for years. The grass was dry and brittle and of course much too long. These old burying-places get scant attention. Skilled men don't want the risk of damaging their tools on concealed stones and moss-grown memorials; even the few flowers that stood in jam-jars and pots were dead. It was as though the departed who lay here had passed utterly out of human recollection.

The church had the same derelict look, and indeed he was rather surprised to find it open. The great main door would have withstood a battering-ram, and you could have knocked a man out with the key. The walls within were crumbling with age and lack of care. Yet someone had cared once, for in one corner were traces of a mural painting of some unidentifiable saint that loving hands had disinterred from the offensive whitewash savagely applied by the puritan hordes. Everything round him spoke of decay. The whitewash on the walls was cracked and discoloured, the great beams supporting the roof eaten with worms. The place was as cold as death. He walked up the nave with its shabby cocoanut matting over uneven stones and marked the place where those same sacrilegious hands had torn a brass from its bed. The pulpit was tall and had a swinging door to prevent a too-ardent preacher from stepping backwards down the eight narrow steps, pitching in all probability into eternity. There was a rubbed brass plate here, and he made out the letters A.M.D.G. and a capital C. But the smaller letters were too rubbed to be legible any more. The Chancel itself looked the most neglected part of the building. The choir stalls were mere benches with what had once been finely carved ends, but these were now so eaten by worms, or perhaps the death-watch beetle that was certainly responsible for the damage to the rafters, that the wood crumbled into fine dust when it was handled. There were three of these pews—two on one side and one on the other, and the seats themselves had been replaced by a local carpenter during the past twenty years. A number of mildewed hymn books lay on a rush-seated chair, the organ was covered with some torn sheeting, the brass of the altar-rails was green. And everywhere, on pillar and pulpit and pew, the cobwebs had gathered. Butterflies that had flown in out of the sunlight had become entangled in these filmy webs and now hung, their bright wings folded and dingy with dust, in every crevice of the building. Feeling that this was the last time he would ever take Timothy Tramp's advice on anything, Crook decided he might as well make a good job of this derelict House of God, and moved very quietly for so big a man up

to the altar itself. The now-familiar shabby sheeting covered the
frontal, and a stained and spotted piece of green linen had been
spread over what was, in fact, an old refectory table, as worm-eaten
as everything else. The linen strip was daubed with droppings from
six wax candles set in dingy brass sticks; there were brass vases filled
with flowers that had stiffened and blackened with the passing of
time. He was not a religious man but a curious sensation passed over
him. He felt himself in the presence of something horrible—something surely more potent than the decay and disorder of the building.
He told himself that he'd often met men who confessed to similar
sensations in unfamiliar buildings, but the explanation wasn't good
enough. He lifted his head and looked uneasily round him. There
was an atrocious window in modern glass above the deserted altar,
and a white patch the shape of a large plate part-way up the wall on
the right. They must have had a picture hanging there, he thought,
but there wasn't any nail in the wall. The credence table stood on the
other side, supporting the brass alms dish, against a background of
tarnished green and gold embossed tapestry hanging from a brass rail.
His gaze came back to the altar itself; after an instant his mind began
working. It was only a trifle but trifles hang people. He'd never forgotten the story of the blood-stained match that hanged the first
trunk murderer. It was one of the candles that had caught his attention. They were made of a white wax that had yellowed with exposure and grimed by a fine coating of dust; but this one was different from the rest. Though the dust showed on one side, on the
other the candle was clean, and the downbent wick was black and
brittle, "as though" he told himself slowly, "someone had lighted it
quite recently." He knew nothing of ecclesiastical usage; it might be
a common practice to light only one candle for a service or it might
be just war-time economy, but surely any man who lighted an altar-
candle would at least have removed the dead flowers whose dried
pollen was sprinkled on the stained green cloth. He touched the
"shroud" of wax that streamed down one side of the candle where
the wick had burned unevenly; it was quite fresh. Someone had
lighted that candle during the last few days. He dropped on his
hands and knees and inspected the dusty floor. Under the edge of

the dirty sheeting he found a spent wooden match, burnt very low, as though the candle had been difficult to ignite.

"It can't have been for a service," he reflected, scrambling to his feet again, "and what on earth do you light a candle in a church for —unless you're looking for something."

But what on earth of any value could a man hope for in these moribund walls?

"All the same, the place smells of death," he said, and he even went across to the pulpit and opened the door. There was quite evidently something dead there, something that had been dead for some time. But it wasn't enough to account for the atmosphere. A terrified bird might hit its head against a pillar and drop on to the pulpit floor and die and putrefy there, but it wouldn't create this sense of horror that was slowly enveloping him. And he wasn't an imaginative man and his profession didn't allow him to be squeamish. Still, the bird was one more piece of evidence that the church hadn't been used for a service for a long while. Clergymen don't hold services and neglect the opportunity of going into the pulpit and talking down at the congregation, and the most absent-minded parson must have noticed the bird's existence.

It was then, as he stood there, the door of the pulpit swinging in his hand, that he saw two things he hadn't noticed before. One was what is known in the country as the parson's bier, a simple affair like a glorified rag-and-bone cart (thought the irreverent Mr. Crook), that stood behind the great door, and the other was a great carved chest standing against the wall. Fascinated, yet scoffing at his fears, he came slowly down. The bier offered no mystery; you could hardly have concealed a dead butterfly there, but the chest that stood against the west wall held his attention. It was a big carved affair, shaped remarkably like a coffin. Crook came slowly down to it. It was ridiculous, of course. If he opened it he'd find vestments or—or hymn books or perhaps some spare hassocks. The one thing he knew he wouldn't—couldn't—find was a body. Because it's only in books these things happen. And besides, it would be too unsafe. The church was open all the time; any tourist might come in and lift the lid.

The lid wasn't nearly so heavy as he'd expected. And when he had opened the chest and saw what it contained he wanted to laugh. And under that impulse was something he couldn't explain, something that made him wish—he who lived on crime—that he'd never left Earl's Court.

CHAPTER FOUR

How now! A rat?
Dead, for a ducat, dead!
HAMLET.

THE FIRST THING he saw inside the chest was an empty beer bottle. It wasn't the sort of thing you'd look for in an antique affair like that. He felt vaguely shocked. For one thing, it was a very new beer bottle, and it was the only new thing the chest contained. For the rest there were some shoddy old cassocks from which the moths rose in a cloud, and some tatterdemalion prayer and hymn books. There wasn't anything like a body. He let down the lid and stood staring at the great rusty stove and the bags of various sorts of fuel that leaned against the wall, not even decently shrouded by a curtain. He felt he should be satisfied now, get out into the fresh air, resume his wrestle with the bicycle. There was no mystery here.

All the same, the beer bottle bothered him. It wasn't so much that it was a beer bottle. Beer, he believed, is one of God's gifts to men and if you can heap the sanctuary with giant vegetable marrows and untidy stacks of corn, why not a bottle of beer? But this bottle had been only put there recently. You couldn't tell Crook much about beer, and since beer zoning had begun in this part of England he had begun to get accustomed to a variety of labels that wouldn't have passed muster in the good days before France fell. Burman was not only a war-time label, it was a new label altogether. That bottle hadn't been there long. And yet he'd swear nothing else in the chest had been touched. And why should anyone go to the trouble to hide a beer bottle inside the chest, when he could easily throw it away in the graveyard? And anyhow—he came back to his first problem—what was a newly-burnt candle doing on the altar and what was a newly-opened bottle of beer doing in the chest?

He got up, shaking himself angrily. It was ridiculous. He was making a mountain out of a mole-hill. Some tramp had left the bottle there—but he didn't believe that. To begin with, tramps don't go into churches like the parish church of Kings Fossett. It's perfectly obvious from a single glance that the alms-boxes won't be worth cracking, and anyway there wasn't an alms-box in sight; and tramps know far too much to expect they'll get any comfort from a church. Churches offer pews for beds and hymn books for pillows. Even an amateur tramp can do better for himself than that. And even a lunatic wouldn't come into a deserted church in order to drink beer by candle-light.

"Well, anyway, it's no business of mine," he told himself, replacing the bottle and going back to the great door. "I'm here for a holiday."

Even now he couldn't throw off the feeling that tragedy was very close to him, but there wasn't anywhere you could hide a body. The font was too small—but all the same he managed to raise the heavy wooden lid. He let it go with a sigh. He'd known there'd be nothing there. There was nothing anywhere.

In the porch a tattered notice informed the parishioners of certain measures to be adopted in the case of enemy aerial action. The date on the notice was more than a year old. He came out into the wilderness of graveyards. If you wanted a body this was where you should look for it. He walked round the church. At the extreme north end there was a second door, closely bolted. Crook examined the bolts. No one had come in this way for a long time. The bolts were rusted into their staples. He stood there for a minute frowning. He was only making a fool of himself; he hadn't a thing to go on— only a hunch. But he felt he owed it to the considerable balance he had in more than one London bank to respect his hunches.

"That's for the parson," he reflected. "Must lead into the vestry. Well, that's reasonable. The chap's got to vest somewhere." He paused. There was something wrong. After an instant he knew what it was.

"Where the devil was the vestry?" he wondered. "There wasn't a door."

And then he realized something else—the meaning of that curious circular lighter patch on the south wall of the chancel. He assumed that a picture had once hung there, though he had been puzzled because there was neither nail nor hanger. Now he remembered that other things in use in a church are round—notably alms-dishes. And wasn't it unusual for the credence table to be on the north wall when there was plenty of room for it on the south?

"That's where the door is," he thought. "And there's no sense blocking that unless there's something that's got to be hidden."

His sense of the macabre and the horrible stiffened. Someone, he now knew, had recently shifted the table and the alms-dish, knowing that while some idle visitor may open an unencumbered door, no one is likely to remove a piece of the sanctuary furniture. He plodded round once again to the south entry.

As soon as he had moved the table he saw something else, a splash of wax on the floor. Behind the curtain was the door, as he had anticipated—and this also was bolted. He wondered for a moment why the bolts should be on the church side; then reflected that obviously the authorities would want to protect the church against thieves. Someone might break in through the vestry, but that wouldn't be much help if the door to the main building were fastened. All the same, so much care didn't fit in with the general impression of neglect and dirt. He was pretty certain by now that whoever had bolted the door and moved the table had wanted to conceal something more valuable than a surplice and an alms-bag. The bolts ran back easily; they'd been used not very long ago. Besides, the candle-wax on the floor was new. The key was in the lock, which was surprising till you'd thought for another minute. After he'd discovered what the vestry concealed Crook understood all right.

Inside the little dark room, lying against the door, so that he had to push it aside as the door backed, was the body of a man of middle-age, and even someone with less experience of this sort of thing than Crook would have known at once that he was dead. Not that Crook was one of your wiseacres; he didn't believe in Jacks-of-all-trades. He was a lawyer, not a doctor, and so he didn't, after placing a finger on the corpse's eyelid, know just how long the body had been there.

But the fists were blood-stained and battered, as though they'd hammered desperately against something that wouldn't yield. The atmosphere of the little den was suffocating; there was no window and the curtain over the door had shut out all the air. Then, too, when he'd taken a further step, he saw a charcoal brazier standing in the middle of the little room. It was cold now, of course, but it hadn't been cold when the poor devil on the floor found himself locked in without a hope of escape. A man in a hermetically-sealed room with a charcoal fire wouldn't have very long to live. He must have known that; that's why he'd battered so fiercely on the impenetrable door. Crook came back into the chancel. He had to get his breath. A dead man in an airless cell is a bad thing to meet on a holiday. For once, he thought, the authorities were right. You'll be better taking your holiday at home this year.

There was nothing to show who the man was. He was between fifty and sixty, Crook decided, and there was money in his pocket, but no sign of identification, no card, no ration book. He was a powerful sort of fellow, he must have died hard.

"That was a pretty devilish thing to do," Crook told himself, looking round the little room. Some sandwich paper and a bottle stood on the little table, alongside a square white cardboard bearing a label from a well-known ecclesiastical furnishing firm in London.

"The Reverend R. Cupit," he read. "The Rectory, Bishops Cleveland, Mereshire." He opened the lid; inside was a white satin alms-bag and a white book-marker embroidered with a gold cross and the letters I.H.S. Bishops Cleveland was presumably the next village, with one parson for the two parishes. Someone, for reasons he didn't yet appreciate, had hidden this fellow here, brought him food and then gone out and bolted the door on the outside, knowing, presumably, no one was likely to enter the church for a month—or even three from the general look of the place.

"I don't seem able to escape the police," Crook reflected, thinking that his first notion was right—that all the major crimes are committed by countrymen. Londoners might hit you over the head, garrot you, push you into an emergency water supply tank or even out of a window, but they wouldn't lock you in a vestry—you'd be found too soon.

36

He shut the door rather reluctantly—he'd have to come back and one experience of that airless room was enough, but it wasn't fair to give some other fellow the sort of shock he'd had—and he couldn't be the only man in England who read Timothy Tramp. He came out and rescued his bicycle. He felt inclined to blame it for this interruption of his holiday. If he'd had the car he'd never have stopped at Kings Fossett at all.

"I wonder if this dead-alive place sports a policeman." He wheeled the bicycle rather crookedly down the overgrown path between the graves. People have to be murdered, of course. If they weren't fellows like himself would be lining up for the dole; but it's more satisfactory when they're polished off quickly with a knife or a gun or the familiar anonymous blunt instrument. It wasn't nice to think of that fellow beating on the door—gently at first, probably, because he wouldn't want to betray his whereabouts, then more stormily and at last desperately, as the appalling truth broke over him that, barring a miracle, this was the end, he wasn't going to get out. It wasn't surprising that no one had heard him; the church stood too far back from the road and anyway, behind that door would anyone hear that parched panic-stricken voice? It wasn't likely. There was only one house of a reasonable size at all near, and as he wheeled his machine up to it, he saw that every window was shrouded in dark blue linen. The state of the steps warned him no one lived there for some time.

"Devil take it, there must be someone living in the village," he exclaimed. Of course the drawn blinds might indicate a funeral, but it wasn't likely. Everyone in the place had probably died long ago. Now that he was back in the empty street, leading his obstreperous bicycle, the body in the vestry seemed to fit in with the rest of the pattern. In fact, it would be more surprising if there hadn't been a body. He looked to the right and saw a crop of giant sunflowers mopping and mowing with their idiot faces over a cottage wall; he looked to the left, and an idiot boy nodded amicably at him over a shut gate. He looked hurriedly at the window of one of the cottages that gave him back his own reflection and was relieved (but surprised) to see that he had straws neither in his mouth nor his hair. But he wasn't much reassured for all that. Even the cottage wasn't quite right. The two top windows were too close together, the eaves overhung them like the brows of the idiot who was opening the gate and coming through, as though at last he had discovered a kindred soul.

"Everything's crackers here," thought Crook. He even began to think there mightn't be a pub. Shakily under the contemptuous eyes of the village zany, he mounted his bicycle and wobbled down the road. He found that if he pointed the wheel towards the right he kept reasonably near the hedge.

It was an endless street; he passed a number of farm buildings and a salvage dump of hundreds of rusty tins and some pieces of broken earthenware and an outworn stove that looked as though they might remain as the village war memorial long after peace was signed, then a Men's Club, apparently permanently closed, and a Methodist Meeting Hall bristling with notices of forthcoming events, including a W.V.S. Sale of work on the previous Friday, and at last fetched up at the village shop.

He abandoned his bicycle to the hedge and went eagerly forward. If there was any one anywhere it would be here. But a neat little notice hung on the blind-covered door.

CLOSED FOR DINNER

Crook gave it up and turned back. He collected the bicycle and wheeled it past some more cottages and a big house in its own grounds—untenanted, of course—and a farm-house decorated with a notice saying Sale of Antique Furniture October 21st 1942, and finally came to the pub. It was called The Man With A Gun, and a reproduction of the Man pointing a villainous musket at passers-by stood at the entrance to the Public Bar.

"Bad psychology," said Crook in judicial tones, feeling better at the mere sight of the sign, even though the place was clearly no more than a beer-house. "Shouldn't try to frighten custom away."

The Man had what looked like a label slung round his neck. When Crook went nearer to see what was written on it he found two words.

SOLD OUT!

CHAPTER FIVE

The Curse shall be on thee
For ever and ever.

SOUTHEY.

CROOK WAS SO MUCH DEMORALIZED by this information that he
abandoned all hope of finding anything as normal as a police constable in this deserted village, and, recklessly mounting the bicycle,
he swept round the corner of the road, paying no attention to a
black and white bull that galloped along the other side of a remarkably frail-looking hedge, bellowing encouragement, and so reached
the next village which proved to be Bishops Cleveland. This formed
such a contrast to Kings Fossett that he began to wonder if he were
dreaming and hadn't really found a body in a derelict church. There
were several shops here, all open, two pubs—he sampled the beer
at both—some cottages with washing blowing in the back gardens,
several cats and enough dogs running under the wheels of his bicycle
to cause him to dismount in his own interest. At the second of the
two inns—The Seven Bishops—he was tempted to confide his diffi-
culties to the lady behind the bar, but decided not. It was a Victorian
tradition that females should stay away from funerals, and if funerals
surely corpses, too. Besides, coincidence in life was much stronger
than any mere novelist dares to suggest, and it would be just luck to
find that it was her husband. Better, in spite of his independent
nature, confide in a policeman. While he was drinking his second
pint, however, the door swung open again and a very tall thin white-
haired man entered. Crook was surprised to see that he wore a parson's collar. An old phrase came into his mind. He shall open his
grief to the Minister—that came out of the service for the Visitation
of the Sick, but if he wasn't sick it was only due to his robust con-
stitution, and anyway in the country generally the parson knew
everyone. If this one didn't it certainly wasn't his own fault, because,

39

before Crook had thought up a good opening—something about the crops or the remarkably handsome nature of bulls thereabouts—the clergyman had edged a bit nearer and was saying cheerfully, "Touring the country? I saw your cycle outside."

"It's not my cycle," said Crook meticulously. "It's borrowed." He wanted to say that he generally went round by car but wasn't sure how it would be received.

"Press?" asked the clergyman, lowering his beer in the manner of an expert. "I've done a bit of writing myself." He put back the tankard to be refilled. "I never can understand why a parish magazine shouldn't be as interesting as one of the women's weeklies."

"Then I'm the man you want to meet," said Crook simply. "What do you generally do with corpses in this part of the world?"

"Bury them according to Christian ritual," said the old gentleman. "Have you—that is to say . . ."

"Yes," said Crook, "I have. Matter of fact, I've been looking for a policeman."

"He's out on his bicycle. I saw him. You'd better tell me, hadn't you?"

Crook told him. He tried to break it gently. "Don't you ever have services there?" he wound up. "What's the good of keeping the place open if it's never used?"

"You mustn't say Never," said the clergyman earnestly. "I admit the position at the moment is a little irregular—but then so are the circumstances of our days. Until about a year ago I had a colleague, an excellent fellow, who acted as curate-in-charge, but he persuaded the military authorities to accept him for work overseas, and since then it's proved absolutely impossible to replace him."

"All work and no pay," suggested Crook cheerfully.

"Man does not live by bread alone," agreed his companion, "but it's difficult to live without it. I try to hold a service there once a month, but sometimes I feel the Earl would do better to close the church altogether—except that that does seem like giving the victory to the Methodists."

"They doin' a thrivin' business locally?" murmured Crook.

"There's a good deal of inter-marriage in these parts," acknowledged the parson, "and the Methodist community is certainly on the increase. Still, I do what I can, though since they took off the local bus in the national interest it's not easy for people to get so far—particularly when they have, so to speak, a church on their doorstep. The ones who have got petrol go to Horsfall in preference."

"Hasn't your Earl got a pet bishop in his pocket?" demanded Crook. "I thought the aristocracy hung together."

"I'm afraid my late colleague was what is called rather High Church, so he naturally hadn't the sympathy of Lord Cleveland who is, in this connection only, as low as the dust beneath Love's chariot-wheel."

"Difficult," agreed Crook, "but of course jam for the criminal."

"Criminal?"

"I keep telling you," said Crook patiently, feeling that at this rate they'd be talking when the Victory Bells rang. "There's a corpse in that church and he didn't put himself there."

"I gathered there was some irregularity," replied the Rector, "but until we know who it is . . . I wonder if I should know. I've been here thirty years. But in a little place like this if a man disappears for a couple of days we all know about it. He might be a stranger, of course."

"Not very probable," objected Crook. "A stranger wouldn't be likely to hide in the vestry of a more or less disused church. If that man was hiding—and no one would go into such a place for fun—he was hiding from someone, and you don't hide from strangers. Besides, someone knew he was there, someone brought him food and drink, someone bolted the door and cold-bloodedly shifted the table against it."

"While he battered on the other side? One doesn't like to think of human nature doing that."

Crook looked at him pityingly. He didn't say anything. There were times when even he felt tongue-tied. He took a good gulp, and decided the kindest thing would be to pretend he hadn't heard the last words. After a minute he went on carefully, "That's why the key was left in, of course, so that if anyone should notice there was a door, it wouldn't strike them as odd. Besides, those are enormous keyholes and the key fitted tight. A desperate man can sometimes open a door if the lock's clear, and there's nothing that blocks the

41

lock so well as its own key. The poor devil's only chance was to push the key out of position from his side of the door and then—but I don't think he could have done it without special tools. Those locks are like bulls. Even Bill (he meant Bill Parsons, his A.D.C. in London, a one-time ace burglar and now working cynically on the side of the angels as personified by Arthur Crook) would have his work cut out. In fact, it may be damn difficult to prove it was murder at all—no sign of a weapon, y'see. . . ."

"It may even turn out that it is not murder," observed the clergyman severely. "Whoever moved the table and drew the bolts may have had every intention of returning and met with some accident. One should consider every possibility."

So innocent an explanation had never occurred to Crook. He wouldn't have believed it could occur to anyone outside Colney Hatch. He began to see why so many sound people have decried charity. He put up his head like a tortoise emerging from its shell.

"What's the black-out time for the church?" he demanded.

The parson—he was the Roger Cupit whose name Crook had found on the little box in the cell of death—understood him at once.

"The church is always open," he said. "There's nothing there worth stealing, and tramps can find more comfortable shelter."

"I'll say they can," said Crook grimly. "You know, if that chap hadn't wanted so much to guard himself he might have got away with it, sworn he didn't shoot the bolts, anything—but the table makes it murder. Come on, let's find a policeman."

"You won't find him here. There isn't much use for the police in a place like this, and they've thinned out the ranks a bit since the war. No, your man is the Deputy Chief Constable—Lord Cleveland up at the Manor."

"They the big noise round here?" asked Crook intelligently.

"The place is named for them." He put some coins on the counter as they left the bar. "There have been Clevelands here for centuries."

"Who was the Bishop?" enquired Crook, wishing he could mount a bicycle as gracefully as his companion, who couldn't be far off seventy.

"He started the legend. I suppose, as you're a stranger here, you

42

haven't heard it. It's known as the Cleveland Curse. The story itself is orthodox enough; the uncanny thing is the way it's fulfilled in every generation. It seems that the Bishop refused to let some beggar into the Palace, as it was then—though what a place this size was doing with a Bishop is more than I can tell you—still, it was a biggish place once. . . ."

He fell into a reverie. Crook avoided a green spotted caterpillar that was drowsing its way across the road. "Don't tell me," he begged. "Let me guess. He was found dead in the snow next day and his real name was the Angel Gabriel."

"Near enough," agreed the rector with a faint smile. "Branch right here. It was then that the Curse was put on the family. They say the eldest son always comes to grief and never inherits."

"Jam being the second son," said the unromantic Mr. Crook. "Mean to say that always happens?"

"It has to date," admitted Mr. Cupit. "One was drowned and one was shot by a resentful husband and one was poisoned and one died in battle and—oh, in one way or another the Curse always operated."

"Of course it did," said Crook robustly. "What else did you expect? Start a story like that and you're asking for trouble. Bring up a man to know he'll never wear his father's shoes and bring up his brother in the expectation of poachin' the birthright and you're hatchin' a murder every time. Why, if anything does happen to the elder brother the whole village says, It was written in the book of words, and lets it go at that. But there it is. Your old families can think up something more damned immoral than any gangster would dare connive at. How about the present heir?"

"He presents a problem," said the Rector, who clearly liked doing the talking. "Though in this case the prophecy's only too likely to be fulfilled. He's twenty-three and in the Army."

"And his brother?"

"There isn't one. That's why I say it's a problem. Apparently it's the first time such a situation has cropped up since the Curse came into force. The old lady—the present Earl's mother, who rules the roost and lets everyone know it—never forgave her daughter-in-law for producing only one son, and then lingering on in a sort of fatuous invalidism for nearly twenty years. When she died she—the dowager, I mean—was all for a second marriage, but the Earl wouldn't. Said he didn't intend to be made a fool of at his age, and it was tempting Providence when he had a son and heir."

"And he was a second son himself, I suppose?" prompted Crook.

"Oh yes. But by a second marriage. There were one son and one daughter by the first marriage. The son, true to tradition, managed to break his neck and the daughter still lives at the Manor, though she's no chicken now, of course. The Earl's nearer fifty than forty and naturally she's older still."

"Spinster?" questioned Crook, and Mr. Cupit nodded. "I don't think I'm giving anything away if I say the two ladies don't get on too well. Not that it would suit the Dowager to have a step-daughter she got on with. Friction's meat and drink to her—gives her a chance to show her mettle. As for Miss Oliver—Oliver's the family name—she says openly that her step-mother always intended her own son to inherit. Why, she even called him Reuben, though it's not a family name, to indicate that he was, as it were, the head of the family."

"And the first son was—eliminated?"

The parson drew his fierce white brows together. "We don't like that word here. He met with an accident. He was an odd, unworldly sort of young fellow. I'd been here a few months when it happened. He liked to go sketching—a regular milksop the old Earl called him —and one of his favourite places was some wild country near a quarry."

Crook groaned. "Some chaps seem born with a suicidal tendency," he observed, "but then it was probably in the family. Besides, if he had any sense of tradition, and they tell me the aristocracy all have it, he'd know it was expected of him to get himself bumped off. Was Sister the only member of the family who had any affection for him?"

"I'm hardly in a position to say that," returned Mr. Cupit more cautiously. "The present Earl was only a schoolboy at the time, too young probably to accept the implications of his own position. There's no doubt, of course, that his half-brother's proposal to marry out of his own class didn't endear him to the family. He was after Elsie Manners, whose mother was originally in the Clevelands' service; she has the village shop now. Edmund pointed out that as no elder son ever inherited it didn't matter if he married a gypsy queen. Anyway the argument didn't lead anywhere, because after a thundering row with the family, during which his step-mother announced that though it might be a marriage in the eyes of God she was more particular, he marched out and went off to his favourite sketching ground and forty-eight hours later he was found with a broken neck at the foot of the quarry. And some time later Mrs. Manners took her daughter away to some place where they weren't known to have a baby whose father the whole village could name. But Elsie didn't come back," he added, "and the old dowager showed her religious convictions by saying it was a judgment on her for loose living."

"I seem to have heard that before," murmured Crook, thinking this young-squire-and-village-maiden stuff was pretty old-fashioned anyway. "Any one decide how exactly he fell off the cliff?"

"There was a lot of talk. There was a fellow called Grigg who wanted the girl, mad about her, in fact. He was Mrs. Manners' nephew and she'd looked after him since he was a shaver, but for all the gratitude she got she might have put him out for the pigs to eat. . . . He disappeared almost immediately after the tragedy and tongues wagged, of course, but nothing was ever proved."

"Gentlemen, these aristocrats of yours," commented Crook, turning through the wrought-iron gates of Cleveland Park and searching the horizon for the House itself. "They do play the game. Though I dare say, if it comes to that, they haven't much choice. What was the verdict?"

"Oh, death by misadventure," said the parson, as if surprised that the question had been put. "He'd been warned more than once not to go too near the edge."

"I bet that came out at the inquest," remarked Crook drily. "All very convenient for Son No. 2. How about the Earl? I suppose he was heartbroken."

Mr. Cupit showed his first sign of embarrassment.

"Oh, people said this and that. The Clevelands aren't exactly popular locally. Too stand-offish. And I dare say the local gossip hadn't endeared Edmund to his father. And everyone knew that

Lady Cleveland was burning to have the place for her son. If she could have broken the entail or bought Edmund out she wouldn't have hesitated. But that was out of the question."

"So the heir's neck was broken instead. How about Sister?"

"She was crazy about her brother to the extent that she backed him against her step-mother, whatever he did. But those two never did get on."

"Still, she's stayed here ever since?"

"I understand she's no means of her own and naturally she wasn't brought up to earn her own living. Besides, she said she wasn't going to be pushed out of her own nest by a cuckoo—that was her exact phrase. I've heard her use it myself."

"Sounds an enlivening existence," suggested Crook.

"There's the present heir, young Simon. She seems to have transferred all her affection to him. I've heard her say quite candidly that though she may not have been able to save the first heir she'll see that nothing happens to the present one, if it costs her her own life."

"Any likelihood that it might?" enquired Crook.

The clergyman took this quite seriously. "I've never heard any speculations as to that."

"And I'd say you didn't miss much," said Crook, kindly. "Is Simon married?"

"He's engaged."

"A local belle?"

"She's a very attractive young lady. I believe they met in London."

"Grandma pleased?"

Really, reflected Mr. Cupit, the fellow had no sense of delicacy at all.

"I'm afraid I don't enjoy the family's confidence to that extent," he said, "This way."

"Though I dare say Simon won't care if she ain't," added Crook, unaware of his blunder. "He can't be cut off with the legendary shilling and even if he were I dare say auntie would come to the rescue."

The old man suddenly unbent again. "Families like the Clevelands don't think of providing for their women," he said. "They look to the other men to do that, and if they don't marry they must expect to reap the rewards of failure."

"Got it all pat, haven't you?" said Crook with genuine admiration. "It's not surprising Sister and Grandma don't get on so well."

"I doubt whether Miss Oliver could lay hands on fifty pounds," said Mr. Cupit skirting a pond with some black and white ducks on it. "Cleveland's not what you'd call a generous man either."

"What does he think about the Curse?"

"Swears he doesn't believe in it. Simon says he doesn't either. But if that's true they must be about the only couple in the village who don't. You should hear old Mrs. Manners on the subject. Believe it or not, she practically crosses herself—and she's no Papist—whenever the Curse is mentioned. I tell you, if half of them believed the Gospel with anything like the zest they believed in the Curse I'd have my name down for a Bishopric."

"And if you'd taken to crime instead of religion," said Crook heartily, "I'd have been delighted to defend you."

The old man tactfully ignored that.

"There are even legends about this church," he went on blandly. "The church at Kings Fossett, I mean. I've never been able to verify the stories, but even if I could prove them all false it wouldn't make a scrap of difference to the villagers."

"What legends?" enquired Crook, kind and sceptical at once.

"They say that some idolators once perpetrated a Black Mass there, and—I don't know if you know the ritualistic details—but actually a girl was supposed to have been murdered. On a windy night you're supposed to be able to hear her shriek right down in the village."

Crook didn't make any comment. Mr. Cupit looked a little embarrassed. "I dare say, living in a town, it all seems incredibly childish to you. Screams, for instance. . . ."

"In a town you have cats," said Crook sensibly. "You don't need to use your imagination. All the same, it's a useful idea. Imagine this poor chap set up a hullabaloo after dark, finding himself locked in and having the wit to know his hours are numbered unless he can get the door broken down, no one would come near the place because they'd think it was the ghost of the murdered girl. That's what X

47

banked on, of course. And the odds are they wouldn't come in the morning either. Ghosts don't function except after dark, do they?"

"You seem to take it all very light-heartedly," said the clergyman with a shudder.

"He didn't look the sort of chap the angels 'ud weep for," Crook pointed out, "and who am I to go one better than the angels? The only thing I don't understand," he added, "is where the corpse comes in? He can't be one of the missing heirs, I suppose?"

Mr. Cupit said curtly that he could not. All the heirs were accounted for. If this were a film, reflected Crook, this would be Edmund Oliver, and when they unearthed his coffin they'd find nothing in it but a lot of stones. But Cupit said that there was a tablet in Bishop Cleveland Church to commemorate him, with the date of his death, April 28, 1912.

"If the quarry hadn't got him the Great War probably would have," said Crook, thinking aloud. "I dare say it isn't so difficult for the Curse to operate as you might suppose."

"This isn't a local man," said Cupit, who was also following his own thoughts. "At least, if he is it's queer no one's been missed."

"It's all Lombard Street to a china orange it's a local murderer, though," Crook pointed out grimly.

"It could be a woman's crime," said Cupit who, unlike Crook, liked to move from step to careful step.

But the lawyer was inclined to disagree. "If so it's a damned clever woman," he said. "Most of the sex are so infernally subtle, and simplicity's the art of crime, and particularly it's the art of murder."

They came to an iron gate set across the path, marked by what Crook called a summer-house and Cupit said was a gazebo. Beyond for the first time the House itself could be seen.

"I'm not surprised they go in for legends here," said Crook handsomely, feeling as though he'd seen all this somewhere before—on a film, most likely. "It's all too feudal for common or garden chaps like me."

"Feudal's about the word," said Cupit, dismounting. "We have to walk our bicycles from here. No one, not even the family, may ride beyond this gate. Don't," he added thoughtfully, "be surprised if they treat you like the man who delivers the meat. It's just part of their old feudal way. Why, they don't even sit with the rest of the congregation in church. They have a separate entrance and a sort of converted chapel, like a glorified theatre box, and they sit on red velvet chairs with tassels, with the tombs of their ancestors behind them, and the coat of arms in front."

Crook, who liked things to be twopence coloured, looked round him appreciatively. It was like something out of a guide-book. On a brilliant pond moved swans looking as though they were made of china; in a paddock a string of red horses with sunburnt manes came streaming down to sniff out the new-comers; the timber was magnificent. Crook wondered how it was they'd kept the axe of the ministerial spoiler off those trees during four years of war, but after all, what's the good of being a seventh Earl if it doesn't bring you any privileges? Nothing was missing but the deer, and he supposed the Ministry of Food had had them.

They stabled their machines at the laurel-framed entrance to the servants' quarters and made their way round to the beautiful front door. A row of wide windows looked over the Park; in the flower-beds bloomed the last roses of the year. A wren hopped experimentally on to the toe of Crook's square brown boot; a toad put up its head and then sank out of sight again, the colour of the earth on which it crouched. It was all in keeping. If you could believe in curses and missing heirs, this was precisely their background.

CHAPTER SIX

. . . One of your antediluvian families;
fellows that the flood could not wash away.
CONGREVE.

THEY MADE THEIR WAY up the long winding drive, that was as clear of weeds, despite the notorious shortage of labour, as though an agricultural Hoover had been used not an hour since. Cupit noticed this and wondered how they did it. More evidence of feudalism, he supposed. Crook was following his own thoughts.

"Suppose the Curse operates again," he enquired, "who comes into the property?"

"There's a cousin, the Earl's contemporary, who's next on the list, assuming that Simon pre-deceases his father and leaves no heir. He's a bachelor, too. He lives with the family at present. He had a big place in Sussex, but the military took it and the Dowager Lady Cleveland, though she's not famous for her affection for her relatives, presumably thought a cousin without encumbrances better than evacuees so he's been here for the past eighteen months."

"Cousin's like love—covers a multitude of meanings," said the graceless Crook. "How does he get on with the other cousin, the sister of the late heir?"

"The moment that man finds himself in a woman's company he's struck dumb," said Mr. Cupit who, decided Crook, would have talked to a bedpost by night if he'd nothing better to talk to—and for all Crook knew he hadn't. "He's like that chap in *David Copperfield*. 'Orses and dorgs is some men's fancy. They're wittles and drink to 'em—lodging, wife and children—reading, writing and 'rithmetic —snuff, tobacker and sleep."

Crook instantly felt that there was one member of the household with whom he would be en rapport, his strong feeling about women out-weighing a mild disinclination for the company of horses.

At last they reached the haughty front door and after they had waited an appropriate time on the step a servant admitted them and left them to stand in the hall. This was, to a connoisseur, a magnificent panelled vista, with stairs stretching upward, apparently for ever, and passages that led to invisible quarters where once armies of scrofulous serfs had been housed (thus Crook who liked everything a bit larger than life). From the opposite wall an arrogant dark face looked disdainfully at the visitors; there were more portraits along the corridors. The place indeed seemed populated with dead and gone Clevelands.

Crook, however, was not impressed. "They could sell this site lock, stock and barrel to an amusement palace," he suggested. "The Hall of the Winds. Odd how it's never possible to be cosy and aristocratic, and I dare say the Earl matches the furniture."

Someone laughed. Crook turned sharply. A girl had appeared

from nowhere, it seemed, and was standing at his elbow. He wasn't easily impressed by women, and he didn't like them. He said they didn't like him either, and that was his luck, but it wasn't true. They mightn't take to him at first sight, because the most besotted mother could never have christened him Romeo, but it was astounding how many females, particularly the elderly and undesired, found themselves thinking comfortably that if Mr. Crook had their affairs in hand they could stop bothering. He never remembered them himself till Christmas came round, and brought a lot of cards signed with names he believed he'd forgotten.

But this girl was different. It wasn't just that she was pretty or even that she was smartly dressed. The world's full of smart pretty girls, coping efficiently, being courageous and gay, and you meet them and forget the next minute. But he knew at once this was the sort of girl you wouldn't forget. She had one of those perfect oval faces you read about and hardly ever see. Her eyes were green under fair smooth brows, and her fair hair was drawn away above her ears and over the back of her head and lay in a little row of curls horizontally along the middle of her scalp. It ought to have made her look like a skinned rabbit, but it didn't. It made you draw your breath rather sharply and look again. She had a pale clear skin, and her mouth was large and pale too.

Crook's reaction was characteristic. "God help Simon," he thought, "if this is Simon's girl."

Oh, she was lovely, but she was strange, too. If you could imagine a beautiful witch, this was the way she would look. There was something about her—without speech or movement she beckoned. She'd take a man's will and his heart and his life; he'd feel them flowing out as you watch water flowing from an overturned jug. Even Crook, who liked to think he was impervious to young women, felt a little uncomfortable.

"Is the Earl in, Stella?" asked Mr. Cupit, who was presumably accustomed to this startling young creature. "We want to see him."

"I expect Bates has gone to tell him. Are you staying here, Mr. . . . ?"

"Crook," said Cupit, doing the honours.

51

"The Human Hyena," added Crook gravely. "No, I'm just passing through and dropping in to talk to the Earl about a matter of local interest."

"Are you a journalist?" asked the young beauty innocently. Cupit had thought the same thing. They had some rum-looking journalists in this part of the world evidently, reflected Crook. Stella was watching him. He had the feeling she was like an archer, her bowstring taut, arrow quivering. Say something she didn't like and you'd find the arrow in your heart. If the old lady really believed in this ridiculous legend you'd think she couldn't encompass its fulfilment better than by letting the heir marry the girl.

"Not exactly," said Crook guardedly, in answer to her question. "I've just been talking to the Reverend about this and that."

She moved, and it was as though an icicle winged through the air and struck your heart. The atmosphere seemed to freeze.

"And I suppose he's told you about the legend and you think it's romantic and would do for a column. Quaint Survivals of our Countryside. Superstition among the Savages. Well, write what you please, but I tell you one thing. However often that Curse may have worked in the past, it isn't going to work where Simon is concerned. He doesn't believe in it and nor do I. When people knew about our engagement I could feel them all looking at me in an odd sort of way —oh yes they did, Mr. Cupit, and you know it. I don't say you believe that legend yourself, because you wouldn't think it right, but even you. . . . If I'd said I was going to marry a man under sentence of death they'd have looked like that."

"Well, pipe down," said Crook sensibly. "Suppose they did? Isn't that just what you are going to do? Isn't it true of us all?"

"I don't say strange things haven't happened in the past," the girl went on passionately, "but if they have it's because—someone— meant them to. And what people mean desperately they generally get. I know that. The trouble was that there never seems to have been any one in the picture meaning just the opposite and meaning it even more hard. That's the difference where Simon's concerned. Whoever is against Simon has got me against them. I don't just sit down helplessly and say, If there's a Curse there's nothing more to be said. I don't believe in the Curse, but if it does exist then I'll show it it can't have things all its own way."

She stopped, breathless, leaving her audience dumb. That girl, thought Crook, could beat Nancy Astor at her own game. Young Simon was going to have his work cut out controlling that. And how infernally lucky for him that she was agin the Curse·and not for it. He wouldn't stand an earthly chance.

A door upstairs opened and someone began to descend. A voice said unemotionally, "Stella, my sister's asking for you. You might see what she wants."

The seventh Earl came into view round the bend of the staircase. He was a strongly-built man rather below average height, with dark hair thinly sleeked across the top of his head; his features looked as though they had been modelled in plasticine and put in the appropriate places. They were suitable enough—the nose was powerful, the mouth long and thin, the eyes sharp, even piercing. But, put together, they didn't, thought Crook in his odd way, make a face; they weren't related; they were like a machine without an engine. He was instantly intrigued by the seventh Earl.

The girl had disappeared as noiselessly as she had come. He didn't even know where she had gone, but he would swear it wasn't upstairs to Miss Oliver's room.

"Anything I can do for you, Rector?" the Earl continued, not offering to shake hands and not betraying by even a glance in the stranger's direction that he realized Crook was there at all.

"This is Mr. Crook," said Cupit placidly. He seemed accustomed to the odd personalities at the Manor. "He's wanting to see you. He's a lawyer," he added, though Crook couldn't remember having told him that.

The Earl nodded. He didn't look interested. His air suggested that some men had to be lawyers just as others were scavengers, and he classed them in much the same category, different in degree but not in essence.

"And the Reverend here tells me you're the Deputy Chief Constable," added Crook, quite unruffled by his mannerless reception.

That did strike a spark.

"Well?" said the Earl sharply.

"Could we go into your study or somewhere a little more private?" suggested Cupit, as untroubled as his companion.

"It's about the church at Kings Fossett," Crook explained when they were all three seated in one of the most soulless and uncomfortable rooms he had ever occupied. "I understand you're the patron."

"Well?" repeated Lord Cleveland impatiently. "I should have supposed Mr. Cupit could have told you anything you needed to know. As a matter of fact, the church is very little used. I'm surprised to hear a stranger has even gone into it."

"Which means you'd be twice as surprised to hear two strangers have gone into it quite recently, and one of them ain't coming out again."

Cleveland moved an ink-pot from one side of the table to the other.

"You mean—a tramp or someone has broken in and . . ." He paused. He meant, "Died of starvation, I suppose," and thought how damned inconsiderate these worthless members of the community are. What are ditches for if not for tramps to die in?

"Don't you ever have any decent chaps in this part of the world?" asked Crook curiously. "Mind, I don't say he wasn't a tramp. He could certainly do with a shave. But tramps don't generally go around with thirty pounds in their pockets."

The Earl moved the inkpot back again. "Mr. Crook, will you kindly come to the point. What are you trying to say?"

"I'm trying to tell you it's a murder," said Crook in his politest tones. "Oh yes, it is. It could have been an accident if it hadn't been for the table in front of the door, but that stamps it. And I don't suppose you like murder any better than the rest of us."

He began to add a detail or two, but he hadn't spoken more than half a dozen words when there was a second interruption, as sudden as the girl Stella's had been, and a deal more noisy. Cleveland had left the door ajar, and while they were talking someone had come into the hall, and now burst into the room. She was a woman of ripe middle-age—she hasn't had to register, was Crook's way of putting it—and she had one of those weather-beaten faces that can never have looked really young. He put her down at once—correctly—as the spinster step-daughter. Her hair was thick and hardly touched

54

with grey but no one had taught her how to arrange it. She was powdered in an abrupt sort of way, wore the sort of clothes you'd expect from her face, and had the large square hands of the Clevelands. No, thought Crook, it wasn't the sort of face he'd want to see over the breakfast-table, and he couldn't imagine anyone trying to hold her hand in the pictures. Looking from her to the Earl he thought it would be a neck-and-neck race, though on the whole it might prove that the female of the species was more deadly than the male, because she had rather less to lose. She swept into the room and stopped in front of her half-brother.

"What are you talking about?" she demanded.

It was pretty obvious to Crook that the Earl was accustomed to indoor fireworks. He didn't change his expression as he said in a forbidding sort of voice, "Mr. Crook came to see me about the church at Kings Fossett."

She didn't even pretend to believe him. Her voice was rather like his, deep and abrupt, and she made no attempt to lower it as she said, "The word was murder. I heard it. You can't gammon me."

"It's hardly surprising he didn't want a third woman in the household," Crook reflected, but he was interested all the same. The anæmic aristocracy that coloured—but oh, how faintly—the Manor's tepid air—gained vitality with the arrival of this rather alarming female.

"My dear Rhoda," began the Earl, but she said again, "What was it you were talking about? All I want to know is—Is it anything to do with Simon?"

Her fierce gaze raked them all. Crook remembered the Rector's story. Simon was the young heir she'd sworn to save if it cost her her own life.

"If you mean the young gentleman," he said in what he intended to be soothing tones, "it can't be him. This chap'll never see fifty again."

"Why didn't you say so before?" demanded Miss Oliver, paying about as much attention to Crook as her brother had done, and staring in a hostile manner at the Earl. "So long as it's not Simon you can murder half the village for all I care. They couldn't be much deader than they are now."

She swept out again. It was obvious that she wasn't interested in the corpse. So long as her beloved nephew was safe she didn't care a button. Crook was often astounded by the lack of enterprise of the well-to-do; lived in a narrow rut and didn't even notice what was going on round them. You'd think ordinary chaps like himself and this fellow in the vestry at Kings Fossett didn't belong to the same world. And probably from her point of view they didn't. He wasn't resentful; he was just damned sorry. People like that missed such a lot of fun. The Earl was staring at the ink-pot as though he was willing it to disintegrate before their eyes.

"Nice sense of family!" suggested Crook politely, feeling it was time somebody spoke.

The Earl looked as though his collar was a bit too small for him. He got up, saying something about the car. He didn't ask whether it was convenient for the other two to fall in with his plans. He felt about them as his half-sister felt about the dead man.

"They're all a bit mad about the Curse here," explained Cupit. "I warned you."

"I notice they're all damned anxious I shall realize they don't mean the Curse to work this time," agreed Crook. I'm beginning to wonder what that means."

CHAPTER SEVEN

Thou canst not say I did it; never shake
Thy gory locks at me.

MACBETH.

SOMETHING HAD HAPPENED during the short interval that had elapsed between Crook's first visit to Kings Fossett and his second. The time had been something under an hour, but in the meantime the village had waked up and almost, said the incorrigible Crook, turned out a royal guard to meet the aristocracy. As the car, driven by its owner, came up the narrow village street, faces appeared at windows and bodies at doors to watch them pass. The Man With A Gun was still

closed, but someone was messing about in the outer yard. The sunflowers quivered in their beds and behind the gate where Crook
had last seen the idiot a flock of cows had collected and gave them the
V sign as they went through.

Only the church seemed utterly unchanged and remote.

The party left the car and wended their way between the untended
graves and came once more into the neglected ice-cold building.
Some chap must have got his notion of a refrigerator from a church
like this, thought Crook, as they walked solemnly up the nave and
came to the chancel. He would have shifted the table, but Cupit,
who seemed suddenly to assume a priestly authority, stopped him.

"I will do that," he said, and the two younger men stood aside and
watched him lift the table—it was very light, an old woman or a
child could have handled it—and withdraw the bolt and pull back
the curtain. There was no dramatic hesitation about opening the
door either. Even when he stood beside the huddled body and noted
the bloodmarks on the wall where the poor wretch had made his last
fight for life, there was no change in the thin intellectual face. He
kept his eyes half-shut, so, if there was any expression in them, his
companions couldn't see it. Crook, with unwonted modesty, hung
back, but Cleveland pushed past and stooped over the body. There
was a slightly puzzled look on his face, but as he straightened himself
he only said briefly, "He's a stranger to this part of the world. It may
have been an accident, after all."

Crook was impressed by that, he spoke with so much assurance.
In London, of course, nine hundred and ninety-nine people out of a
thousand whom you meet are strangers, but in the country Lord
Cleveland, though he didn't give you the idea of being a sympathetic
or friendly person—nothing cosy about him any more than there
was about his house—knew his people as he knew the pictures on his
own wall. Cupit, on the other hand, looked thoughtful. It was
obvious that here, at least, he knew more than his temporal lord.

"How the devil we're going to find out who the chap was—unless
he's got any identity marks on him," Cleveland continued, and
Crook interrupted, "None. That is, no cards or letters. I don't know
about birth-marks."

Cleveland was emptying the pockets. "He wasn't without funds, that's one thing. And whoever shut him up here didn't do it for theft . . . Looks like a sailor. . . ."

"Ever met a sailor with over thirty pounds in his pocket all this way from a pub?" enquired Cupit. "Besides, even in the munificent days of war we don't pay our merchant seamen on that scale. Also, a man with that much in his pocket doesn't go to bed in an empty church." He spoke grimly. He was on all the War Committees—the British Legion, S.S.A.F.A., S.S.H.S., C.A.B.—he didn't believe that hearts just as brave and fair may beat in Berkeley Square as in the purer air of Seven Dials. To him Seven Dials would always be a lot nearer the Kingdom of Heaven than Park Lane

"We ought to get the police," said Cleveland, pushing the dead man's possessions back into his pocket. His voice said that a man who claimed to be a lawyer should have thought of that in the first place. "I'll ring up Horsfall and ask for Isaacs. After all, it's for them to find out who the fellow is."

"Just a minute," said Crook, who had been watching the third member of the party. "I fancy the Reverend may be able to tell you that without bothering about fingerprints or anything. Now then, Padre, out with it."

"What?" murmured the Rector. He looked vaguely surprised, as though he had forgotten there was any one there.

"You heard," said Crook.

"It was so long ago," explained Cupit. "I might easily be mistaken. All the same, I think I'd better get Mrs. Manners." He didn't offer any further explanation, just turned and left them there, walking back down the nave, a long thin slice of a man with an odd impression of strength for all his physical fragility.

Cleveland, who clearly didn't believe in wasting words, watched him go, and then ostentatiously forgot Crook's existence. Crook wondered if there was time to slip out for a quick one, then remembered this was the village's drinkless day and anyhow his companion would doubtless put the worst construction on his action, and stayed where he was. He didn't have long to wait. After about a minute the Rector returned, accompanied by a little creature who looked as though she moved by clockwork. She was very small—like a little black bird with downbent head and old, old hands holding a big black bag. When she got nearer and he saw her face he knew—because he could recognize fear in all its guises—how desperately afraid she was.

She came up to the body and stood staring for a moment, one black-gloved hand over her mouth. Then she whispered, "Ay, it's Tom all right. But how this could have happened. . . ." Her voice died away, choked by a sort of passionate despair.

"Did you expect it to be Tom, whoever Tom may be?" demanded Cleveland, and Crook's mind said quickly, "Leading question! The dirty dog!"

Cupit said in a calm voice, "I asked you to come here in case you could help us by identifying the body," and she said, "It's my nephew, Tom Grigg. He came back last week and hid here. . . ."

"Why hid?" demanded the Earl.

"He was in a bit of trouble. He thought I might help him. But I had my grandson with me, so I couldn't keep Tom in the house."

"And you hid him here? Knowing he was wanted by the police—because that's about the size of it, isn't it!"

She said, "Yes, sir," so simply you'd have thought Cleveland might have softened, but you'd soften cement before you'd melt him.

"That's accessory after the fact," said the Earl sternly, and Cupit, who might fear God but certainly didn't fear the peerage, broke in, "As you observed just now, my lord, all that's a matter for the police. It came over me this might be Tom Grigg—he left the neighbourhood soon after I came here—and thought we might as well make sure. That's all."

Cleveland said, "I've heard the name, of course, but I shouldn't have known him. I was at Eton when he left the neighbourhood, and of course he's changed."

"Mrs. Manners and I remember him better than you do," agreed Cupit, taking the old woman by the arm as though he was afraid she would fall. None of them took the smallest notice of Crook. The clannishness of village life had never been more apparent. To them he was a Londoner, the townee, the common or garden tourist who couldn't listen to the Government's appeal to make this a stay-at-home holiday, but had to go prancing out into fresh woods and pastures new, and so had blundered on to something that was going to make trouble for more loyal citizens. Crook could read all that with his eyes shut.

Cleveland, who had no intention of being put in his place by a mere clergyman, continued his inquisition.

"You admit you knew he was here. When did you last see him alive?" he demanded.

"Thursday in the middle of the day. I went to bring him some money. That was what he wanted and then he was going."

"How much did you give him?" The words rattled out like machine-gun bullets."

"Thirty pounds," whispered Mrs. Manners. "It's all I could spare. I had Ted to think of, you see."

"And—er—Ted. He knew—or at least guessed. . . ."

"He didn't know anything," she defended quickly. "Why if he had he'd have gone straight to the police. You could always count on Ted to do his duty."

"I see," said Cleveland, who might have been the original robot. "Well, there's clearly only one thing to be done."

"Sure," agreed Crook, jumping in where any angel might be forgiven for fearing to tread, "find out who saw Mr. Grigg after his auntie did. A chap like that probably had more enemies than just the law."

"The law?" said Cleveland, and Crook replied simply. "Don't you ever see the papers? This is the chap they wanted for the stabbing affair at Swansea."

"That's not to say he did it," Mrs. Manners defended the dead man. "Oh, I know what they think. But before—there was trouble when the heir got himself killed. People talked, but it was an accident. The Crowners Quest said so."

"Then you can be darn sure it was—an accident, I mean." Crook supported her heartily. "Take the word of a man who knows. You can spread your evidence on the table as plain as sausages in a pan but if the Court don't choose to be lookin' the right way—well, the pan's empty. . . . Edmund Oliver died of a fall, the Reverend himself told me so. Well, what's that got to do with a man bein' found dead in a vestry?"

Cupit alone of the four seemed to realize at this juncture where they all were.

"I take it, my lord, we shouldn't meddle with things till the authorities have been informed," he said, "but I don't know that we need go on discussing this very tragic happening just here."

"We shall attract considerably more attention if we discuss it anywhere else," replied Cleveland in the same unemotional voice. "But we'll come down to the bottom of the church, if you like."

They walked down in single file. Cleveland went first, then Cupit, then the old woman, then Crook. As they stepped into the nave over the ragged carpet that covered the three steps leading out of the sanctuary, Mrs. Manners stumbled. Crook caught her by the elbow.

"Take it easy," he said. He felt her body stiffen with fierce resolution.

"She's as scared as a hen," he reflected. "I wonder how much she knows and how much she's going to tell."

Coming alongside, he said out of the corner of his mouth, "I'm a lawyer and what I say goes. You don't have to answer any questions you don't want to—see? This is a free country and considerin' what we're payin' to keep it free someone may as well draw some dividends."

But she could be as impenetrable as Cleveland himself. Gently she withdrew her elbow from Crook's firm grasp.

"Thank you, sir," she said. "I hope I know my duty. Of course, I should never have agreed in the first place. . . ."

Cupit said over his shoulder, "We can talk in the porch. No one's likely to see us there."

Cleveland thrust his hands deep into his pockets. Crook, watching him curiously while Mrs. Manners told her story, saw that the fingers were bunched together into tight little fists. He was able to put two and two together as the recital went on. This chap, Ted, was clearly related to the Manor crowd, on the wrong side of the blanket.

"You wouldn't want him brought into it," added Mrs. Manners when Cleveland seemed inclined to do some brow-beating on his own account. "Not seeing who he is."

Cleveland straightened himself. "I see no reason why he should be involved, since you assure me he knew nothing of your nephew's

61

return. Naturally, if I had any cause to doubt that statement I should not be able to exclude him from the case." In such a mood, thought Crook, had the Grand Inquisitor sent men to the auto-da-fe. The chap wouldn't recognize compassion if he saw it served up on toast. Mrs. Manners' face hurt you to look at. That was on Ted's account not Tom's. It occurred to him that they had a sort of obsession about young men in this part of the world—Miss Oliver with her darling Simon and this old lady with her precious Ted.

"Was it you who sent the police to the Manor?" enquired Cleveland suddenly. "On Wednesday night, I mean."

"I said I didn't think it was likely he'd come that way, only it was your father helped him before. After Mr. Edmund died, I mean."

Cleveland drew a sharp breath. "I know nothing of any of that. I was at school at the time. You do realize, of course, you've put yourself hopelessly in the wrong concealing Grigg's return from the authorities?"

She hadn't any answer. Crook, who wasn't accustomed to being overlooked, said, "Oh come, my lord, the black sheep's never been the most welcome guest. I don't know that you and I would go out with open arms to meet the family skeleton."

The Earl looked at him with suspicion and anger. "Is there any particular significance in that, Mr. Crook? Are you suggesting that my family had any reason to fear this man's return?"

"I wouldn't know," said Crook simply, "but I thought all bang-up families had a skeleton." He rose from the mossy stone slab on which they were seated. "It's a bit cold on this tombstone or whatever it is," he explained.

"We had better go along to Horsfall," agreed Cleveland, rising also. "You had better accompany us, Mrs. Manners."

But the old lady surprised them all by saying, "I'm sorry, my lord, but I can't leave the shop any longer. It's not as if I can tell the gentleman any more than I have already."

"You'll have to make a statement to the authorities," argued Cleveland impatiently.

"Then they can come to me," said Mrs. Manners, firmly. "The Labour Office has taken my only girl, and you can't expect people to go without their rations because I've gone gallivanting into Horsfall."

"Your duty," said Cleveland, but she interrupted him in her gentle, obstinate way, "My duty, sir, is to my customers. I've got to be getting back now. The police'll know where to find me."

Crook wondered what she wanted to destroy, whom she wanted to warn.

"You'd better lock the church, Rector, and we'll take the key with us," Cleveland continued. "We don't want any other tourists coming in and making inconvenient discoveries."

The look he gave Crook was sheer poison.

CHAPTER EIGHT

1 Corinthian, a lad of mettle, a good boy.
KING HENRY IV.

1

"THERE'S MORE IN THIS than meets the eye," reflected Crook, who was partial to a cliché. "Still waters run deep. I might do worse than watch that old dame."

He had been to Horsfall and repeated his story, agreed to be present at the inquest the following day, returned to the Hall and collected his bicycle, said good-bye to the Earl without regrets on either side, seen his wan hopes of being offered a drink dwindle and disappear, and now he and the parson were cycling back through the Park.

He was aware that he hadn't created a favourable impression in a single quarter. When he picked up his machine he had had a glimpse of the old lady, as fierce as the old Queen and as proud as Lucifer; the alarming Miss Oliver was with her, and they were examining the grass that bordered the drive as though they intended to count every fallen leaf and assess its probable value as leaf-mould in days to come. Miss Oliver towered above her step-mother, yet there wasn't much doubt which of them ruled the roost.

"A jolly household," suggested Crook in heartfelt tones as they left the sacred precincts behind them and emerged on to the right of way. "Don't the ladies ever give one another a clear field?"

63

"It's like a steeplechase," confessed the old man. "Naturally old Lady Cleveland thinks she owns the village. Everything that's being done must be done under her ægis. In a sense, it's her war in these parts. She's the head of the Red Cross and the Savings Society and the Salvage Committee and the District Visitors and the R.S.P.C.A. Miss Oliver does her best but she has to go further afield. Now, she has the W.V.S. in Kings Fossett, though the old lady would take that away from her, too, if she could. But though she's game she's past cycling and of course petrol's rationed, so Miss Oliver goes swinging out practically before breakfast every Friday and puts the fear of God into all her volunteers and really gets some work done, and when she comes back she nearly drives the old lady mad telling her what they've achieved, until, of course, she has to stop for breath and then the old lady has an innings. She gets her own back by saying what's she done locally and if she can upset a plan of Miss Oliver's she feels she's scored a bull's-eye. I should think young Simon will find the Middle East a rest-cure by comparison."

Crook, who'd fought in France in the last war and didn't in his heart think much of a race that had had four years to put a bullet in him and had missed him every time, didn't agree. You could say this and that about a war, but you couldn't pretend it was a picnic.

He and the Rector parted a little later; Crook thought he might have been offered something, if only a cup of cold water, but it was evident that his luck was out. He pedalled sturdily home, reflecting sagely that if he'd walked he'd only have had himself to carry, whereas now, most of the time, since the road lay up hill, he was carrying the bicycle as well. It was a relief when he found himself sitting snugly in the bar of the Duck and Dragon, talking to the landlord's father, a hale old gentleman of eighty who, he assured Crook, had known Tom Grigg as a boy. It didn't take him long to realize that the Old 'Un had an imagination that wouldn't have disgraced a novelist, while the bare mention of the Cleveland Curse set him off like a drunkard on the slippery slope.

The story of the discovery of the dead man was all over the village, and Crook was looked at enviously as the chap who had found him. Crook, who was used to publicity, and who had got it into his obstinate head that the two mysterious deaths were linked, was pumping the old boy for all he was worth.

"I mind 'un," declared the informant, nodding a head that wouldn't have disgraced a Roman coin. "Everyone round-about know about that. Every generation it works out true as the Book. And this 'ull be the same, no matter what they say up at the Manor."

"They don't believe in it, in spite of all the evidence?" suggested Crook, saying, "Same again," to the lady behind the bar.

"I reckon his Lordship thinks the Almighty wouldn't set Himself up agin him, but he'll learn. Never the eldest son inherits, that's the Curse and he won't, you mark my words."

Crook couldn't help thinking it was uncommonly likely, seeing the expectation of life of the average young man in wartime. But he only said, "And it's always accident, isn't it?"

The Old 'Un picked up his glass, looked at it thoughtfully and drained it at a gulp.

"What has to be has to be. And no one can be sure about accidents, can they?"

"I can see Caution is your middle name," Crook congratulated him. "Still, just between the two of us—take the last accident now—the one who fell into Lost Man's Quarry—what do you think of that?"

"I think there's times a body feels he might lend Providence a hand," ventured the Old 'Un.

"Any particular body?" pressed Crook.

"I wouldn't know," said the Old 'Un, "but 'tis no use flying in the face of Providence, and if Providence says a chap won't step into his father's shoes, then he never will. There's no bringing a man back from the dead, and everyone knew it was bound to come."

You couldn't, Crook decided, argue with that sort of mentality. He felt like an ardent missionary confronted by an equally ardent heathen; there was no making any headway either direction.

"There's a rumour that Tom Grigg had a hand in it," he suggested slamming down a trump card.

"If so tes Providence," said the old man calmly. "But if Tom Grigg killed a man for the sake of a lass like Elsie Manners he's more of a fool than I took 'un for. Everyone knew she was goin' with the young gentleman. . . ."

"Including Tom Grigg?"

"She never had a fair word for him. Mind you, she'd not have took him nohow. I'm sure of that. She was never my choice. I like a gel to be soft and kind of pretty. Elsie was a little bit of a thing as full of spirit as a Dartmoor pony. And the way she'd look at Tom, as if she had to wash her face when he'd been staring at her. I reckon it riled him."

"You presumably are a bit riled before you push a gentleman off the edge of a cliff," said Crook.

"No one saw 'un," protested the old man. "And I reckon Tom's neck was worth more than any gel to him. He could take his pick hereabouts, but the silly chap must fix on Elsie Manners. And anyway I don't believe it was him."

He stood up as he spoke. It was clear the gentleman wasn't going to be good for a third drink and there might be a more generous fellow in the other bar.

"Who are you backing for the Murder Mile?" Crook enquired as he reached the door.

The old man looked balefully over his shoulder. "Who benefits?" he demanded. "That's what I always say, Who benefits when the young gentleman was killed? And who benefits by Tom's death? You tell me that and I'll tell 'ee who killed 'un."

He shuffled noisily out. Crook absently called for more beer.

"That's a true bill," he told himself. "Well, who does?"

He didn't know much. Mrs. Manners had said the present Earl's father had paid Tom Grigg to clear out; that might mean something. Still, if Tom committed the murder it didn't seem probable that the family would reward him financially. That looked as though he knew a bit too much and had been putting the screw on. And who benefited now? The old lady, of course, to some extent, but mightn't it be that someone else benefited still more? If he'd had a secret when he left the country thirty years ago, he might hold that secret still. And though time wears out many things secrets are like first editions —they're often more valuable when they're thirty years old. He thought he might be able to find an account of the heir's death and the inquest in the local paper if the records went back so far. Because it didn't occur to Mr. Crook that he could be in at the beginning of a murder story and be elbowed out of it before the end.

2

The inquest had been fixed for the following afternoon; the police had wanted it in the morning but the coroner couldn't get over. The Methodist Hall, so often the centre of good clean fun in the shape of whist drives and jumble sales, was fixed for the occasion. At about twelve o'clock Crook wheeled out his iron steed, as Timothy Tramp affectionately called a bicycle, and went over to call on Mrs. Manners. She had closed the shop at midday as a mark of respect, and he found her already wearing her severe black straw hat and her black and white silk scarf, waiting to start for the ordeal. When she saw him she looked surprised—surprised and helpless. She had already had one visitor that morning—the Reverend Roger Cupit.

"If there's anything I can do to help be sure to call on me," he had said. And she had stared, because when life's at its worst no one can ever do anything about it. When Elsie was dying, when young Ted had scarlet fever and they didn't think they'd pull him through, at every crisis in life you stood alone. And what Mr. Crook wanted she couldn't imagine. She was more tired than she had ever been in her life, and yet she was glad it was him. Every time any one went by she thought it might be young Ted, and what good could he do coming to the inquest and being a further witness to her perjury. Because what she'd told the two policemen that night was as good as perjury and you could get put in prison for that.

"Don't freeze me out," begged Crook, wishing she'd taken him into the kitchen rather than the parlour. He was never at home in parlours; he said they made him feel like someone wearing a suit a size too small for him. The old lady was watching him, looking like something out of an etching, as clear-cut as though she'd been shaped with a pair of scissors. "I want to give you a bit of advice," he said. "Remember, I'm the professional. You're new to all this. Not had much to do with the police in your time, I take it—apart from Ted."

67

She said with a dignity he found rather moving, "I've always kept myself to myself," and he thought, "Yes, but that's what you all say. It can't be true of you. Everyone knows about your daughter and the heir. You can't have enjoyed that much."

"Look here," he said aloud, crossing his pudgy legs, "you're in a spot. You do realize that. Oh, you can look like Queen Victoria's twin sister till the cows come home, but it won't help you, not when you're in the witness-box."

She sat bolt upright, so still that she shook. "I don't understand you," she whispered.

"That's what I say," explained Crook, leaning forward and putting out one huge hand towards her as though he offered her security on its palm. "You ought to have a solicitor to watch the case for you. If you're thinking a good conscience will see you through take the word of the man who's never wrong—it doesn't work that way. What the world's going to say is 'Could he have done it himself?' and we darn well know he couldn't. Then they'll say 'Could it be an accident?' and your jury's goin' to be even more chuckle-headed than most if they believe that. Then, don't you see, they'll say 'Who wanted him out of the way? Who was he dangerous to?' and—well, even a country jury can add two and two when it's written out in front of them on a slate."

"You mean, you think they'll say I—why, I wouldn't have done a thing like that to a living soul. And in a church and all."

"The jury's job will be to find someone with more reason for wantin' Tom Grigg out of the way and what's more with the chance to do it. I dare say it wouldn't be hard to find the first, but the second's another matter. If you could show that someone else knew where you'd hidden the chap. . . ."

"I can't," she said. "Is it really as bad as that?"

But she didn't seem to take it in, even now. "I'm a lawyer," he pointed out, "I know my onions, so if there's anything I can do later on—I know the police and their nasty sneakin' ways. All that matters to a policeman is to make a cop. He don't care if it's the King of England or a nark from Shore-ditch. His reputation depends on how often he gets his man and his promotion depends on his reputation, and his pay depends on his promotion—like the steps of Jacob's ladder," he added a little hazily.

Mrs. Manners had already recovered her self control. The moment of terror was past.

"It's very kind of you, sir," she said, "but I don't need to pay a man to help me to the truth." Crook caught back a quick exclamation. Truth may make the devil blush but that doesn't mean the devil doesn't frequently get the best of it. "That's all I need to do," the poor woman went on, knowing no better. If looks were hatchets the coroner would have had a second inquest on his hands by the time he reached Kings Fossett. "So it's kind of you, but I'll do nicely, I'm sure."

"It don't do to be proud," Crook warned her sadly. "You know what they say about advertised goods—look at the trade mark and buy the stuff that lasts. I dare say you think a lawyer's got to sport white slips to his vest and dangle an eyeglass on a monocle to be any good, but it ain't so. If you can deliver the goods you don't need all that fancy-dress. I aim to please—the client, see? And there's only one way of pleasing a client and that's by provin' he didn't do it, even if he thinks he did. And," he added gracefully, "seeing I started this racket—I'm like the elephant's child, insatiable curiosity, you know —this'll be on the house."

He grabbed up his brown bowler from under the chair where he'd put it when he came in, and left her. She looked a bit dazed and he wasn't surprised. But he didn't think she was thinking of her own safety, as any ordinary selfish, decent person would have done. All she was worrying about was how it was going to affect Ted.

3

Everyone who could get away came to the inquest. It was like a free show. The old men came because they remembered the young Tom Grigg and had most of them prophesied that he'd come to no good; others came because they knew Mary Anne Manners or because they wanted a glimpse of Crook, who'd livened up the village as it hadn't been livened up in twenty years. The Cleveland family came in force, presumably because they felt they should support the head of the family. They filed in solemnly with as much gravity as though they were assembling in their familiar private chapel in the church and it seemed natural that they should be given ring seats. Lady Cleveland came first, in dead black, seventy-two and as tough as new-killed meat, looking as though she were attending Divine Service and was doing the Almighty a favour by consenting to be present. The Earl followed her, outraged because it was Tuesday and he always went to town on Tuesday. It seemed to him fantastic that they couldn't postpone the inquest by twenty-four hours at the bidding of a man who was both an Earl and the Deputy Chief Constable, but it appeared that the ridiculous English law favoured the coroner, a fact that put his Lordship in a shocking temper to start with, a fact that became increasingly obvious as the inquest proceeded.

After the Earl came his half-sister, mannish and scowling, muttering in her deep masculine voice to the cousin, who came next, and ignoring the strange disturbing girl who needn't have come at all.

The cousin was a tall slightly stooping man, his hair thinning a little on the top of his head, wearing excellent clothes and having a manner that seemed to set him apart from everyone else. He looked, decided Crook, like a spectator, and all things considered the lawyer respected him for being able to create such an impression.

The case went with a swing from the start. The coroner, a disagreeable man called Hackworth, made no bones of his dislike of all the witnesses in turn. He examined Crook with great suspicion, purporting not to understand why he should have been in the church at all. Crook courteously explained about Timothy Tramp; the coroner consigned Timothy Tramp to the outer darkness with the dogs and idolators. He wanted to know why Crook had felt suspicious and Crook said that it was what was known as feminine intuition. The coroner snorted, and Crook said it was like being a publisher and knowing which book to publish and which to refuse, even though it might be difficult to give reasons for your choice. A sixth sense warned you. The coroner said icily that some publishers didn't heed their sixth sense.

The doctor said that Grigg must have been dead for some days—two or three anyway—and since Crook had been in London all the previous week even the coroner had—albeit reluctantly—to drop him out of the list of possible murderers. But you could see he suspected that a man with a gift of the gab like Crook might conceivably be in two places simultaneously. But nothing really spectacular happened until Mrs. Manners was called. The atmosphere was instantly flavoured with excitement. No matter how respectable she might appear or how honest a record she possessed, there was no getting away from the fact that she had deliberately bamboozled the law. They didn't blame her for it—the Law like the Treasury is most people's natural enemy—but still, she had hidden away a man the police were seeking and sworn she'd never seen him. The fact that you, obviously, didn't betray your own flesh and blood was not permitted to affect the issue. None of the villagers believed their kith and kin could be wanted by the police for murder.

Crook had wondered how his prospective client would take the mannerless staccato of the coroner's examination, but he need not have been afraid. Mrs. Manners wore her usual dignified air and she answered everything in a slow simple way—no attempt to score off her questioner or be subtle. Just as she stepped into the improvised witness-box there was a slight disturbance and young Simon Oliver entered the court, wearing uniform. He caught his father's eye, nodded and dropped into an inconspicuous seat at the back of the hall. The coroner, after a cold glance, returned to his questioning. The villagers were thrilled. Something must be in the wind to bring a young man back from military duty at such a juncture of the war.

Mrs. Manners faced her ordeal with a courage that even the hardened Crook found moving. She admitted recognizing the dead man, she admitted concealing him in the church; yes, she knew the officers were after him, but what else could you do? Yes, she'd told them she didn't know whether he'd come to Kings Fossett or not, but you couldn't give up your own blood. Yes, she was aware it was against the law, but her voice and her manner said there was an older law yet, and that law you obey with your instinct and your heart. She hadn't thought he would be there more than just that one evening; she'd taken him the money the next morning and she'd hoped that was the end of it. While she was speaking she folded her hands like the paws of some little animal, a mole or a field-mouse, over the back

71

of the chair. Her smallness and fragility were an asset; you got the sense that forces were being too brutal for her, and in their hearts the villagers were admiring her for standing up to this fellow. He was a stranger from Horsfall, and they didn't care for him. Thank God, thought Crook, we're a sentimental race.

The coroner, however, seemed to be the exception that proved the rule. He was like Cleveland in that. He fired question after question at the exhausted old woman, dragging the whole story out of her; she hadn't, Crook realized, wanted to admit the spoliation of her cottage, but she'd no chance against Hackworth.

"What do you suppose Grigg was looking for?" he inquired.

Mrs. Manners hesitated. Crook could almost see the dreads and speculations moving behind the frail barrier of skin and bone. How much to say—how much it was safe to deny. After a moment she whispered, "Money, I suppose, sir. What else would he want?"

"Did he find any?"

"There wasn't any to find."

The coroner leaned forward. "So your suggestion is that, not having found whatever it was he wanted, he went back to the church. Why should he do that?"

"I couldn't say, sir. I never saw him again to speak to. But I dare say he was afraid of being seen and recognized."

"Was there anything missing from the cottage—anything that wasn't money?"

"Not that I could say, sir."

Crook pricked up his ears. She wasn't a fool, she knew she was in desperate danger, though whether he and she had the same danger in mind he couldn't be certain. She had a grim sort of courage that he admired, but it angered him all the same, because he knew courage isn't nearly such a powerful weapon as cunning when you're fighting for your life. Besides, she was tiring. It made him angry. He'd never been able to understand how grown men in hosts could enjoy running a fox down and chasing it from stopped earth to stopped earth.

"Well." The coroner was off again. "He went back to the church. I suppose it didn't occur to you to follow him?"

Damn Cleveland, thought Crook. He ought to stop this. This

chap's going far beyond his rights and the fellow knows it. But Reuben, Seventh Earl Cleveland, was sitting well back in his seat, his arms folded on his pudgy little chest, looking more than ever like a man hearing someone else read the Lessons in church, while knowing he'd have read them far better himself. Reuben didn't care if they hanged the old woman by the neck till she was dead; he didn't care about anything but his own reputation. He didn't want Ted's name introduced because of reviving an old scandal, but that was all. His terrible old mother, sitting alongside, was just the same.

The last question got through Mrs. Manners' guard. She hesitated—fatally. The coroner didn't miss a thing.

"Well?" he demanded aggressively. "Did you? Or don't you remember?"

"Not—not then," faltered Mary Anne Manners.

"But you did later?"

"Yes, sir."

"When was this?"

"A little after six. I had to make sure he'd really gone."

"You're quite sure about the time?"

"Yes, sir. I stopped to hear the news. . . ."

The coroner looked incredulous. "You mean, with your home torn to ribbons and your nephew concealed nearby, a man suspected of a capital crime, with the police after him, you still stopped to put on the news?"

"The neighbours would have thought it odd if I hadn't. You can hear everything in these little houses."

"You didn't forget much, did you?" He laughed unpleasantly. "Well?"

"He wasn't there," said Mrs. Manners flatly.

"Oh come," said the coroner, "that doesn't make sense. He was there at midday and he was there next morning, but . . ."

She interrupted sharply to say, "I don't say he was there next morning. I don't know. I only know he was there yesterday when the Rector called for me to see if I could tell him who he was. But he wasn't there between six and half-past on Thursday night. It was quite dark in the church, I know, but I took my torch, like I always

73

do if I have to be out in the black-out, and I went up to the vestry door, that was shut, and I remember I stood there a minute before I durst open it."

"What were you afraid you might find if you did?"

"Tom was always a bit violent when he was roused. I thought maybe he'd be put out at not finding what he wanted at the cottage."

"You mean money?"

"Yes, sir. I spoke his name twice and then I opened the door and shone the torch inside, but he wasn't there. There was just an empty bottle and some paper, but no sign of Tom. I thought then he must have gone back to London, like he said he meant to."

"H'm," ejaculated the coroner, "it's a pity you can't find anyone to back up your story."

She looked at him mutely. She'd done her best, but it was no good. He didn't believe her, and she hadn't anyone to help her. She flung one glance at Crook, but his face was like a block of wood. No admittance even on business, it seemed to say. Nothing but will-power kept her on her feet.

Then, just when it seemed she must break, deliverance came from a totally unexpected quarter, something that wiped the look of triumph off the coroner's grim hatchet face.

Young Simon Oliver had risen slowly and was speaking out of turn. He was a very tall young man, more like his cousin than his father, except that he was fair, so fair that his pale gold hair looked almost silver. He wasn't, thought Mrs. Manners, wondering what he was going to say, how many more of them she'd got against her, near so handsome as her grandson, but all the same he had something indefinable, a queer casual charm that couldn't be gainsaid.

He took a long time getting to his feet, moving languidly, slowly, yet he conveyed a sense of power. An interesting, enterprising, possibly even a dangerous young man, decided Crook. Galahad on roller-skates, that was his number.

"That's all right," he said in his slow attractive voice. "Tom Grigg couldn't have been in the vestry at half-past six on Thursday evening, because at that time he was talking to me in the grounds of the Park."

CHAPTER NINE

Always suspect everybody.
OLD CURIOSITY SHOP.

1

If a snake had reared itself in their midst and hissed them into appalled rigidity, the court could not have been more dumb. Even the ruthless coroner was silenced. Mrs. Manners looked less startled than most, possibly because, secure in the knowledge that she was telling the truth, she had expected Heaven to provide her with a witness, but more likely, thought Crook, because she had reached such a pitch of exhaustion that no development, however staggering, was likely to move her greatly.

The coroner was furious at the interruption; so was Cleveland. A quick mutter broke out in the body of the hall.

"If you've evidence to give," snapped Hackworth, "you should do it in the proper way. This is most irregular. . . ."

"I couldn't get here earlier," explained Simon. He didn't seem in the least intimidated by the coroner's jutting chin or angry manner. Which was as it should be, thought Crook. A fellow—a Captain in the army, too—who could be frightened by that little legal rat wouldn't be much use when it came to panzer divisions and dive-bombers.

"You'd better go into the witness-box," said the coroner, looking defeated, and Simon moved out of his place and took the oath.

"You say you know this man?"

"I didn't know him, but I recognized him. I saw his picture in the paper with an account of what had happened, and I realized he was the fellow I met last Thursday evening. I got leave to come down at once in case I could be any use. I'm late because trains aren't very good, and then I had to see the body first and be quite sure I was right."

"What business did you have with him?" Hackworth demanded.

75

"I was coming through the grounds on Thursday evening soon after six when this fellow appeared from behind a tree or a giant sunflower or something, and asked me if I was the heir. I thought he was a bit wanting, but I said I supposed I was. Mind you, he meant nothing to me, I'd never seen him before. I asked him what he wanted, and he said he used to work on the place as a young man and he was home on leave and he was just taking a look round. I pointed out that actually he was trespassing and asked him why he hadn't come to the door in the usual way. He said well, none of the servants would remember him, it was so long ago, and he asked if my grandmother was at home. I said she wasn't available, and that everyone else was out—I remember he asked particularly about my aunt—was she still living at the Manor? Well, she was out, too, down in the village, and if she hadn't been I don't suppose she'd have particularly wanted to see this chap."

"You're not being asked your opinions," snapped the coroner. "If you can tell us anything else relevant . . ."

The young man hesitated. "Not precisely relevant," he said.

That aroused everyone's curiosity. Crook thought, "Damme, he ought to be on the stage, an actor like that," and then, "And if he were he'd knock 'em all in the Old Kent Road."

The coroner was saying waspishly that he ought to tell them anything that had a bearing on the case, and the young man seemed to hesitate again, and then said, "Well, it shows he knew the legend, anyway. He was talking a bit about the place, just to show me he knew his way about, I thought, unless, of course, he was one of a gang of burglars come to spy out the land, and suddenly he said, 'You're the heir, aren't you?'"

Crook looked at the family to see how they were taking that. The old lady sat very stiff, her small plump hands clenched; the Earl looked more indifferent than you'd have thought possible in a breathing creature; Miss Oliver was watching her nephew as though he'd vanish if she looked away for an instant. The girl was smiling a little, that odd smile that even a woman might not understand. Simon met her glance and smiled back, silver-fair brows lifted. The cousin had clasped his hands between his knees and was staring at the floor.

"Well?" snapped Hackworth.

"He touched me on the arm and said, 'You can laugh at the legend if you like. There have been others who laughed just the same as you, but they're not laughing now. Take my word for it, you're in danger.' I said, 'Who from particularly?' not counting the whole German Army, of course, and he said, 'You look out for your cousin. One of these days, if you're not careful, he'll stand in your shoes.' "

The effect on the court was electrical. The cousin turned brick-red and put his head right down till it was almost between his knees. The Dowager said clearly, Stuff and nonsense. No guts. And the Earl looked like someone whose child has been sick in a crowded carriage. The young girl, Stella, put her hand to her heart in a gesture so spontaneous and so innocent that even Crook was touched.

But Hackworth was scowling more blackly than before. "You mean to say you take that sort of old wives' tale seriously?"

"Oh no," said Simon. "But I was giving evidence and you asked me what this fellow said. As for the legend, I was sung to sleep with that—not inheriting the estate, I mean. Well, I daresay I shan't. I dare say by the time it's my turn there won't be any large estates left. I may be allowed a bungalow on the site. . . ."

The coroner interrupted in a voice that was almost a shout. "You are here to give evidence, Mr. Oliver. This is irrelevant."

"I thought it was," agreed Simon slowly, "but I also thought I should repeat everything he said in case it had some significance that wasn't apparent to me." He spoke so seriously that Crook felt his interest quicken again.

"Is that all he had to say to you?" demanded the coroner.

"I said to him, 'If you're out for money you won't help yourself by talking like that,' and he said, 'Oh, there's a lot you don't know, things that happened before you were born.' I said, 'Have you come to remind the family of them?' and he said, 'They don't forget, you mark my words.' I said, 'Why not come into the house and make sure?' but he moved away, said after all he'd got to be going. I said again, 'Why not come up in the morning?' and he said, 'The morning's no time for seeing ghosts. Besides, I have to be getting along.' Then I walked with him as far as the private gates and left him."

"And when you went indoors you told your family all about it?" Hackworth suggested.

"As a matter of fact I did mean to ask my father if he knew who the fellow might be, but when I came in I found the telephone ringing, and it was my C.O. My leave was cancelled, I had to go back at once. That drove every other thought out of my head. As I told you, all the household was out, except my grandmother and Miss Reed. I said good-bye to my grandmother, and Miss Reed came in the car with me as far as the gate."

"You intended to make the entire journey by road?"

"There wasn't a train that would have got me back to my station that night. And I had my C.O.'s permission and the petrol. Priority licence," he added.

The coroner, who had his own brushes with the Local Petroleum Officer, emitted a snort. Like a lot of other men he didn't, he said, so much mind the inconvenience of having to make use of what the authorities pompously called "alternative transport," but he did object to having to stand in queues, to waste hours of time that even a modest man, he felt, might consider valuable waiting for the bus to arrive, to have to straphang, with consequent more or less severe attacks of dyspepsia, when young men like Simon Oliver were permitted by the authorities to dash recklessly about the countryside using petrol with utter abandon. This was the kind of thing that engendered bad feeling. The nation was constantly being told that this was everybody's war, that we were all in the front line, but the fellows in uniform got the privileges just as they got the food. He felt prejudiced against the witness.

"How long should you say it took you to get ready to leave?" he enquired.

Simon considered. "Ten minutes, say. Perhaps a quarter of an hour."

"And how long would it take a man to walk to the Park gates from the private gate?"

Crook saw what this was leading up to if Simon didn't. But he couldn't help.

"Oh, about twenty minutes—perhaps a little more in a bad light.

78

That path wants something doing to it, but, of course, in a war the labour's lacking. The land proper has it all, and quite right, too."

The coroner sniffed again. He knew that. He'd been quite a well-known amateur horticulturist before the war; he was developing a tulip that might make history, he shouldn't wonder, and now the nosey Ministry of Agriculture came down demanding that he should plant turnips or some such nonsense.

Privilege again.

He continued in level tones, "So that presumably you would over-take this man before you reached the gates? Offer him a lift, perhaps?"

For the first time Simon looked disconcerted. "I ought to have done," he agreed, "but the fact is, I didn't. But that might be be-cause I stopped just before I got to the gates. My aunt, Miss Oliver, had just appeared on her bicycle. She'd been down to the village of Kings Fossett to see about some special W.V.S. Fête they were hold-ing there next day. A sort of dawn to dusk affair it was. My aunt had been out the whole afternoon getting things ready. I stopped the car to tell her what had happened."

"Did that take long?"

"Oh, only a minute or two. I hadn't any more time. I'd heard it strike seven a minute or so before."

"And did you happen to say anything to her about your mysterious visitor?"

"As a matter of fact, I nearly ran her down. Her cycle-lamp had petered out and I didn't see her at first in the dark."

"And you say you didn't mention this man's visit."

"I've told you I didn't. It didn't seem important." He paused. "To tell you the truth, I'd almost forgotten about him."

"But she spoke of him, perhaps?"

Young Captain Oliver fell headlong into the trap. "Oh, no, why should she? She hadn't seen him."

"I thought you said she'd come up from Kings Fossett."

"So she had."

"Then she must have seen this man either before she met you or later; and it could hardly have been later or you'd have overtaken him and you say you didn't."

79

Miss Oliver, a fervent believer in the divine right of kings and probably the most rigid opponent of the Beveridge Report that the country had produced, here called out indignantly, "If you want to know who I saw or didn't see, why don't you ask me myself instead of trying to trip the boy up? As a matter of fact . . ."

But the coroner, who didn't like the Beveridge Report either but loathed the divine right of kings even more ardently, spitefully called her to order. She would, he said, have an opportunity of giving her testimony, irregular though the whole affair appeared to be, in due course. He turned back to Simon.

"I shan't need to detain you more than a minute, Captain Oliver," he said. "I think you told the court that this man didn't give you a name."

"That's so."

"And it was between six and half-past on an October evening?"

"Yes."

"And you had never seen him before?"

"No," said Simon again.

"And you didn't tell any one you'd seen him and no other member of your family saw him?"

"Not so far as I know."

"And yet when you saw his photograph in the paper—a picture of a man you'd seen once in a bad light—you recognized it at once."

"I couldn't be certain, of course, but when I saw the body . . ."

"You knew it at once?"

"I knew it was the same man."

"Though he had been dead some days, and he was a stranger to you?"

"I'm giving evidence on oath," Simon reminded him stiffly.

"I'm glad you realize that, Captain Oliver. Now, although you didn't know who he was, you do know the last witness?"

"Mrs. Manners? Well, of course. She was my nurse when I was a kid."

"I see. But you didn't know she had a nephew?"

Simon considered and shook his head. "I never heard her speak of one, but then, in all the circumstances, would you expect her to?"

The coroner let him go after that, and Miss Oliver took his place. But she had little to tell the court. She confirmed meeting her nephew on the public road through the Park on the Thursday evening, but had to admit that he hadn't mentioned the visitor to her. She added, however, that there really hadn't been time, and what was a tramp to her anyway compared with the fact that the authorities had cancelled Simon's leave? She'd only had a dozen words with him before she mounted her machine and rode up to the house.

"And it doesn't strike you as strange that you didn't see this man?" Hackworth enquired.

"It would be easy enough for him not to be noticed in the Park," snapped Miss Oliver. "And he may not have wanted to be seen."

"And yet he specially asked for you, according to Captain Oliver's evidence."

"He'd hardly recognize me after thirty years. Besides, it seems pretty clear that my nephew sent him away with a flea in his ear. Once bitten, twice shy."

"The jury may think that point worthy of consideration." Hackworth plugged obstinately on. "The fact remains that this man was subsequently found in the church, to which presumably he returned after his visit to the Manor, and yet although there is only one path to the gates no one saw him from the instant he left the private gate. We know he got back to the church. . . ."

"I don't know anything of the sort," snapped Rhoda Oliver. "All I know is he was found there some days later, but that doesn't mean he spent Thursday night there. And don't ask me where he did spend it," she added threateningly, "because I can only assure you it wasn't with me."

2

Simon Oliver's evidence had upset the jury badly. Up to this moment—that is, up to the moment when he made his dramatic incursion into the case—everything had seemed straightforward enough. Mrs. Manners had admitted a series of damning facts; everything pointed to her as the murderer, and, more important still, nothing pointed at any one else. Clearly she would want Tom out of the way, for so long as he was at liberty he was a menace to her, and if he was caught he was a disgrace. Only she had known of his presence at Kings Fossett, she had hidden him, fed him, lied about him, robbed herself for his sake. The case had seemed perfectly clear. And now here was young Mr. Oliver blurring the whole affair with his senseless story of meeting a stranger in the grounds at just the time that Mrs. Manners declared the vestry was empty. It all fitted together neatly, too neatly for the jury.

Since there was no suitable place into which the jury could retire to come to a decision the public was cleared out of the hall, and stood about outside, in awkward groups of two and three, whispering among themselves. Crook, with his usual good sense, remarked, "They won't make up their minds on that in a hurry," and went across to the local, taking Cupit with him.

"I hope," said the clergyman, taking his beer absent-mindedly, "this isn't going to mean more trouble for young Simon. I wouldn't care to be in his shoes." He looked anxious.

"You and me don't have to worry," Crook assured him. "The jury's goin' to tell us what happened—that's what juries are for. Now, if you'd said you were glad not to be on that I'd have felt for you."

Cupit gave him an odd look. It classed him as an outsider, a fellow who doesn't understand tradition. Crook wasn't dumb; he knew just what it meant, but he didn't care. He wasn't much of a betting man in the accepted sense of the word, finding it poor fun to stand on the side and watch a lot of horses make the running, when you might be doing a bit of running yourself and making a lot more money, but he did know enough of the sport of kings to realize that outsiders sometimes come romping home at the head of the field.

They had another round and then Cupit, who seemed a bit on edge, suggested going back to the Hall. Crook knew it was too early, but you have to let these fellows have their head sometimes, so he put down his tankard and they trailed back and stood staring at the idiot sunflowers till they were summoned back to hear the verdict.

The verdict, which Crook had expected but which seemed to floor Mr. Cupit, was Wilful Murder against Mary Anne Manners.

CHAPTER TEN

And hence, one master-passion in the breast
Like Aaron's serpent swallows up the rest.

POPE.

1

WHEN THEY LEFT the Mission Hall a few minutes later Cupit's face was stupid with surprise.

"How could they reach such a decision in the teeth of young Simon's evidence?" he demanded.

"What the soldier said ain't evidence," returned Crook in his blunt emphatic way. "Who's proved Simon Oliver's story? Tell me that."

He said the same to the young man himself as he came sliding through the swing doors of the Duck and Dragon that evening. The bar had been open almost an hour; the air was blue with smoke and pleasantly redolent of beer. Simon ordered a pint and carried it to the table where Crook was sitting.

"I'm told you're a lawyer," he began, putting down his first card with a firm hand. "I want some advice."

"Six-and-eightpence-worth?" enquired Crook.

"More, I think," replied Simon. "Quite a lot more. Tell me, don't the jury believe my yarn? And if they believed me, why did they find old Mother Manners guilty?"

"You testified that you'd seen the chap at six-thirty and packed him off with a flea in his ear and a quid in his pocket. And though various members of your family seem to have been out and about none of them met him. And you didn't see him again, though you were pretty well bound to pass him in your car. And Miss Reed didn't see him. The only person who admittedly wanted him out of the way, and knew where he was staying and could have put out his light was Mrs. Manners. Q. E. D. I don't see myself how they could have found any other verdict."

The young man pushed aside his untouched glass of beer. "Look here," he said, "this is all wrong. You don't know Mrs. Manners, but—she wouldn't do a thing like that. This chap was almost the nearest relative she had."

"The little more and how much it is," hummed Crook. "She had a grandson who was the apple of her eye and the whole place knew it. Every man on the jury knew it. And women ain't like us. It's not their fault, it's the way they're made. Men can think of half a dozen things at once. Women can only see one. And I'll tell you another thing," he added, swallowing his beer with a gulp of enjoyment, "women, take it by and large, are morally short-sighted. All your Mother Manners cared about was her grandson. He was right and therefore anything that threatened him must be wrong. Tom Grigg threatened him—don't ask me how, because this ain't my case to date and I don't know—but she thought he might hurt her darling, and a rattlesnake would be child's play compared with a woman like Mrs. Manners on the warpath. Y'know," he went on, while Simon watched him, fascinated by the absorbing spectacle of a man who could drink and talk simultaneously at such tremendous rates, "women are so constituted—and here I speak by the book, not just by hearsay—that by this time, supposing she did do it, she could justify herself that it was the right thing, even if no one else agrees with her. God help poor devils of lawyers if women ever sit on the judge's bench. The poor chaps won't know where they are, because every woman's a law to herself. What d'you want me to do? Get her out of jug? And talkin' of jugs . . ." He nodded significantly at his companion's glass.

"Well, no, not for the minute," murmured Simon, and Crook wandered across to the bar to have his tankard refilled.

"I gather you had suggested taking a hand if it were necessary," urged Simon as his companion rejoined him. He was like Crook's conception of women—as single-minded as a one-way track. "And it looks as though someone's got to jump in and do something smart before it's too late. Though, of course, if you think she's guilty. . . ."

"If I think she's guilty?" Crook stared. "Who the hell cares what I think? It's what the jury thinks, and the jury'll think what they're damn well told to think. And the chap who'll tell them will be the chap who conducts the defence, and the chap who conducts the defence will be guided through the valley of righteousness by the chap with the facts. And the chap with the facts in this case is going to be me. Same like the House That Jack Built."

"I'll swear she's innocent," said Simon, earnestly.

"She'll be innocent if I take the case on because my clients always are. And truth, in case you haven't recognized the fact, is what you can persuade the other chap to believe. And a snake-charmer with a pipe and a python hasn't got anything on Arthur Crook, take my word," and he opened his uvula and swallowed his second pint as neatly and completely as a python would swallow a rabbit.

"The police are great believers in coincidence, if you're right," suggested the heir, still moving along his single-track. "How do you explain the fact that Mrs. Manners mentioned the one time during the day that the church was in fact empty?"

"Don't you see, because she knew. That'll be their line. She knew her nephew was goin' to try to make a touch up at the Manor and she knew when he was makin' it. It was pretty safe to say that the church wasn't occupied at six or whenever it was. But they'll also suggest that she knew he was comin' back—to report to her most likely. Now, if I was preparin' the case for the prosecution that's how I'd argue it. I'm goin' to see what the gentry are good for, auntie, he says and off he goes. The grandson's off with his girl till late, so the coast's clear. And no one was likely to call because she didn't have visitors at night, and anyway the black-out puts a stopper on that sort of fun, especially in the country." He sighed, thinking of Earl's Court, where life never stops, despite black-out and restricted transport. To and fro in these dark streets people moved, secretive, determined, furtive, or just amorous or tired after the day's work. Life never slept in those shabby by-ways.

"Is there no way of proving that isn't true?" If this young man was acting it was a shame he wasn't in the West-End, where, Heaven knew, they could do with a few first-class men what with the war and mumble-jumble technique and the emasculation of humanity generally.

"Only one way," said Crook, "the way I'd take if I were dealing with the case."

"What's that?" enquired Simon.

"Find the chap who's responsible," returned Crook, as though that were the simplest thing in the world.

"Any idea?" murmured Simon.

"Just a hunch or two," said Crook.

The young soldier looked up sharply. "You can't imagine any of my people are involved."

Crook put out his big hand and caught his companion by the shoulder.

"Now, talk sense," he said. "Why are you here? Because you want me to show your old Nannie couldn't have committed a murder. If I take this case on, then she didn't commit a murder. If she didn't someone else did. It's nothing to me—get this into your head—who the other person is. All that matters to me is that it isn't Mrs. Manners. Mind you, I don't say your family is involved. I don't know. I promise you one thing—I won't manufacture evidence; after all, I've got a reputation to guard, too. But if I take it on and it does get one of your lot into the soup, you can't squeal and say it isn't fair. I like," said Crook, with a great deal of candour, putting his hand back on his own knee, "to put my cards on the table. If now you don't want me to take on the job just say so. But if I do, then I have a free hand. Roll, bowl or pitch, every time a blood-orange or a good cigar."

He folded his arms and leaned back; his big intelligent crafty face glowed. He looked about as soft as a hunk of mahogany and as conscious of his own worth as the Bank of England.

Simon did not answer for a while. Then he said, "You're clever, aren't you? You've tied my hands. I couldn't refuse, even if I wanted to."

"Do you want to?"

"I don't know." Simon spoke slowly. "But I do know that I haven't any choice."

2

No one seeing Arthur Crook would have put him down as an imaginative man. His great red face, his cocksure manner, his hard

brown bowler, all spoke of the man of steel. It was only people like
Bill Parsons, his invaluable A.D.C., who ever saw the reverse side of
the medal and knew the real reason for Crook's crashing success.

Mr. Crook was a firm believer in the saying that what a defence
mainly requires is all the evidence, which he can then arrange to suit
himself. No one was better at making intricate patterns than Arthur
Crook, but he wasn't a miracle man; he couldn't make bricks without any straw at all. He decided that the first thing to be done was
to have another chat with Mary Anne Manners, so, having made the
necessary arrangements required by a fussy legislature, he went along
to the prison. He preferred men clients, just as he preferred men in
every other situation in life, but if they had to be women he wished
they wouldn't look like Whistler's old mother. Self-respect is a very
fine virtue, but it doesn't save people from the gallows.

"Look here," said Crook briskly, as if they'd been interrupted by
a telephone call, "I don't want to badger you, but just tell me one
thing. What was it Tom Grigg was looking for in your cottage that
afternoon?"

Whatever she'd anticipated, it hadn't been that. She tried to look
away from those small bright eyes, that big intent face thrust dramatically close to her own. Crook's hand came out and closed like a vice
over her knee. He got the impression that if he tightened his fingers
her brittle bones would crumble into dust under his touch.

"Now, listen here," he said. "Throw dust in everybody's else's eyes
all you like, the more the better. Make 'em water, blind 'em, but
don't try any of those games on me. You see, we're partners in this.
We got to work together."

She said in that little voice that hadn't faltered even when she was
being hectored almost past endurance by the little squirt of a coroner, "It's very kind of you, sir, but I'd rather you didn't. I mean, I
don't mind . . ." The old lips trembled, and she folded them tightly.

"You don't mind!" ejaculated Crook, looking hurt and outraged
simultaneously. "Hell, what about me? My reputation's at stake as
well as yours and mine's worth a hell of a lot. Why, I'm like a young
gel looking towards the marriage market. My good name's all I live
on. Besides, there's justice. You may say you don't care, but how
about that precious grandson of yours? What's he fighting for, if it

87

isn't justice? No, no. If he were here he'd tell me to go ahead and do my damnedest. He can't do anything himself, being otherwise occupied. . . . Well, come on, what was it?"

Even Mrs. Manners wasn't altogether proof against these shock tactics. "I—I told the court—that is, what I guessed. . . ."

"I don't care what you told that old Buster," said Crook, "but don't try to pull the wool over my eyes. He wasn't looking for money and you know it. Why, you told the court so yourself."

"I told . . ."

"You said that when Tom Grigg turned up on Wednesday evening asking for money you told him he'd have to wait till the next day when you could draw something from the bank man. Now, if you'd had any money in the house you'd have paid him off right away just to get him off the premises. You wouldn't have risked keeping him in the neighbourhood even if nobody does risk going inside the church, not if you could have got rid of him that night. And the only way you could hope to get rid of him was by giving him money, so it stands to reason that if you'd had money in the house you'd have given it to him. No, no, it wasn't money he was looking for and you know it. Come on, what was it?"

She shook her obstinate head, "I couldn't say, sir. It must have been money or else why would he have gone up to the Manor?"

"He didn't stand much chance of getting anything out of that crowd of tightwads, unless he took a gun with him." Crook expressed himself with his usual lack of elegance. "He had something that could squeeze money out of them and that something was what he was looking for in your cottage."

Her face seemed dead now. Nothing lived but her eyes. She said again, "I don't know, sir, but it doesn't look as though you could be right. I mean, he didn't have any money but what I gave him. . . ."

"They're probably like you, don't keep wads of money in the house. No, that would explain why he went back to the church. He was to wait there till next day when the money would be brought to him. And the next morning whoever it was didn't bring the money, just brought death," added Crook, with conscious melodrama.

"I don't like to think anyone at the Manor would have done that," said the old woman simply.

"Well, damn it all," exploded Crook. "I know we're a barbaric nation and all that, but even so we don't go round stifling people for fun."

But she only said, "We don't really know much, do we, sir? It might have been someone we've none of us thought about."

"Oh, it might," agreed Crook, in what was intended to be a resigned voice, "but if the chap isn't sporting enough to come to the surface how does that help us?"

But it became obvious that he was going to play dummy's hand as well as his own. She didn't say a word.

"All right," said Crook, playing his last trump—admittedly a small one—as he rose to his feet, "I won't grill you. But just tell me this. Did he find what he came for?"

But she only said in that maddening way of hers, "If it wasn't money, sir, how should I be able to tell you?"

And for the moment he had to leave it at that.

CHAPTER ELEVEN

Wake not a sleeping wolf!
KING HENRY IV.

THE EVENINGS at the Manor House had a certain statuesque quality. When dinner, served at 7.30 in deference to the wartime servants, was over, the family assembled in the library for what remained of the evening. Lady Cleveland, while deploring everything modern— in her young days wars were fought in other continents and there was no radio to harass your nerves with hourly reports of how the battle was going—was tolerant enough to allow the nine o'clock news to be put on, though she seldom had patience to listen to the postscript.

"We really can't be expected to take an interest in what some stranger thinks," she would remark.

After the wireless had been switched off, the ladies carried on a sedate conversation while their fingers busied themselves with needles of every kind. They all sat together, no matter what their mood or business, in order to save fuel, and long experience had made them all capable of remarkable concentration. Only the young girl, Stella Reed, seemed a centre of disturbance, for all her silence and her down-dropped lids. Seeing the others, you might momentarily forget the world was at war. You could never forget while she was there, though she wore no uniform and indulged in no military phraseology. Lord Cleveland, a small absorbed figure, looking like his own bailiff, sat at a large desk so far from the fireplace that even when there was an economical blaze its heat never reached him. The cousin, who never felt either heat or cold, sat as far as possible from everyone else and read Horse and Hounds or made out fantastic mathematical problems on slips of paper. There might be a world war on, he might have been rejected because he had brought back a stiffish leg from the last war, but he didn't intend to have his entire life disrupted. Most people couldn't afford to continue breeding horses or hadn't the time; he was lucky in having a considerably bigger fortune than his cousin, and no wife or mother to teach him how to save. He had put his estate under the plough, had acquiesced when the military requisitioned his house, but nothing stopped him buying horses in anticipation of the day when he'd be able to show them again. Cupit was right. Horses were his love. The girl to whom he had once been briefly engaged had said that Gregory would sooner bed down with one of his own mares than the Venus de Milo. He was looking troubled to-night. All was not well. His brow was like the hour before the dawn.

The silence was broken suddenly by Rhoda Oliver, who said in an abrupt voice, "Will they hang her, do you think? Mrs. Manners, I mean?"

Cleveland who was doing estate accounts with his back to the rest of the room's occupants, looked over his shoulder to say, "She hasn't been tried yet. They may not find her guilty."

"Hope not," ejaculated the cousin in jerky tones, looking up from his preoccupation. "An old woman like that. Bad as Poland." Like many bachelors he entertained chivalrous notions about a sex who terrified him. This made him looked at askance by the average husband.

"You should study history, Gregory," said the Dowager in a dry voice. "There are plenty of crimes committed by old women. In France and in America I am told that leaders of the most ferocious gangs are frequently women."

"Yes," agreed the cousin in the chuckle-headed way of men who know more about horses than humans, "but they were French or American."

The Dowager looked as though she'd like to scratch his eyes out. "Women are the same all the world over," she declared.

The cousin digested that for a moment. "No," he assured her, when the period for reflection was past, "that's not right. I went to Paris once. Quite surprisin'. You should go to Paris, Victoria. Not now of course. Out of the question. But I tell you, I was surprised. . . ."

"And anyway you can leave the verdict to the chaps who'll be called upon to give it," added Cleveland in tones of deep disapprobation. Simon said he'd never known a fellow who could even put his voice into black like the governor.

"Shouldn't think she did it, though," laboured the cousin. "I mean to say, she'd know she'd be the first person to be dropped on. Means, motive, opportunity. That's how the police work. Read it in a book. Book by a chap. One of the Big Five. C.I.D., you know. Besides, as Simon says, this fellow was up at the House. . . ."

"It's unfortunate for Mary Anne,"—that was the Dowager again, of course—"unfortunate that Simon didn't see fit to mention the fact before to-day."

"He didn't have a chance." Stella defended him quickly. He wasn't there to defend himself. He'd had to go straight back to his unit. "He only saw me—to talk to, that is. He wouldn't be likely to tell me that an ex-gamekeeper had tried to borrow money. He wouldn't think it important."

"He saw me," said the Dowager coldly.

"But you had someone with you. He couldn't speak."

"He saw me," flared Rhoda. "But I suppose I don't count." Her deep masculine voice was full of resentment. The Dowager looked at her with something too like contempt to be distinguished from it. As though to assert herself Rhoda pulled out a packet of cigarettes and stuck one in her mouth. No one offered to give her a light—neither of the other women smoked and the men weren't the chivalrous sort—so she had to produce her own matches from her pocket and look after her own needs.

"Simon never had any sense of proportion," continued the Dowager, ignoring her step-daughter as usual.

"And Simon's sure that Mary Anne isn't guilty," continued Stella, ignoring the Dowager in her turn.

"Simon," riposted the old lady, "does not represent the law."

"Mr. Crook does," said Stella.

"Crook!" exclaimed the two older women simultaneously, but their surprise and displeasure was drowned by Lord Cleveland's furious exclamation of "That shyster! It's intolerable the way that chap pushes himself into everything. He's nothing but a tout and he . . ." He stopped abruptly, aware of the curious glances of his kinsfolk. "What does that fellow think he can do, anyway?"

"Simon's asked him to act for Mary Anne."

"Highly improper," snapped the Seventh earl. "Why, he was a witness in the case."

"Simon says that will make him more interested. It's not as though any one could suspect him of being guilty. Anyway, he went to see Mrs. Manners before the inquest. I suppose he realized how things were going to go."

"It all sounds damned fishy to me," said Cleveland.

"He's a lawyer," Stella pointed out, and for all the gentleness in her voice there was something stubborn too, something that wouldn't be gainsaid.

"And does he think he can prove she didn't do it—knock up an alibi or something?"

"Oh no. Simon says his head's pretty hard, but it's not as hard as that. I suppose he'll find out who really did do it."

Rhoda Oliver's normally pale face had turned a dusky mottled colour. "You fool!" she whispered. "You little fool! Can't you see what you've done between you?" A needle dropped out of her knitting, but she didn't even notice.

"What are you saying, Rhoda?" demanded the old lady.

Rhoda turned her furious disfigured face to the old woman. "Can't any of you see? Suppose Crook persuades the authorities that Mary Anne is innocent, they'll start looking for another criminal and who are they going to pick? Simon, of course. He's the only other person who would admit he knew Tom was in the neighbourhood. He says he didn't know where Tom was spending the night but no one can prove that."

"No one can prove he did," returned the old lady icily.

"No one can actually prove Mary Anne bolted that door, but they found her guilty for all that. Law doesn't rest on inalienable proof; it rests on probabilities, and if this man, who looked as dishonest a creature as I ever set eyes on, can make people believe she didn't do it, he won't care who hangs."

Stella broke in, her beautiful voice a tone deeper than its wont, "You don't seem to care if an old woman hangs, even though she is innocent."

"Of course I don't care, so long as Simon's all right," cried Miss Oliver. "What's Mary Anne Manners to me. That family's done us enough harm in its time. And why do you call her innocent? You don't know—of course you don't."

"Who put this insane idea into Simon's head?" demanded Simon's father.

"I suppose in a way I did. I couldn't bear to remember that old woman's face. I said to him we were responsible."

"We?" The guillotine itself could hardly have been more cold, more final, more cruel than the Dowager's voice.

"This House is the head of the village and Mrs. Manners was your servant once. It does carry obligations. . . ." Stella was clearly no more democratic than her prospective aunt by marriage. "Simon felt the same," she added.

"Simon would feel whatever you told him to feel," retorted the Dowager impatiently. "Well, my dear Stella, no doubt you had your reasons, though it may not be easy for the rest of us to appreciate them. All the same, I find it surprising that even you, a comparative stranger, failed to realize what the outcome of this—madness—

would be. You know this community is as superstitious as an Indian tribe. They will recall the legend of the Curse, remind one another that it has always operated, and if anything should happen to Simon . . ."

"Nothing of the kind you mean will happen to him," cried Stella, scornfully. "Why, what motive would Simon have? Anyway, we don't believe in the Curse, he and I."

"You may not believe in the Pyramids, but that doesn't alter the fact that they exist."

Gregory Oliver said in his jerky way, "It doesn't do to laugh at everything you can't explain. People would have laughed at wireless once. Black magic they'd have called it. We know better now."

"Is that what that man meant when he told Simon to look out or his cousin would stand in his shoes?"

"He won't," said Rhoda, impervious to the cousin's outraged feelings. "Simon will be the next Lord Cleveland whatever any one may believe. I'd kill any one who stood in his way."

"There's no need to be melodramatic," said the old lady.

"And if you're threatenin' me," said the cousin, going a dusky red, "I'd rather have Redacres any day."

"Redacres!" sneered the old lady. "It's just a glorified villa."

"It's got twenty-two rooms," protested Gregory Oliver.

"Compared with the Manor, it has neither tradition nor antiquity."

"Nor is it saddled with a Curse."

"Still, even a Curse benefits someone," put in Rhoda, her voice deeper than ever. Her half-brother stiffened, like a hunter scenting danger. "They say God moves in a mysterious way . . ."

"I should hardly care to say that He was responsible for your brother, Edmund, being such a fool he went too near the edge of a notoriously dangerous quarry."

"We're not altogether certain that he did," suggested Rhoda in the same deadly voice.

"Mr. Crook thinks that that death may be linked up with this one," intervened Stella. "I told Simon I should tell you. Because he may come down here asking questions."

"I'll give instructions he's to be sent to the back-door," said the old lady, quick as lightning. "I'll have no tradesmen coming to the front at the Manor."

"One thing he specially wants to know," continued Stella, refusing to be silenced, "is why this family gave Tom Grigg money to go away?"

The old woman broke into a fierce coarse laugh. "Really, Mr. Crook seems as fond of melodrama as Rhoda. If he is so anxious to know you can tell him that my husband helped Tom Grigg to leave the country because he was a source of too much attraction to the young women of the neighbourhood and Rhoda's father thought it was money well laid out."

"Here, dammit," said the cousin helplessly, after the manner of bachelors, wishing, not for the first time, that he'd accepted the War Office suggestion to retain a portion of Redacres for himself and let the military have the rest. It would have been much less nerve-racking to listen to dummy machine-gun bullets than to be the helpless audience of the Cleveland family when it was at home.

Rhoda herself made a desperate effort to save the situation. "Tom Grigg was after Elsie Manners, his cousin," she said. "Everybody knew it. Just as everybody knew Edmund was mad about her. That's why when Edmund met with his accident there was some talk of foul play."

"He didn't marry her when he had the chance," said Cleveland dourly.

"She wouldn't have him," said Rhoda.

"If she wouldn't, she showed more sense than some I could name," chipped in the old woman meaningly. "Not that he wasn't a handsome young man in his day. I've still got a picture of him somewhere."

"You?" The word jumped out of Rhoda's mouth like the frog from the lip of the fairy princess.

"I found it when I was clearing some papers. No one seemed to value it any more, and I put it by for interest's sake." She rose with surprising liveliness and moved to a big ugly set of drawers that stood against the wall. "It's somewhere here." She rummaged among some papers. "Here it is," she added after a moment, with malicious triumph. "It's not so difficult to understand young women losing their heads over him in those days." She handed the picture to Stella. Across the bottom was written "With love from Tom."

The two men were horribly embarrassed by the turn the conversation had taken, and had begun an irrelevant conversation from opposite corners of the room. Stella took the picture and looked at it.

"Tom Grigg!" she said. "So that . . ." She broke off.

"Don't you think he's handsome?" demanded Rhoda, truculently.

"He must have been very good-looking then," Stella agreed. Her voice told you nothing, and she laid the picture back on the table.

"Rhoda thought so," said the wicked old woman. "But Elsie Manners had no use for him, though he was crazy enough about her. But she looked higher. She followed Edmund round everywhere. She meant to have him."

Her voice made the two men shudder, but Stella said simply, "You can't blame her, it's what we all do. She wanted Edmund Oliver just as I wanted Simon. I suppose individual happiness doesn't seem very important if you set it against the background of contemporary life, but it's terribly important to the people concerned. You only have your own life to gamble with and if you lose that you lose everything. She wanted Edmund and she played pretty high for him. She lost, it's true, but if you're a gambler you know you take the chance, and you always hope you'll win. I don't know if I'll get Simon, and I know the cards are stacked pretty heavily against me, but it won't stop me playing high for him. Most women do. You must agree there."

Her earnest gaze met that of the enraged old lady. As for the men they didn't know where to look. Rhoda was fascinated with horror.

"Young women nowadays allow themselves a good deal of licence," snapped the Dowager. "We learnt restraint when I was a girl."

"I dare say the results were the same," returned Stella.

"All the same, Victoria," Rhoda broke in, "you'll have to find some better answer than that for Mr. Crook. I hope you can."

There was so much venom in her voice that Gregory Oliver won everyone's gratitude by getting up and saying he was goin' to turn in, and going off with a sort of equine grunt to the company at large. It had been a pretty grim evening, he reflected, shutting himself into his room, worse than most. Sometimes he wondered which were the more deadly, the evenings when they talked, all (with the possible exception of Stella, though she, being a woman, was doubtless no different from the others at heart) with the poison of asps under their tongues, or those other evenings when they sat like so many smouldering braziers till the very air was charged with their unspoken hates.

It was enough to make any sane man curse Adam, who didn't know his blessings and yearned, like a fool, for a companion in what Gregory would have found utter Paradise, snakes and all.

CHAPTER TWELVE

And dye conjecture to a deeper hue.
BYRON.

1

STELLA WENT UPSTAIRS with the rest. She was glad to be away from the sound of voices, the scarcely-repressed bitterness of Rhoda, the malicious triumph of the old woman, the acerbity of the Earl, the undisguised discomfort of the cousin, and her own inward dreads. It was a strange house and certainly not a happy one. Only when Simon came into it did the shadow lift for an instant, for he brought gaiety with him and kindliness and a sort of innocence that defeated the ghosts by whom the dark inhospitable rooms were peopled. She had never contrived to establish much contact with Gregory, but she felt that in his place she, too, would prefer Redacres. Spectres and legends, ancient hangings, and panelled walls might be romantic enough and a fine setting for a film, but an ordinary girl preferred something less macabre, less menacing. If Simon need not inherit she wouldn't mind, but not if his only way of withdrawal was by the dark highway of death.

She sat at her window, the light extinguished, the curtains drawn back, looking at the sky. There was no moon but in the sable heavens

97

the stars were thick as dust, silver dust that gave its own light. If Simon looked up he would see the same stars, know the same sky sheltered them. Yet she could find no comfort even in the thought that he was comparatively near. Most women mourned the absence of husbands and lovers in distant lands, under tropical skies, knew them to be facing enemy fire or prison bars; yet she felt in her senses and her blood that none was in greater danger than he. Laugh at the Curse as you might, dismiss it as an old wives' tale, speak airily of coincidence and a morbid family strain, but you could not laugh away the atmosphere of the old house, the dark faces of the dead in the hall, and the watchful sinister faces of the living everywhere.

"I should never have come," she thought, "and yet—this is Simon's house. This is where his children will be born. To go away now is to give the house the victory. For their sake as well as his and mine I must stay."

Her meditations were disturbed by a soft hand at her door, and Rhoda's voice saying breathlessly, "Stella, you're not asleep. May I come in?"

"Wait till I draw the curtains," she said in a quick voice, as though the simple action of covering the windows was coupled by a symbolic covering of her own heart.

"You're sitting in the dark," said Rhoda, and her voice was an accusation. "You shouldn't do that."

"It wasn't dark really; there were stars."

"All the same, you'd better not. This house is too dark, anyway." She closed the door and came forward. Her long hair, hanging to her waist above her blue dressing-gown, had scarcely any grey in it, but the face above gave her more than her age. "Stella, I've come to ask you something."

"Yes," said Stella. She didn't even sound interested.

"It's about Simon. You can make him do anything, can't you?"

"Oh no," said the girl simply. "I couldn't make him change his mind once he's made it up, if that's what you mean. I couldn't make him say he believed something he didn't or agree to anything unless he approved of it."

"You're going to find him a very difficult husband," exclaimed Rhoda, with a flash of angry humour.

"Perhaps. Only if he weren't like that he wouldn't be Simon, and then I suppose I wouldn't want to marry him."

"If you're not careful you may not get the chance." The words snapped out and in spite of herself Stella gave a little shiver.

"If you're referring to the Curse again . . ."

"I wasn't, though in a way it does come into it. Does it occur to you that whoever is responsible for Tom Grigg's death may have realized that things would work out exactly like this?"

"You mean, that Mary Anne would be arrested?"

"And that Simon would try to get her off."

"I still don't think I understand."

"Are you surprised at the way things have turned out?"

"Surprised that Simon should do what he can for an old family servant? Why, it's what you would expect."

"Exactly."

"I still don't understand."

"You're so sure of yourself, you think you can play a lone hand against the entire family. That's because you've no idea how dangerous they are."

"I'm not playing a lone hand," protested the girl.

"You're too sure of yourself. Everyone is when they're young. I was once. There's a kind of pride behind it. But pride goes before a fall. I found that. It isn't pleasant learning. And it isn't pleasant," she added more slowly, "to have this family against you. I speak from experience."

"I can see you're not happy," began the girl more gently, but Rhoda broke in, her bitterness like a river bursting its banks, "Do you suppose any one's ever happy in this house? I tell you, I've lived here all my life. It's like living in the shadow of doom. My mother wasn't happy. She died when I was quite small, but I remember her, a thin, nervous-looking woman who never seemed quite to understand where she was. I suppose being Lady Cleveland sounded very well; she couldn't guess what the reality would be like. I can remember how she would come into my nursery when I was a child and sit and play with me rather timidly, as if she were afraid of getting into trouble if anyone found her there. After Reuben's mother came to the place as governess she came to the nursery less and less and quite soon she never came at all. She just seemed to fade away."

"Reuben's governess?"

"Didn't you know that's who the dowager was? She was a Miss Grant, and she came to look after Edmund and me, just a sort of servant in the house. But it was obvious from the first that she meant to be mistress. From the very first."

"You don't suggest . . ." began Stella, but Rhoda interrupted roughly. "I don't suggest anything. I can only tell you that from the instant she set foot in the Manor she meant to own it, and from the moment Reuben was born she meant him to inherit. When women like my step-mother make up their minds about a thing, it happens. Don't forget that, Stella. I remember when I was a schoolgirl, standing in the hall at the Manor and looking up and seeing her peering over the bannisters, and I'll never forget the look on her face. A woman like that has powers and capacities you can't understand."

"Are you suggesting she's Simon's enemy?"

"She would be the most implacable enemy of any one who threatened Cleveland—and to her Simon is simply a part of Cleveland."

"Then you're warning me?"

"Yes," said Rhoda fiercely. "I don't want you to know the sort of life I've known. And if she's your enemy—oh, it's no good looking like that. You're not as strong as she is, you can't be."

Stella stood up and moved across the room. Rhoda seemed to her like a fire, fierce and destructive, but achieving nothing. Rhoda for her part felt her heart twist at the sight of such casual grace, such untroubled courage. That was what love had done for her. It hadn't been like that for the unfortunate Miss Oliver. Her love had turned to ashes. "Ashes!" she said aloud, and the girl turned in surprise.

"What is it you want me to do?" she enquired patiently.

"I want you to use your influence with Simon to call off this Mr. Crook."

"It wouldn't be any use. He doesn't think Mary Anne is guilty."

"Suppose she isn't?" cried Rhoda, in a sudden rush of words that seemed to sweep away every vestige of self-control. "Does it matter so much? One old woman's life, which is practically ended anyhow?

100

They won't hang her, of course they won't. They may find there isn't even sufficient evidence to convict her. It's quite likely. Why can't you let sleeping dogs lie? Why can't you wait and see what happens?"

"Why should we wait?"

"Because it's dangerous for Simon. I can't tell you why, but you must take my word for it. You think you're a match for Vicky. You're not. You'd have a better chance against a boa-constrictor. And Simon must be mad to want to dig up all the family skeletons."

"Then there are skeletons?"

"Every family has them. But it's better to leave them in their coffins."

"Tell me one thing," said the girl. "Why did your father give Tom Grigg money to go away?"

"I don't know," said Rhoda flatly, "except that it isn't the reason my step-mother gives. There was never any idea in Tom's mind to marry a girl whose family would have cut her off without a penny. And they'd have been glad. There isn't much money, you know. I've never had more than a few pounds at a time all my life."

"You were in love with him, weren't you?" said Stella gently. "I'm sorry."

"Do you think I'd ever have looked at him if we'd lived a normal life here? Of course not. But Vicky never took any notice of me. And forty years ago girls didn't count. Modern women think they're badly treated having to earn their own livings. They don't know. And if it's been hammered into you since you were young that you're plain and unattractive, naturally you've no self-confidence. I had none. Tom was the first person to treat me like a human being. Of course I responded, even when I realized it didn't mean anything."

"But Lady Cleveland . . ." Stella began.

"Victoria wouldn't have minded. She'd have been only too glad to have me out of the way." Despair was making the woman reckless. "I was a mouth to feed, a responsibility, some one alien to herself and Reuben. She wanted Cleveland for them, she meant it to be like—like a prison, every one else to be kept out. Now there's

Simon. To her he isn't a person with likes and dislikes, he's her grandson, the heir to Cleveland."

"And that's why you say she's my enemy? Oh, I could see at once that she wasn't going to like me. We have too much in common."

"You and the Dowager?" Rhoda was frankly incredulous.

"Oh, yes. You see, we've both come in from outside. My aunt, who brought me up, was a sempstress. She worked day and night to keep the pair of us. Money has a sort of magical meaning to people like us, because what's just a little coin to you may be a meal or a fire. We see things in different terms, have another scale of values. Lady Cleveland felt like that when she first came here. Oh, I don't pretend I like her, but I understand her. I even sympathize with her. She was Miss Grant earning perhaps forty pounds a year and her keep. She hadn't any right to stay here once she ceased to be any use; she'd no place of her own at all. You can't imagine what that feels like, to be the person looking in from the street. You think you hadn't got much, but you had a roof and food and clothes. That's a good foundation. People who talk about lilies of the field don't know anything about reality."

"And that," Rhoda's face was dark with fury, "that's why you're marrying Simon? So that you shall have a place?"

"Oh, I'm lucky," said the girl, with the careless insolence of youth in love. "It would be awful if I didn't care for Simon, but even if I didn't I might still fight to keep him, because of what he stands for. You say there isn't much money, but being Simon's wife would spell security to any woman."

"We don't know anything about you," muttered Rhoda, "except that Simon met you in London."

"Oh, you know much more than that," said the girl. "All the things you've decided I am. You know, for instance, I lived in France until the occupation, you know my aunt was a sempstress, you know we were poor. In a way, it's history repeating itself. Your brother fell in love with some one unsuitable. . . ."

"And died," said Rhoda harshly. "I don't qualify that, I don't know anything. But—he died. And his son won't inherit Cleveland."

"And you're afraid that something will happen to Simon if he chooses someone—unsuitable?"

"I'd give my life," said Rhoda, "if it would help Simon. I'd do anything. I haven't anything worth keeping any more, except Simon. To me, he's almost like the son I never had. And he's got to be happy."

"You're afraid I won't make him happy."

"I don't say you don't care for him, but if you do—as much as you say—then you'll let him go. Oh, it's no good. You can't mix people, however romantic you may feel. What good came out of Edmund's infatuation for Elsie Manners? Or mine for Tom Grigg?"

"It's something to remember," said the girl, slowly.

"Remember? Do you think I want to remember I ever cared for any one like that? When he went away I think I was glad—at least it meant Elsie wouldn't have him and it's easier to bear these things when there's a continent between you. When I heard he'd come back I couldn't believe it. And it was harder still to believe I'd really cared for any one who looked so—gross, so—ruined by life. I suppose that's how Vicky always saw him. People in love never see straight."

Anger burned up like a clear flame in the girl's heart. The implications were too obvious. One day, that bitter voice assured her, Simon will see you like that. He'll wonder how he could ever have been in love.

"I don't think so," she said softly, and her gentleness was like the deathly quiet that precedes the storm. "Simon knows about me. He knows how Aunt Frances and I fled for our lives before the Germans marching in, just with what we could carry. He knows how we hid in ditches and behind hay-stacks, and how it wasn't any good, after all, because they were angry by the way we blocked the roads. We couldn't help it. Old people and children move slowly, and fear was spreading. When they brought out their tanks it became panic. They didn't care. They wanted to get us out of the way. Some people died because of the tanks and others because of the dive-bombers. Aunt Frances died. I was with her, but I couldn't stop. It was death to stop, and I wanted to live. In spite of everything I wanted to live."

Even Rhoda was silenced by the look on her face, a look of such recollected anguish, such misery as defied speech. She wasn't an imaginative woman; when London was being bombed she had convinced herself that people got used to that sort of thing, that there were shelters where you could be safe, that townsfolk don't mind crowds and squalor as country people would; she even made herself believe that the horrors were exaggerated. But you couldn't doubt Stella. Oh, no wonder she had infatuated the young, romantic Simon, this beautiful, mysterious girl.

She said harshly, "I understand. At least, I think so. But don't think it would advance your cause with the Dowager to tell her this. It would only be another weapon in her hand."

"You speak as though I had no armour," said the girl, "and no weapons, either."

"You'll need them. It won't be nice for you if your grandmother and your father-in-law refuse to come to the wedding, or even to acknowledge the bride. Simon has nothing until his father dies, you know. Or perhaps you didn't. And Reuben may go on for twenty years."

"I'm not your step-mother," said the girl. "It isn't Cleveland that matters to me. It's Simon. And the whole army of you can't separate me from Simon. You see, I know . . ." She stopped, smiling at her knowledge. There was in that confident smile on the lips of one who had been derelict and was even now far from safety something so assured that the older woman felt her heart would burst. She had loved the rascally Tom in her youth, but never with gaiety, with a conviction of love returned, a certainty of mutual delight. Always she had timidly offered and Tom had taken what he wanted. And he hadn't wanted much of her, when all was said and done. Elsie was what he had wanted, Elsie whom Edmund had wanted, too. . . . It was like a twisting knife.

"You know so much, don't you?" she heard her dry lips say.

"More than you guess," said the girl. Suddenly her face changed; the light went out of it; she looked tired beyond all words. "You can tell the Dowager from me, if it was she who sent you, that whatever she does I shall have Simon." She paused, and added in an odd voice, "Have you ever heard of secret marriages? They're just as binding as the other kind."

She stopped. Rhoda was looking at her in amazement. "You mean you'd even stoop to that to get Simon? That proves you only think of yourself. If you thought of him . . ."

104

Stella stood up. "Please, will you go now? There can't be anything else for either of us to say. I've told you, I'm desperate and I shall stop at nothing—nothing—to get what I want."

2

Rhoda went back to her room, braided her hair, tied her dressing-gown cord round her thick waist, gave one glance at her face, was apparently satisfied with what she saw or despaired of any improvement, and went along to her step-mother's room. The Dowager Lady Cleveland was sitting up in bed, a small erect figure with her hair in two small stiff grey plaits standing well away from her head. She scorned shawls and boudoir caps, just as she scorned unguents and lotions; her face owed nothing to artifice and was (as the graceless Mr. Crook had already remarked), nothing for Nature to write home about. She wore a hand-crocheted fawn-coloured dressing-jacket of solid texture over a white cambric nightdress lavish with feather-stitching and starched frills. Open on her knee was a large book, with an embroidered marker tucked between the leaves. Rhoda recognized it at once. It was a volume of sermons of trenchant dogmatic content, written by a downright divine at the beginning of the century.

"No shilly-shallying with Heaven," had been his motto. Lady Cleveland approved of it. She had never shilly-shallied herself, holding that those who have a living to earn have no time for the more delicate entertainments of existence.

"You are ill, Rhoda?" she enquired, looking about as welcoming as a refrigerator.

"No," said Rhoda, shutting the door and coming to stand in a state of earnest excitement at the foot of the bed, "but there's something I have to say to you."

"Could it not wait until the morning?"

"No, Victoria, it can't be. I've just been with Stella, talking about Simon. . . ."

"Do you ever talk of anything else?" enquired Lady Cleveland, with a kind of resigned contempt. "Those last two words were superfluous."

For once Rhoda ignored the insult. "You and I, Victoria, have often disagreed about things. . . ."

"Have we?" murmured Lady Cleveland, indifferently, turning a page.

"But all the same, our interests where Simon are concerned are identical," Rhoda blundered on. "Stella's determined to take him away from us—from Cleveland, too, if necessary." Hastily she began to outline the conversation she had just had with the girl.

Lady Cleveland stopped her after a minute. "My dear Rhoda," she said, "do you seriously imagine I'm not a match for a girl like that? Did you ask her, by the way, where she had met Tom Grigg?"

Rhoda looked like something checked in headlong career. "Tom?" she stammered. "And Stella?"

"Didn't you notice her face when I showed her the photograph? But you never did see things right under your nose, did you, Rhoda? What we want to find out," she added, her face hardening, "is when she saw him. Was it some time ago or was it the night he died?"

"The fact is we don't really know anything about her," burst out Rhoda.

"That can be remedied," said the old lady, "and now, unless you have anything fresh to tell me, I must return to Mr. McCorquodale and his doctrine of the sins of the fathers. Unpalatable but unfortunately only too often borne out by facts."

3

After Rhoda had returned to her own room Lady Cleveland pulled a bell by the side of her bed that rang in her son's room. A few years earlier when the Dowager had had an illness that some (though never Rhoda) had thought might be mortal, this bell had been installed, so that at any hour of the night the Earl could be summoned. She used this bell very seldom and only at times of great emergency. Her son, who liked to get full value for every minute of the day, just as he liked to get full value for every penny in the pound, had taken his accounts up to bed and had been working on them when her bell disturbed him. He had put a dressing-gown over his dinner-jacket—war or no war the Clevelands remembered their duty to tradition—for his room was chilly and a fire in a bedroom not to be thought of in times of war—and looked more like his own bailiff than ever.

"You are ill?" he said quickly, coming in and closing the door.

The Dowager, who had more concern for his appearance than for her own, ignored that.

"Reuben," she said, "Rhoda has been here. She is a fool in many ways, but like most fools now and again she stumbles on something important."

"What has she found out now?" enquired her son.

For a minute the old woman did not speak. Then she said, "It's useless trying to move Simon when he's made up his mind. We must find some other way of preventing this marriage. I'm convinced it would be disastrous."

"The important thing is to convince Simon," suggested Lord Cleveland drily. "Do you think you can buy her off?"

"No. I had hoped—but I can see that's impossible. But there are other ways."

He said sharply, "Be careful," and she gave him a look of grim contempt.

"Your father would have mortgaged this place if I'd let him," she said, "and who do you suppose makes it possible for us to live here ourselves, rather than let it to some *nouveaux riches* who'd use it like a museum. And I haven't done all I have to date to lose it now. Simon is going to inherit Cleveland in due course. I'm resolved as to that."

"And so he mustn't marry Stella Reed?"

"I'm glad you understand," said his mother sarcastically.

"She's attractive," murmured Reuben. "A good many men might think so."

"She is at liberty to marry any other man in the world."

"And you think you can turn Simon against her?"

"There are certain things that impulsive young men like Simon expect in a wife, certain things they won't accept. . . ."

"But you've no evidence that this girl . . ."

"As you say, my dear Reuben, I have no evidence. But I shall think very poorly of the Clevelands if within a few days the necessary evidence is not forthcoming."

"How you hate her!" exclaimed Lord Cleveland involuntarily.

"She? She's nothing. It's Cleveland I think of. If your poor wretch of a wife hadn't tired of her duty so early . . ."

Cleveland turned away with a shrug. "They might all have been daughters. Very well, my dear mother, you will, as usual, take your own path, but for once I shall not be surprised if you find you are too late."

CHAPTER THIRTEEN

I'm eyes, ears, mouth of me one gaze and gape,
Nothing eludes me, everything's a hint,
Handle and Help.

ROBERT BROWNING.

CROOK'S HEAD was like a foolproof money-box. Once put anything into it, and no amount of coaxing and cajoling could get it out. He had made up his obstinate mind that the two deaths, though thirty years apart, were linked, and not all the judges on both sides of the Styx could have disabused him of the notion. As for the facts—if they weren't discreet enough to back his theory, then he taught them discretion. Having ruled off Mrs. Manners from his list of suspects since, being his client, she could not conceivably be guilty, he was left with the household at the Manor, and here, he felt, he had a pretty wide choice. His main difficulty was motive. The fact was he didn't know enough and since to get reliable information it is generally thought wise to go to the fountain-head, he ran through the list in the hope of finding one member who might be cajoled or bullied into giving him some information. The Dowager he discarded at once; she thought him dirt, and if he attempted to call on her she'd treat him like dirt—ring for a servant to have him taken away. As for Reuben, he might as well try to break into the Bank of England with a pair of scissors as make any attempt to get past that stony façade. Miss Oliver wouldn't help; she was the kind that really sees blue moons because it means to, and the girl wouldn't know enough. There remained, therefore, the horsey cousin.

While he waited his opportunity to tap him Crook considered the scanty details he had.

"Who stands to profit?" the old man in the Duck and Dragon had enquired, and "Who stands to profit?" demanded Crook of his own soul.

There are two main reasons for murder—passion and greed. Edmund Oliver had been killed—or at all events had died—because he'd got two possessions coveted by others—Elsie Manners and the estate. The proof of the pudding, Crook assured himself, being used to self-communion on the ground that he liked to hear a clever chap talk and a clever chap reply, is in the eating. Grigg didn't get Elsie Manners, and Lady Cleveland did get the estate. Add to that the fact that Grigg was known to be in the neighbourhood at the time, and almost immediately after the death of the heir he went abroad on Cleveland money. What could an enterprising chap like Crook make of that? In fact, he made very little. It was like a lock and a key that didn't match. As obstinate as Beth-Gelert faced with the wolf he hung grimly on to his conviction that the answer lay somewhere in Cleveland Manor. The casual seaman Grigg had knifed down in Swansea didn't come into the affair, except as providing a reason for the exile to return to his own neighbourhood, but he wasn't an essential cause. Grigg, knowing the police were after him, knowing they would probably identify him with his earlier self, because the police aren't suckers, whatever amateurs may believe, wouldn't have come back to a place where he might so easily be recognized unless he was pretty desperate. He'd come for two things, a roof over his head and money in his pocket. And the first was only important until he'd achieved the second. He'd come first to his aunt, but she'd only been a second string. He had had his eye on the big House. If he hadn't been pretty sure of his ground he'd never have risked going up there, being recognized, a wanted man creeping up to the back door of the Deputy Chief Constable. Since he'd asked for the old lady he must have been pretty sure of his onions. He knew the police were after him, knew, too, that you could squeeze lemon-juice out of a china friut before you'd find tenderness or pity in that fierce heart. And yet, for some reason she'd parted with money thirty years ago, she who counted every penny, and the fact that he had gone back to her, like a homing pigeon, lent colour to the idea that whatever the nature of his hold over her a generation earlier, it hadn't weakened with the years.

"The fact is," Crook confided to his tankard, "I'm like the chap in the poem who cried for More Light."

And as he put the tankard down the door of the pub swung open and the cousin marched in.

Gregory Oliver moved to the bar like a man deep in anxious thought, as indeed he was. He appreciated his relatives' uneasiness about this matter of Grigg's death, and the old woman's danger, but he thought it a little unreasonable of them to behave as though there was no other form of trouble in the world. He had plenty of worries of his own, chiefly Pyrethrum. That was enough to keep a man awake of nights. She was young and strong and she came of a good strain; there was nothing to account for her poor physical condition. And now he was warned he might lose her. It didn't bear thinking about. When the barmaid gave him his beer he carried it over to where Crook was sitting and took a place beside him. Crook thought it was a friendly act and darn nice to a stranger till he realized that if Gregory had been sitting next to Adolf Hitler he wouldn't have noticed the difference. Preoccupied—that was the only word for him. Still, here was a chance you couldn't refuse, so after a minute he picked up his tankard and said in his chatty way, "You'd never believe, would you, that some chaps find our war-time beer too strong for them? A bath of this wouldn't make me want to sing."

Gregory's eyes slewed round. For a minute they remained blank. He had a single-track mind and his thoughts had been fully occupied with other considerations. Then he seemed to discover something familiar in the square cheerful figure and he exclaimed, "Hallo, weren't you the chap that found the body? Yes. . . ." And then he stopped abruptly, because it occurred to him that this must be the man Simon was hiring to solve the mystery. Somehow it wasn't in the least what he'd expected. A private enquiry agent, which was how Gregory thought of him, ought to be an unobtrusive slight furtive person, not a great burly man with red eyebrows like the spines of a hedgehog and a voice like a bull of Bashan.

"You'll see a lot more of me before you're through," Crook assured him. "How's tricks?"

The cousin brooded. "Worried about my filly," he confided.

Crook looked astonished till it occurred to him that Gregory was probably one of these literal chaps who, when they say a filly, really mean a little lady horse.

"No wonder you're anxious," he observed in sympathetic tones, though he knew rather less about horses than the average district visitor.

His companion warmed a little. "Saw her sire win the Derby," he explained with real enthusiasm. "That was a race. That was a horse, too. Mind you, there was some queer stories about him. He'd savaged one of the lads at Colley's stable and that sort of thing doesn't do a horse any good."

"Doesn't do the lad any good either," suggested Crook.

"Colley sold him after that to a chap called Lemaire, and he put him out to stud. I bought four of his foals. Petunia, Polyanthus, Pansy and Pyrethrum. Bit of a gardening expert Lemaire is. Calls all his foals after flowers. The first three are all right, but something's gone wrong with the last."

"Bit of a matrimonial slip-up?" suggested Crook, looking like a sympathetic alligator.

"I've just been over to Burke's place," went on the cousin, passing over Crook's badinage like the gentleman he was. "He tells me. . . ." He embarked on a spate of professional detail. "Though, of course," he added when he had talked himself dry, "if you're not a betting man . . ."

"Betting?" repeated Crook, and his eyes were like the eyes of the dog in the tower, as large as mill-wheels. "Why, I'm England's champion gambler. Matter of fact, I trot a very nice little mare myself, though she don't always run quite true to form."

"Mare?" You could almost see Gregory's ears prick.

"Name of Murder," explained Crook, finishing his second tankard at a gulp.

111

The cousin came back to reality. "Of course. You're the fellow young Simon's put on to get the old girl out of the jam."

That was the sort of language Crook understood. He felt at home at once.

"That's me," he acknowledged.

"Never understood much about sleuthing myself," said the cousin, looking a little uncomfortable. "But I suppose you've got ideas."

"I can supply the ideas all right. What I need are the facts. I don't say all the facts but enough to build a foundation. Too many facts are sometimes as dangerous as too few. I've known conscientious chaps make 'emselves a rope necktie out of facts. You know what they say about discrimination. The little more and how much it is. It's like brandy in the Christmas pudding. Too much is a waste. . . ." The cousin looked at him anxiously. Words and ideas were both scarce in his part of the world, and a man who poured them out like beer flowing from a jug aroused his caution. "The truth is," continued Crook earnestly, who wasn't half the fool people sometimes thought, "I'm still looking for the missing link. Why did your crowd pay Grigg to get out thirty years ago?"

Gregory looked more uncomfortable than ever. "Lady C always gave out that there was a bit of trouble between her step-daughter and the fellow," he mumbled. "I wouldn't know. I dare say there wasn't much in it. Though, mark you, you can't be sure. They were a queer couple, she and the boy that died. No moving either of them when they once made up their minds, no matter how unreasonable they were. Edmund was always a bit of a thorn in his father's side. Didn't seem able to take his responsibilities seriously. Used to moon off and daydream. The old man wanted him to marry a girl with a bit of money—they can do with it, y'know. I used to come and stay now and again, but—well, Edmund and I didn't seem to talk the same language. You'd have said an estate was wasted on a chap like that."

"You don't seem to have been the only one who thought so," interposed Crook drily.

"Oh, it don't do to believe everything you hear," the cousin warned him. "He wasn't the first young man not to hit it off with his step-mother. Of course, any one with half an eye could see she was dyin' to get the place for her son."

"Includin' the dreamy Edmund?"

"Oh, he knew all right. What's the use? he'd ask his father when the old man got rorty about this and that, 'Why don't you take Reuben around with you? You know the heir never inherits.' Well, the old boy couldn't say much to that, because he'd had an elder brother accidentally drowned. It made his father wild though. The old lady couldn't stand him either. She can say what she likes about the Curse, but she'd never have forgiven it if it hadn't operated in Edmund's case."

"Nice household it must have been," commented Crook. "Not surprisin' if Sister did go on the rampage."

"Oh, I dare say there wasn't much to that, and I've always thought old Lady C was to blame. Never gave the girl a chance. Treated her as if she hadn't a right to be alive. Naturally Rhoda took any bit of fun that was going."

"Just so," agreed his companion. He hadn't been a lawyer for thirty years without knowing the quite incredible lengths to which disappointed, infatuated young women will go.

"What I don't get," he added, "is why this chap, Grigg, still thought he could milk your lot. Because he obviously did, or he wouldn't have chanced comin' up to the House. Cleveland's the Deputy Chief Constable, he knew the police were after the fellow, and Grigg must have known he knew it. Yet he chanced his arm. Don't you see, he must have known they wouldn't dare give him away. It isn't every secret that's like the caterpillar—improves with keepin'."

"We-ell." Gregory gulped down some beer. "There's some feelin' that it's a bit odd no one but Simon saw the fellow. Mean to say, we were all around that evening. . . ."

"I thought you were all out," expostulated Crook.

"Yes, but we were all on our way back by that time. You'd have thought one of us would have set eyes on him. There was a Home Guard practice, and Cleveland and I were both in it. We had orders to stop any one, drivin' or walkin', and though the exercise was over at half-past six, even so we'd have seen the chap if we hadn't stopped him."

"And neither of you did?"

"I didn't. And if Cleveland had he'd have backed up his son in court."

"I suppose you couldn't have passed him without recognizing him? It was a dirty sort of night."

"Not likely," said the cousin. "I was goin' slow because of the weather. I remember thinkin' I hadn't seen a soul all the way from Bridget St. Mary."

"You came by car?"

Gregory nodded. "You get petrol if you're in the Home Guard," he said. And then he grinned for the first time. "I'm Local Petroleum Officer," he observed.

"Shouldn't have thought a chap who cared for horses like you do 'ud have had much use for a car," suggested Crook, wanting to show he, too, could be matey.

"I haven't," said Gregory Oliver promptly. "That's what makes me such a damn good choice. My idea is to keep cars off the road."

It wasn't surprising, reflected the philosophic Mr. Crook, that no other nation really understood the British. They had a national logic about as easy for other races to comprehend as Chinese to a Cabinet Minister.

"I suppose you're pretty successful," he offered.

"Well, what can these chaps do if I refuse? Write to their M.P. And what does he do? Writes to the Minister of Petroleum. And what does he do? Writes back to me for my comments. He has to take my word for things, of course, because if he don't how's he going to justify my appointment?" The cousin got quite warmed up as his logic expanded. "Naturally, I give way now and again as a matter of policy."

"And that," agreed Crook, "is what's known as horse-sense." He began to have a new respect for horses.

To his surprise the cousin turned an uneasy red. "Come to think of it," he confessed, "there's just the chance I could have missed this chap. I've just remembered I did stop off for about ten minutes coming by Burke's place to ask about my filly. Didn't like the vet's report and that's a fact. I had to go practically past the door anyhow."

"No idea of the time, I suppose?" suggested Crook.

"Oh, it was after half-past six. The exercise wac actually over. And I didn't stay long because the old lady's fussy about meal-times. They have dinner at seven-thirty and I was back in time to change into civilian gear before the gong went. Cleveland just beat me to it and Miss Reed told us about Simon when we came down. It was a gloomy sort of evening, anyway. The girl was brooding a bit—but then she's always quiet. The old lady was annoyed with her step-daughter, because she was late for dinner, and didn't have time to change out of her W.V.S. uniform. She's always inclined to make fun of anything Miss Oliver does. She'd like to have the whole bag of tricks to herself. But that wasn't anything unusual. They were always at loggerheads, those two. No Cross, No Crown, that's their motto. Cleveland added to the gaiety of nations by saying that if we did have invasion God help the country if there were as many fools everywhere else as there are in Mereshire, which he supposed was the county set aside in the old days as a kind of national lunatic asylum. His mother said something about patriotism—and the cook had let the water get in the pudding. You could have stunned any invader with that."

"I hope you told the Dowager so," said Crook cordially, but the cousin only said in a gloomy voice, "Any one can tell you live in a bachelor establishment," and sighed for his own lost liberty.

"So, if Cleveland didn't see him—is there any other road this fellow could have taken?"

"He might have gone through the woods."

But Crook said he thought not. Any one who ploughed through the woods on such a night would have got his shoes coated with mud, and though Gregory suggested lamely that he might have cleaned it off, Crook told him gently not to teach his grandmother to suck eggs.

"The church floor must have borne traces," he said. "Dead leaves and whatnot. No, he came by road all right."

"If he came at all," the cousin agreed.

"Oh, he came all right," said Crook. And left it at that.

The cousin wanted to ask more questions, but while he was trying to summon up courage the bosomy lady behind the bar called "Time, gentlemen, please," and he lost his opportunity.

CHAPTER FOURTEEN

We traced her footsteps to the bridge
And further there were none.

WORDSWORTH.

1

IN SPITE OF HIS HABIT of self-assertion Crook was, in many ways, a modest man. He wouldn't have dared lay claim to intuition which, as everyone knows, is a feminine monopoly, but he did sometimes have hunches which often came off, and one such now told him to hold his horses and retreat to London. Retreat at this stage of the war was according to plan, no matter which side retreated, and the general public said, Oh yeah? and wondered why the authorities thought the man in the street was bound to be a fool. But Crook believed in himself as dipsomaniacs believe in whisky and he was convinced—this was the form this particular hunch took—that once he was out of the limelight things would begin to happen again.

He had made a special virtue of patience and he knew how to wait, a thing all successful lawyers and all successful criminals must learn. And three weeks after the inquest to the day his expectations were fulfilled.

Stella Reed came to see him.

She arrived unannounced and without any effort to make an appointment. She was wearing black which might make her look a little older but certainly added to her air of remoteness; she walked in looking as delicate as a deer and as timid as a lioness.

Crook didn't like women, but Noah greeting his dove with the

116

olive branch in her mouth couldn't have felt more encouraging than he when Bill Parsons brought her in.

"In trouble?" he asked cheerfully, offering her a chair which she accepted and a cigarette which she didn't. "That's fine."

Her delicate brows lifted. "So you'd heard? But . . ."

"Be your age," invited Crook reasonably. "I didn't suppose this was a social call. What is it? Letters?"

"Post cards. So you expected this?"

"It has happened before. How many?"

"Three." She opened her bag. It was a nice bag. Simon had given it to her. "I thought you might be able—and willing to advise me. Simon told me to come to you if anything developed."

He liked the way she came to the point at once. Earning a living may rub the gilt off the gingerbread but it has its advantages. It does teach young females not to waste words.

He picked up the cards. "Pre-war standard," he observed. "What's known as ivory laid. Anything else?"

"One thing. Mr. Crook—are you having me followed?"

"Why should I?" asked Crook simply, "if anyone else is mug enough to do it for me?"

"Then they are?"

"I don't know. But it could be. Mind you," he added, "I'm like a Member of Parliament. I never leave any avenue unexplored. But I haven't put the dogs on you. No scent," he added inelegantly. He took up the cards. "Horsfall. That mean anything?"

"It would be easy for any of the family to go into Horsfall."

"Always supposin' it is one of the family."

"But why should a stranger write to me?"

Crook looked a little sad. "You'd be surprised. Jealousy—love of mischief—no reason at all. Like that recipe for easy drinking." He saw she didn't catch the illusion and kindly supplied it.

> "There are five reasons I do think
> Why men should something something drink,
> Good wine—a friend—or being dry—
> Or that I might be by and by—
> Or any other reason why.

"Still, it's just as likely to be one of your prospective in-laws. Any idea which?"

She sighed. "They're all hostile. I understand that, of course."

"Of course?" His bushy eyebrows, like red hedges, climbed up his imposing forehead.

"If you were the Seventh Earl you'd want your son to marry someone of distinction, wouldn't you?"

"And isn't that just what young Simon's proposin' to do? Who does the chap think he is, anyway? The Archangel Gabriel?"

"I didn't mean that. I meant—they're all democrats, or so Lord Cleveland said in his last speech in the Lords, but they don't want their sons to marry girls who've been in cabaret shows on the continent."

"Y'know," observed Crook, with a great air of tolerance, "it's a darn pity virtue's so exclusive. I mean, ninety-nine times out of a hundred it hasn't got a thing to say to any of its lesser lights—little things like charm and good looks and—well, you get me. I suppose, though," he added, with a yet greater air of being impartial, "if it had, it 'ud leave everything else at the post."

"Not that there's actually anything about my personal history in the cards," the girl went on. "They just—hint."

"I dare say they'll come to it later," Crook assured her. He took them up in date order. The first read:

You will never marry the heir. Get out while there is still time.

The second ran:

Don't think ,ou will be Lady Cleveland for all your scheming. Take a friend's advice and go back to where you belong.

The third said darkly:

Watch out for the cousin. He may be dangerous.

"You see," pointed out Crook, not in the least shocked or surprised by this development, "this chap gets a little nearer the root of the matter with each effusion. The second is an advance on the first and the third on the second. By the time you reach the twenty-second he'll probably have come to the point. What is it, by the way?"

"The point? Oh, I suppose that they don't mean me to marry Simon."

"You're surely not going to let a little thing like that stop you." Crook did look shocked now. "They haven't got anything on you, have they?"

"From their point of view, yes. I've earned a living on the stage—what I'm sure the Dowager would call the illegitimate stage—I don't know who my father was—and I knew Tom Grigg before he came back to Bishop Cleveland."

"You don't do things by halves, do you?" said Crook. She had spoken very quietly. With the same lack of emotion a man may light a fuse that will, within a minute, blow half a landscape skyhigh; but being nobody's fool, he appreciated the involuntary flexing of the muscles, the tightening of the delicate lines round the jaw, the way in which the thin fine hands—where did such a girl get hands like that? The Dowager and Rhoda had short stubby fingers and so had Reuben. Probably the unknown father was responsible—closed round the arms of her chair.

If Stella had anticipated an explosion she was disappointed.

"That would be when Grigg was interested in the entertainment business back in '38," murmured Crook. He looked at the girl speculatively. She couldn't be above twenty or twenty-one now. That made her about sixteen when she met Grigg, and though Crook wasn't a romantic man, he didn't like the idea. He had taken the trouble to look up a bit of the dead man's history and it wasn't savoury reading.

"Did you know that, too?" asked Stella.

"About you? No. Does the family know?"

"I'm not sure about the Dowager. You can never be sure with any one like that. She made a point of showing me a photograph of him as he used to be. I recognized that, because he used to use some of his early photographs when he was in the cabaret business. People used to joke about it. They didn't really think he was the same man."

"Thirty years changes most of us," Crook pointed out. "Some for the better—some not."

119

"Miss Oliver said how much he'd changed. Poor thing, she was trying to defend herself, but she doesn't have to. I can see what the Dowager might do to you if you were defenceless."

"If?" prompted Crook.

"I have Simon," she said.

"How much does Simon know?" Crook enquired.

"Not about Tom Grigg. Well, how could I tell him? Imagine what everyone would think. That he had more cause than any one to want Tom's mouth shut. After all, it was Simon he spoke to that night, Simon who wasn't born when he went away. People would say there was some reason for that."

"And so there might be," Crook acknowledged. "You know, honey, he's got you in a spot."

"That's why I came to you," said the girl simply.

"I had an idea that if I delved far enough into that chap's past I might find something to his credit. Most chaps have done one kind deed once in their lives. But he's the notable exception."

"He wasn't worse than the rest," said the girl, and there was a coldness like death in the voice that could on occasion sound like a gong of gold. "These men who organize cabaret shows in the provinces are very much alike."

Crook wondered if she thought he didn't know. "Give me a decent vulture for choice," he agreed. "Were you doin' stage work when you met young Oliver?"

"Oh no. It was just after France had fallen. I was lucky to get over here. It wasn't a good time for girls to get stage engagements, even if they were known, and of course I wasn't. They hadn't started to conscript women, and the raids on London were just beginning. I had to get a living somehow and jobs were hard to come by, but eventually I found work as a waitress in the Cornwall Hotel."

"Jam for you!" commented Crook, who knew a good deal about the Cornwall. It is, indeed, said of it that the only bar to its chromium swing-doors is the possession of marriage lines. In spite of government regulations, it has made its fortune during the war.

"That's where I met Simon," continued Stella Reed. "He was with a party and I had the fish trolley. I wheeled it to their table. You live mostly on commission at the Cornwall, the wages were

120

nominal. The food they gave the staff was terrible, but at least it was security of a sort. But Simon made me leave it. He said he couldn't bear to think of me working there."

"I get you," said Crook. "Folk like the Clevelands think you can't have that kind of a job and be a good girl."

"They should try it themselves," returned Stella with spirit. "Let them see what they feel like at midnight, when you've been on about twelve hours and you've got to catch the last tube home."

"I believe you. That's why the middle classes—meaning you and me—have to be moral. They've no time to be anything else. The immoral world's bedded down for the night by the time we knock off. Does Grandma know you worked at the Cornwall?"

"I don't know what Simon told her. Anyway, by the time I met her I was doing canteen work down at the Docks. It was just as hard as the Cornwall, and the pay, all told, was worse, but I was glad to be there. I felt the people whose food I was serving and whose dishes I was washing were doing something in the war, just as Simon was. At the Cornwall every woman had a fur coat and half the men . . ." She made a little gesture of disgust.

Crook nodded sympathetically. "There's more fur-bearin' animals than ever came out of the Zoo," he agreed. "I wonder if whoever wrote these cards knows all this."

"It depends, I suppose, on how much enquiry agents can find out."

"If they're any good, as much as the Recordin' Angel," Crook told her promptly. "More, in fact, because if they're smart they can find out all the things that didn't happen."

She didn't answer that. Crook was silent, too, reflecting that a girl like this, who had learned too much about life too young, might well shy at making a present of her history to a lover like Simon Oliver.

"As for the cards," the girl went on, "I didn't know what to do about them. I thought you might be able to take action."

Crook cocked a red eyebrow at her. "Who d'you think I am? Maskelyne and Devant? Why, you said yourself it might be any of them."

Her disappointment was so intense he could have laughed if she hadn't been so distressed.

"But I thought—I thought they'd help," she persisted.

"Oh, sure they help. In fact, they're just what we wanted." He turned one over. "This your London address?"

"Yes. It's what they call a flatlet, which means a room with a lock on the door and a share in the bath."

Crook repressed the retort that that's as much as most married women can expect and more than many of them ever get. He felt marriage might be rather a delicate point with this girl.

"What do we do now?" Stella continued. She wasn't as cool as she looked. Under the surface dignity, anxiety raged like a storm.

"Ever read the psalms?" enquired her man of law. "Well, there's one about the fowler spreadin' the nets and fallin' into them himself or somethin' of the kind. It's a pretty good rule, when you haven't got proof and you can't manufacture it, to sit back and let your criminal weave his own rope. Y'see, what most people can't stand is suspense—no joke intended. Wait long enough and they'll hang themselves from the sheer longin' to be safe. I tell you, half the murders that are found out might go unsolved if it wasn't that the murderers get cold feet and give themselves away. You know how they tell you that murderers return to the scene of their crime. Well, it's true. They keep feelin' they've blundered somewhere and they come back to make sure. Or if nothin' happens they can't believe their luck. They're darn certain the other chap's workin' against them in the dark and they forget that he's got to prove they're guilty, they haven't got to prove they're innocent, and they go round fabricatin' evidence to show they couldn't have been in at the death, and the fellow that knows his onions—in this case—sits back on his hunkers and waits his turn. Ever played poker? Then you know just what I mean. A poker face is better than brains ninety-nine times out of a hundred."

Life had taught Stella not to waste words. She stood up, collected her umbrella—another of Simon's gifts—from the chair where she had laid it, and held out her hand.

"You'll let me know if there's anything for me to do?" she suggested.

Crook beamed. "Sure, honey. And you keep in touch with me. Have you got my number? Here." He scribbled it on a bit of paper and watched her stuff it into her pocket. "You'll lose it," he began to say, and stopped. Experience had taught him it was no good trying to tell women things. They didn't believe you, or if they did they didn't take any notice.

"Nasty night," he said, going to look out of the window. It wasn't night really, but the rain had set in with fog coming up behind it. Even Crook, who loved London, wondered what it looked like to chaps from overseas; but he reminded himself that it was like no other place in the world, and they could console themselves with that thought.

"I'm glad I came," said Stella in her gentle way. "I like to feel you're on our side. And I'll tell you if I have any more cards."

"Don't let them worry you, sugar," Crook advised her. "You leave all the worrying to your Uncle Arthur."

"Nothing will make any difference to me and Simon, whatever they may think. They can't defeat me there. But I'm pleased you know everything. It makes me feel safer."

And how should either of them guess that by coming to his office this afternoon she had virtually signed her death-warrant?

2

After she had gone Crook sat deep in thought for some time, his big stubborn chin cupped in a huge freckled paw. He was brooding on Stella Reed's last words. She had a good deal of assurance, he thought, for a girl with no money, no background, no social position. She must know something to stiffen her backbone like that. And suddenly light broke over him, so that he forgot the misery of the day beyond the smudged window-panes.

"Good Lord!" he exclaimed. "Suppose there was a secret marriage! That would answer everything, would explain . . ." He lifted up his voice and yelled for Bill Parsons.

"Get a chap to go over to Somerset House," he said. "He'll have to be damn quick to get there before they shut for the day."

Bill didn't ask any unnecessary questions. Like Stella, he had learned not to waste words. Crook was scribbling down a note in his big shapeless hand.

"I can only give you an approximate date," he explained, "because

I can't be certain the marriage is an actual one." But if it isn't, his voice said, it's going to upset all my plans.

Bill glanced at the slip of paper. "The heir is putting one over the Curse?" he murmured. But Crook said, "Getting married isn't a free ticket to the Kingdom of Heaven. A lot of times it just balls things up so that you wonder Providence hasn't thought of a better way of carryin' on the human race."

He was so pleased with himself for the notion that he lighted a cigar in office hours.

"A bit of luck that girl coming in this afternoon," he said. "I might never have thought of it. . . ."

But when he said Luck he was thinking of himself and not of the consequences to Stella Reed.

CHAPTER FIFTEEN

A House—but under some prodigious ban
Of excommunication.

HOOD.

1

THE LONDON into which Stella emerged had the appearance of a veiled and forbidden city. A grey drizzle had begun to fall and the town-dwellers went past with heads invisible under spread umbrellas or downbent against the cheerless rain. Already lights had sprung up in a number of windows but these had a naked and cheerless appearance; the omnibuses splashed through the mud in the gutters; the trees were bare and black. The only sounds were those of muted traffic and hurrying feet. The girl had the strange sensation that everyone was hurrying not towards some hopeful destination but away from something sinister.

This part of London had suffered heavily during the bombing; ruined buildings stood naked and untenanted, with boarded windows and shattered steps; railings had been torn down and little or no attempt had been made to clear up the attendant dereliction. Something had gone out of the atmosphere that normally lightened the world; joy and purpose had disappeared.

"Aunt Frances was right," Stella told herself scornfully, "working people can't afford temperament. That is a luxury for the rich."

She made her way toward a tube station with the intention of instantly returning home, but the crowds were thronging the steps and as she stepped aside her eye was caught by the lights of a cinema. The film on view was not a new one; it was one of those little intimate cinemas where the seats are one-and-sixpence, and if you have seen the picture before you can at least relax in the comfortable dark. On a sudden impulse Stella rejected the little cheerless room she called home, and walked into the lighted hall.

That perhaps was her second mistake.

But even inside she couldn't altogether put the memory of those post cards out of mind.

"You will never marry the heir," the sender had assured her. She laughed abruptly, the kind of laugh cinema-goers don't care about. The man next to her strained to see who she was, but Stella didn't even realize his existence. Odd, she reflected, that she had believed, by becoming engaged to Simon, she had discovered security. All she had done was to break into some private park where everyone regarded her as a trespasser and intended to get her turned out.

Donald Duck came and went unperceived. After him aeroplanes dive-bombed cities, ships were launched, tanks raced through the desert, Mr. Churchill gave the V-sign, the Minister of Food put in a good word for dried milk, someone behind Stella said, "Enough to make the cows laugh, isn't it?" and then the big picture began.

And at about the same moment, while Crook was having his inspiration, someone came out of a telephone booth and decided to call it a day. The girl had been to see Crook and that was the end of it—for her. There are some risks no one can afford to take.

2

It was nearly six o'clock when Stella opened the front door of the gaunt house where she had an apartment on the top storey. As she

125

began to mount the steps she heard the far-away clangour of a telephone. Telephones that remain unanswered seem to ring with a peculiar poignancy, like a cry for help—or a warning perhaps. . . . As she got nearer she realized it was the instrument in her own room, and she hurried her steps, knowing the panic of all those whose human contacts are few that it should cease ringing before she could reach it. In her heart sprang the thought, It might be Simon. . . . Another minute and it would have stopped, but that wouldn't have helped her really, because the voice at the other end would have tried again and gone on trying until success crowned its perseverance.

When she had snatched off the receiver, however, it was not Simon's voice that greeted her.

"Are you Mountbar 9191?" enquired a voice.

"Yes. I am."

"Trunk call coming through," said the voice. "Six minutes."

Then it stopped and after a moment a deeper voice took its place. She didn't recognize it for Gregory Oliver at first.

"Thank Heaven you're back. I've been trying and trying. . . . This is Gregory Oliver here."

"Where are you?" she asked, breathlessly.

"The Manor. I can't talk more than a minute. You know how public things are here."

Stella knew. There was only one telephone and it stood in an exposed position in the hall. Old Lady Cleveland said that if people had private business they could transact it by letter. Telephones were for emergencies, such as summoning doctors or ringing up workmen if the boiler burst and, since for such occasions a servant was the most suitable emissary, she had had the instrument put in the least comfortable and confidential spot in the house, in the big windy hall where anyone coming or going could overhear your conversation. No wonder Gregory's voice sounded so guarded.

"I'm here," she said. "Is it Simon?"

"So you'd heard?" No disguising the surprise at the other end of the wire . . . But it wasn't astonishing really. Being in love did that to you, though, she reflected, Gregory could hardly be expected to realize that.

"No, nothing. What is it? Nothing's—happened?"

"No, no. But he rang up here about an hour ago. He thought you might be down here."

"Why should he think that? I write every day. . . ."

"He'd been trying to get through to you and couldn't get any reply."

Her conscience smote her. For the past hour and more she had been sitting in a meaningless cinema and all the time Simon had been calling and getting only nothingness for his pains.

"I said I'd try and contact you and tell you that he's got twenty-four hours leave and is coming up to London."

"Coming here?" Joyfulness warmed her voice at once.

"He's got to go to the family's London house in Chapel Row. Something to do with a War Damage Commission claim. The place was knocked about a bit in the blitz and Cleveland's trying to recover something. Simon suggested you might meet him there. There's a caretaker on the premises."

"Chapel Row? But, Gregory—I mean, it sounds so unlike Simon. If he wanted me to meet him and he couldn't come here, why not a restaurant?"

"I don't know. As a matter of fact. . . ."

"Yes. Oh, Gregory, please!"

"Look here, Stella, I can't stop here any longer. The place is bristling with curiosity. I told Lady Cleveland I had to ring up Burke but I dare say she didn't believe me. Rhoda, too—you know how it is . . . ?"

Oh yes, Stella knew. She could imagine the old lady, hidden in shadows, eavesdropping from the landing above, Rhoda's face peering through a half-open door, even Cleveland finding some excuse to cross the hall.

"The number's twenty-six. He said about eight o'clock. I must ring off. . . ."

"One moment, Gregory," she pleaded. "I know it sounds desperately melodramatic, but—you're quite sure it was Simon who rang up?"

She expected to hear him laugh, solid unimaginative Gregory to whom two and two would never make more than four and who'd never be caught out with posers about the number of beans that make five. But to her discomfort there was only silence at the other end of the line.

"Gregory," she whispered, and a rapid furtive whisper came back.

"Stella, I didn't mean to say anything. It seems so absurd, but then everything about this household is a size bigger than life. So— no, I'm not absolutely sure. I keep telling myself that telephones alter voices—yours doesn't sound quite natural—but even so I can't be certain it was Simon speaking."

Before she could say anything else there was a little click and she realized he'd gone. She sat for some time in the cold room, oblivious to the gathering dark and to the fact that it was time to do the blackout. She was thinking, "Not Simon? Not Simon?" and the inevitable question followed, "Then who?" The answer, of course, was the writer of the anonymous post cards, translating threats into actuality. But to what end? She put out her hand to the telephone.

"Keep in touch with me," Crook had said. She might at least ask his advice. Somehow Chapel Row, with a stout Mr. Crook in attendance, would be robbed of all horrors. But, her hand on the instrument, she paused again. How absurd he'd think her! And what evidence had she that Simon wasn't, in fact, coming to town? If she rang up his unit she could find out for herself. She lifted the receiver and dialled Tolls.

At Mexford someone told her in a sharply military voice that Captain Oliver wasn't available.

She said gently, "This is Miss Reed speaking. I wanted him rather urgently."

The voice said, "Hold on," and someone else came. "Miss Reed? I'm afraid Simon's not here. Got twenty-four hours' leave suddenly and said he was coming to town. He ought to be up pretty soon. I expect he'll be ringing you. In fact, he was putting through a phone call just before he left."

"Oh yes," she said quickly. "I was out. Thank you so much."

It wasn't thinkable that one of Simon's brother officers could be in any plot against her. The weight lifted from her heart. Delight took its place. She understood it all now, Simon was going to see some official of the War Damage Commission in the morning, and before the interview took place he wanted to look at the house, esti-

128

mate the extent of the damage. There was a caretaker there, so it wasn't so odd as it had sounded at first. She hurried into the other room. She had plenty of time if Simon had said about eight. She changed her dress, brushed her hair till it was like silk; her hands trembled with excitement. But on the threshold, pausing for a final glance, the thought came to her that there was, after all, no harm in just letting Crook know where she was going. It didn't seem to matter now if he laughed. With Simon so near nothing was very important. But when she dialled his number she could hear the bell ringing in an empty office. If she'd called him when the notion first came to her she'd have caught him, but at this moment Crook was sitting in a comfortable bar—The Bag of Nails in Merton Street—telling a new client that his idea that he was guilty was all moonshine.

"I only defend the innocent," he was saying. "When I die they'll find that carved on my heart."

"It doesn't matter," said Stella, putting the receiver back.

But it was a pity all the same. Crook knew that incredible things can happen, but even he wouldn't have swallowed that rendezvous like a nestling opening its mouth for a particularly outrageous worm. As it was no sixth sense warned him that a girl without a guardian angel, was slipping out into the wet streets, going to meet death in the dark.

Chapel Row is one of those narrow streets in Belgravia that are so shut off from the general flurry of life that they seem altogether remote from it. This part of London also had suffered from German bombing. No. 26 had a desolate, even a sinister appearance. A fire-bomb had wrecked the roof, blast had blown out the windows; on the ground and first floors the wavering beam of Stella's torch picked out shutters drawn close over the damaged window-frames. Black railings enclosed steps leading to an impenetrable blackness that was the basement; the front door had once been a cheerful yellow but now the paint was darkened and chipped and an air of indefinable squalor hung over the whole building. The houses on either side were empty, great red "E" labels proclaiming the fact. The lock of No. 26 was loose as though burglars had made a half-hearted attempt to break in and had desisted through sheer boredom—and indeed the house offered no encouragement to the most enterprising thief. Seeing this deserted barracks all her fears returned to torment her. Surely, surely, reason urged, Simon, who lived in the daylight, would never have chosen this haunted place for a rendezvous. It was, indeed, a strange house to be the town headquarters of such a family as the Clevelands, but the fact was that the Clevelands never resided in town. The Dowager's predecessor had been an invalid for many years before her death and, there being no daughters to launch on a successful social career, the family had tended to vegetate on their country property. As for Simon, he provided his own entertainment and without much obvious effort had contrived to go his own way since his Eton days. If there had once been an imposing town residence, no one seemed to know anything about it now. This narrow house, forming part of a narrow life-line between two lively squares, had been bought by a former Lord Cleveland for the convenience of his private life, a life he had contrived to carry on with great efficiency and satisfaction to himself for a good many years. After his death the family used it as the middle classes use their week-end cottages, for brief relaxation but never for solid living. In the last hundred and fifty years at all events no child had been born here and the only death known to the family had been that of the lady for whom the property was originally purchased. It had not, therefore, anything to recommend it romantically and the German bombers had simply completed a desolation that history and the Clevelands had begun.

While Stella hesitated at the foot of the three steps leading to the battered front door, she heard heavy steps approaching her in the rainy darkness. The steps were on the farther side of the street but she heard them crossing towards her, slowing down. Hurriedly she went up and pulled the old-fashioned bell. It was presumably typical of the Clevelands that, although electric light had been installed, the bells were the old-fashioned variety that hang in a row in the kitchen and jangle discordantly in due season. The new-comer wore a policeman's helmet and a shiny black cape streaming with water. The rain was now descending in a steady downpour. Suspicion betrayed itself in every movement as he drew nearer. In his experience people didn't come visiting in this deserted byway. Stella pulled the bell so ener-

getically that both listeners could hear the reverberation. The policeman could see nothing but a slender figure under an open umbrella.
He hesitated. Then:

"Don't think you'll find any one at home, miss," he offered.

"There's a caretaker," said Stella quickly, without turning. "She's
expecting me."

The policeman nodded and moved on. Might as well be a rat and
be done with it as live in that perishing basement, he thought. He
was a family man and it was comforting to remember his wife and
five children to whom he'd be returning as soon as he came off duty.
They spent part of their time in a basement, too, having stayed in
London all through the raids and feeling basements were safer for
children, but his basement was as different from this as chalk from
pre-war cheese. He didn't altogether like the position—the girl
looked very young—but these young women know how to look after
themselves, he reminded himself, and stifling his suspicions he
moved on. It was a relief to find himself in the comparative cheerful-
ness of Chapel Square.

And that, too, was a pity. Because if he'd given imagination rein
for once things might have turned out very differently.

After the echo of the bell had died away, Stella stood on the
cracked steps hearing the footsteps going farther and farther into the
gathering fog, which seemed to deepen suddenly, closing round her
like folds of blanket; silence came down like a blind between her and
the living, breathing world. Only the thought of Simon, who was life
itself, sustained her.

Inside the house nothing seemed to be happening. Perhaps the
caretaker had gone to the pictures, or was blind drunk in the basement—and who, in such surroundings, could blame her?—or perhaps
she had died days ago and no one had found her yet. Traditionally
bottles of milk accumulated on the doorstep and aroused the suspicion of the neighbours, but nowadays plenty of people fetched their
milk and there weren't any neighbours. She thought, "I can still go;
it's not too late. I can tell Simon I came and no one answered. He'll
understand."

But her need for Simon was like her need for air, and her imagination, sensitive and treacherous, pictured him at that very instant

hailing a taxi—Simon could conjure taxis even out of fog—driving here, waiting and waiting, wondering why the deuce she didn't come. She couldn't understand even now the tremendous gulf that yawns between those who have always been secure and those who don't know how to spell the word.

"I'll ring once," she decided, "and if no one comes I'll go."

She put out her hand to the bell. This time instead of the former bold jangle no more than a tinkle resulted. "No one will hear that," she thought. "No one will come."

She prepared for flight, but it was too late. She had had her last chance and had thrown it away. She could make no more mistakes, for no more opportunities were to be hers.

Her second summons, faint though it was, had aroused the life that lurked in the black house. Lingering, ears astrain, hearing at first nothing but the drumming of the storm on the roof of her umbrella and the swirl of water in the gutters, presently she discerned another sound, the slow approach of footsteps not this time in the street but from within. A deep voice muttered indistinctly, "I'm coming. Don't be impatient. I'm coming." That voice startled her. She'd expected a woman. Now the caretaker was wrestling with bolts and chains, muttering the while.

"I wasn't expected," thought Stella. "It is a trap. No one was expected." Then she remembered that the message had said eight o'clock. Simon wasn't expected till eight, and it wasn't much after seven.

She heard herself whisper, "I'll come back," but the mysterious creature on the other side of the door replied, "Wait a minute, wait a minute. It's this lock. It sticks." Like someone in a nightmare she knew she had heard an echo of that voice somewhere, but couldn't remember where. The rain, that had been heavy before, now came down in a sudden deluge. It slashed down the sides of the umbrella the girl was attempting to close, ran in icy streams down her neck, soaked her ankles. In the gutters it broke into spray. The whole world seemed as deserted as in the days of the Great Flood.

The caretaker seemed to abandon the unequal struggle. She heard an exasperated mutter of "Open the flap. Open the flap." She put out a chilled hand and pushed the heavy letter-flap inwards. As she did so she remembered a film Simon had taken her to see, in which a poisonous snake had been introduced into a house through a similar flap. However, it was no snake that now made its appearance, but a Yale key, thrust up at her by a cold hand. She took it dazedly.

"See if it'll open from the outside," she was ordered. "It jams or something."

Stella took the key and tried to thrust it into the lock, but partly because her hands were shaking, partly on account of the dark and the rain, and partly, too, because the lock was loose, she was no more successful in her efforts than the caretaker had been. In her nervousness the key slipped from her fingers, and she stooped and groped on the wet step. Now that she no longer had the protection of her umbrella she felt as though the rain were soaking into her very bones.

"Well?" said the voice impatiently.

"I've dropped the key," she stammered. Then she found it and renewed the struggle. But it was no good.

"The lock's loose," she said in despair. "Isn't there any other way in?"

"There's the basement, but the steps aren't any too safe in the dark. Mr. Simon won't like that."

At the mention of his name her heart leaped again. "Then you are expecting him?"

The voice immediately sounded suspicious. "Didn't you know? I thought you were here to meet him. There was a telegram. . . ."

"I am, I am." A more logical creature might have paused to wonder how a telegram could be delivered at a house whose door was bolted and barred, but she was beyond logic. The voice said, sounding farther off as its owner retreated, "I'll have to come up the basement way and let you in. They won't come these days and do anything for you."

Stella gave a final furious wrench to the key and without warning it turned and she was almost precipitated into the dark hall. The caretaker had disappeared. Stella could see the glow of a torch descending the stairs.

"It's all right," she called. "I'm in."

It was pitch-black in the hall, and she felt for her torch. It came on for a second, revealing emptiness, uncarpeted boards, unhung walls, then, as surprisingly as the key had moved in the lock, the battery expired and she stood stock-still in the dark.

"Come on down," called the caretaker.

"My torch has gone out," whispered Stella. "I'm afraid of running into things."

An arm came round the top of the stairs and a powerful light was flashed in her face. She put up her arm to shade her eyes; the next instant the beam lowered, lying like a pencil of light on the stained parquet floor. Stella followed the moving shaft; like a snake it was creeping along the boards.

"Take care of the steps," warned the voice. "They're stone and very steep."

Her foot felt precariously round the curve of the stairs, her hand was outstretched for a rail.

"You'll have to come down another step." The torch was lowered suddenly leaving her in darkness. A hand caught hers. "Straight down," said the voice. Her foot caught in something, her hand tried to pull itself clear. But she hadn't a chance. That other hand pulled mercilessly. She gave a despairing cry. "Simon!" Someone laughed.

"Save your breath!" said the contemptuous voice. "He's not coming here."

As she fell she knew where she'd heard this voice before. This was the voice that had spoken on the telephone, bidding her come to Chapel Row, the voice that proclaimed itself Gregory Oliver. That was all there was time to remember; she had the sickening experience of falling through space, felt a crashing pain in her head and then even the torch went out and everything was as dark as death.

3

The darkness hadn't abated one jot when Stella fumbled her way back to agonized consciousness. Her head reeled and as she moved it the pain was so great that she whispered under her breath. Memory did not return in a flash; first one detail and then another served to remind her where she was. Shakily she put her hand to her eyes, for surely they were bound. But the darkness was the natural darkness of an underground room whose windows are securely boarded. Her languid hand moved along the floor; she was apparently lying asprawl without so much as a cushion under her head. She had supposed she might be in a cellar, but the floor was paved with wood, so it was presumably a room of some kind. Painfully she recalled the events of the evening, her arrival at the house, the mysterious caretaker, her tremulous descent of the stairs, the firm hand on her wrist.

"Is this where I fell?" she thought, and sat up somehow, her head throbbing as though weights swung from her eyes.

Common sense, however, assured her that if the stairs had been made of stone the passage to which they led would be stone also. No, clearly she had been moved into a room of some kind. She felt for her torch, then remembered it was useless. There remained, then, only her sense of hearing and her bare hands—for, since she didn't smoke, she carried neither lighter nor matches. She put her hand into her pocket to find her handkerchief, and to her surprise encountered something unfamiliar. It was small and smooth and she knew it by the feel. It was one of those books of matches you get out of slot machines.

"That wasn't in my pocket when I reached the house," she told herself, forcing her aching brain to think. "So—someone put it there. But why? So that if I did come round I could strike a light. But that doesn't make sense. Why not leave a light burning, if only a candle. And anyway, why should they want me to see where I am?"

The natural instinct of the human creature, to illuminate darkness, made her tear a match from the little packet. But, hand uplifted, she paused once more. When she stood on the steps waiting for the key to be passed through the letter-flap, a little warning bell had pinged in her brain. Don't—go—in, it had pealed. Don't—go—in. And she had paid no heed. Now for the second time that mysterious sixth sense that most people are content to ridicule whispered, Don't strike a light! Don't strike a light!

She couldn't imagine why her instinct should urge her thus until, her head clearing, she was aware of another sensation, a growing sickness, a difficulty in breathing and, as she listened intently, a slow faint hissing scarcely audible above the steady downpour of the pitiless rain.

When she began to understand she stumbled to her knees, rose shakily and felt her way round to the door of the room. But she felt in vain for the handle. It had been removed and the keyhole had been stuffed with something hard, like cement. She lay down and tried to peer under the crack, but whoever had put her here had made a thorough job of it. The crack was securely blocked from the outside; and the window was boarded up, not a vestige of air could leak into the room, while the place was slowly filling with escaping gas.

"That's why the matches were put in my pocket," she realized sickly, leaning against the wall. "I was meant to strike one and then . . ." Then nothing would have mattered much. She didn't know how long she had been here, but probably some time. She had a watch on her wrist, but she could see nothing. Then she remembered the tiny luminous clock she always carried in her bag and kept beside her bed at night. Perhaps they hadn't taken that. But when, on all fours, she felt feverishly for the bag, it had gone. The murderer wasn't leaving anything to chance. There wasn't to be any way of identifying her, even if the gas took effect without her regaining consciousness. She remembered a recently-reported case in the press about a deserter who strangled himself in an empty house and whose body was not discovered for four months. It might easily be the same here. No one ever came to this place. She'd be a handful of bones and rotting rags before they stumbled on her.

Horror of this type is cumulative. The victim cannot accept all the implications of his position at once; it must swell like the incoming tide, gathering force with every wave. But when at length she could appreciate her situation panic assailed her. She ran desperately from wall to wall, beating against them, crying out in the futile hope that she might be heard above the shouting of the rain, as though her feeble voice could penetrate the thick boards that covered the space where once glass had been. She hammered on the door, scrabbled frantically at the boards as though she could dig her way out like a mole. . . .

After a minute reason began to return. All this was a mere waste of energy, a tossing away of any feeble chance that might remain. Her first task was to locate the gas leak and if possible stop it up. The air was bad, but not yet choking, though common sense warned her that even if she could prevent any further supply of gas entering the room, a place so hermetically sealed could not provide sufficient oxygen to sustain life more than a strictly limited period.

"Oh Simon!" she whispered again. But how on earth would Simon think of looking for her here? Even Crook, whose mind ranged the fantastic in the course of his professional activities, would never think of this.

A careful examination of the walls revealed the fact that there was neither fire nor tap to account for the gas-flow. She straightened herself and moved slowly, erect, round the room. She must depend upon hearing now and every moment was of value. Despair, it is true, whispered, "Why bother? What's the use? Even if you turn off the gas you'll only starve or choke to death. Gas is kinder, quicker. . . ."

It would be quicker still to light one of the matches. She had a hazy impression that she need only do that for the whole house to rise and crumble to dust like something in a fairy tale. Lest panic should overwhelm her she took the matches from her pocket and flung them away from her. It was not so difficult, after all, to discover the leak. Once, a long time ago, gas had been used to light this room, and an old-fashioned bracket still stood stiffly out from the wall. Someone had wrenched off the tap and turned on the gas from outside the room, and struggle though she might she could not shut it off at the source. She wrenched at the bracket, but it was firm in its place, and anyhow, wrenching wouldn't help. It would only release an increased flow of gas into the room, hasten her end.

And now she knew she was lost. Once as she listened she heard footsteps going by outside, and she screamed and battered on the boards, but no one came. No one heard that voice, no louder than a kitten's, or heard those little fists battering out their grim cry for aid. Another memory stirred in her and she thought, Yes, this is what Tom Grigg felt, battering on another door, choking as I'm choking now, and she knew that whoever was responsible for the first crime was responsible for this one, too.

As her senses clouded over and the gas forced itself into her lungs she thought, "Now Simon will never know," and then, "The writer of those cards wins, after all," and she thought of Crook whose motto was "Crook always gets his man," and she laughed, a silly lightheaded chuckle, because he might get his man all the same, and the fact that she'd had to die to secure him the necessary evidence—assuming that her death was of any value at all—wouldn't bother him. Facts were what he liked—facts and puzzles and problems—not human beings and their tragedies and their hopes. And she knew, if he could get through to her in some other world, he'd only say reproachfully, "I told you to keep in touch with me, sugar. You didn't give me a chance."

CHAPTER SIXTEEN

Twice one is two and twice two is four,
But twice two is ninety-six if you know the way to score.

G. K. CHESTERTON.

1

P. C. TRIPP looked distastefully at the narrow mouth of Chapel Row. He didn't like these little streets—furtive was his word for them. Furtive was a pretty good word for the people who lived here, too. You didn't look here for normal family life, prams and fairy cycles and all the outward signs of normality. No, in Chapel Row gentlemen kept their janes—what an earlier generation had called doxies—and all kinds of odd rackets went on behind these narrow-chested front doors. Since the war and especially since the blitz the Row had been mostly deserted. It had taken a caning from Jerry, and anyway the lovely ladies were rounded up these days by Mr. Bevin, and though a good many of them had slipped through his net, because there are some professions even the Ministry of Labour won't touch, they'd found other hunting-grounds these days. The black-out protected them, too. Probably made a good thing out of it with all the lonely chaps there were going round London.

It was queer, he reflected, to see that girl there this drenching night. It was the first sign of life he'd seen for a long time. He wondered if she'd got in, after all. With a feeling of repugnance he turned sharply and walked past the blitzed houses. On the other side of the street the rain sucked pitilessly at the leaves in the gutter, an odd gasping noise.

"Here, hold on!" P. C. Tripp admonished himself, "you'll end up a flicking poet if you ain't careful, and then what'll happen to the missus and the kids?"

Resolutely he began to patrol the Row. "Where's your blinking ambition?" he asked himself sternly. This was just the sort of street where you'd expect to find a ghost—or a corpse—and though he'd never seen a ghost and wasn't interested anyway because you can't bring a charge against a spirit, a body was what every police constable likes to find, provided it's dead enough and is a victim of foul play. Thinking of corpses made him think of the girl again. Had she got in? So far as he could remember he hadn't seen a sign of life in the house where she was ringing, not all the time he'd patrolled this beat. It would be easy to recognize it by its yellow door. Snapping on his lantern he swung it from house to house. He didn't really expect to find anything and, seeing the windows were boarded up, he didn't know how he could hope to tell whether she'd got in or not. Anyway, it was probably Chapel Square she wanted. Chapel Square was a nice cheerful thoroughfare, all the houses inhabited, radios going in the kitchens from morning till night, dogs barking and cats streaking up the basement steps. . . .

He reached 26 and stopped dead. Because there in the beam of his lantern was the evidence not only that Stella had got into the house, but that she hadn't come out.

All he had to go on for this daring assumption was an umbrella.

It stood propped against the brickwork by the front door, a handsome ladies' umbrella, covered in the sort of silk you can't get any longer, a long elegant umbrella with a crook handle and a gold band. It wasn't quite closed, as though whoever had put it there had been in rather a hurry, and the rain not only streamed down the shining silk sides, but had gathered in a little pool inside.

"Shocking for the ribs," mused P. C. Tripp severely, picking the umbrella up. There might be a name on the band, but as it happened there wasn't. When he gave it to her, Simon had said to Stella, "Might as well wait and have your real name put on it," by which, of course, he meant Stella Oliver and not Stella Reed.

139

"Something fishy here," reflected P. C. Tripp stolidly. "Funny leaving the brolly on the step anyway, brollies not being so easy to come by these days."

Still the lady inside might be the spinster kind who doesn't want a wet umbrella dripping over her hall. Though most people who are as funny as that have umbrella stands or bath-rooms. . . . And what sort of a girl was she that she was prepared to leave it outside? One thing, continued Tripp, his thoughts moving steadily onward, she wouldn't have come out and left it there, not on a night like this. No, dang it all, she wouldn't have left it there anyhow, just getting ruined in the rain. Which sounded all right, only—there the umbrella was and the young lady wasn't.

Tripp hesitated. An ambitious chap—with five children—doesn't want to make a fool of himself to his superiors, and breaking into someone else's house is the act of a lunatic. On the other hand, a man who isn't prepared to take chances usually ends up where he began. It was a problem and no error.

He examined the front door again. That knocker and letter-flap hadn't seen polish these twelve months, he'd take his davy, and his old woman 'ud throw a fit at the sight of the steps. Clean steps are a sign of respectability throughout the United Kingdom, and these steps hadn't seen water, bar rain, since the New Year. There was something screwy about the lock, too. P. C. Tripp's father was a locksmith, and he'd taught his son a bit about locks. Honest or dishonest trade, he used to say, knowing something about locks is a help. If there'd been any one living in the house they'd have had that lock put right, Tripp reflected. Ergo, there wasn't. And yet you had the odd situation of a girl knocking at an empty house and getting in and not coming out again. He flashed his lantern lower. As he expected, the basement windows had gone, and no attempt had been made to replace the glass. Tripp remembered something else his father used to say when he was teaching his son cricket.

"Play careful," he told him, "but remember now and again it pays to swipe. Blocking balls can keep you in all afternoon, but it's runs that win the match."

"Here goes," said P. C. Tripp and he rang the bell and thundered on the knocker, till it was a wonder the fire escape didn't come dashing to his assistance. If any one was inside he'd simply hand in the umbrella and say he'd found it on the step. Either way he was covered. He stood there forming the words he was going to say. But he might have saved himself the trouble, because nobody came.

"So you're still there, are you?" commented the police constable. "Living or dead." And then wished he hadn't added that. A person would have to be pretty dead not to hear his summons with bell and knocker. "What next?" P. C. Tripp wondered. He couldn't go on standing there all the blooming evening holding someone else's umbrella. If any one else should come this way they'd think him nuts. "Go back to the station p'raps," thought P. C. Tripp. But he didn't much fancy telling the Super what he thought. Go on, Ernie, take a chance, he told himself. One good swipe.

Breaking into the house was much easier than you'd have expected. The lock gave almost at once under his bullock pressure, and he came slithering into the hall. It was immediately obvious that someone had been here before him, someone coming in from the dripping night, because there were muddy footprints on the parquet. In spite of the dull surface and the general air of abandonment, they showed clearly enough, and he was careful not to foul them. The stairs leading upwards were uncarpeted, and since there were no footmarks there it seemed fairly clear that the girl had gone downstairs. Besides, the footprints led in the direction of the basement steps. They were a steep flight and very dark. He went down carefully and about as quietly as an elephant. There were electric switches everywhere but when he pressed them nothing happened. No one had been living here for a long time, just as he'd thought. He didn't like it a bit.

Half-way down the stairs he stopped and shouted "Any one there?" but there was no reply. He charged down the remainder as noisily as Crook himself could have done, and stood taking stock of his surroundings. There was a number of doors painted a kind of varnish-red and he opened the nearest, which led into the kitchen. There was a great cooking-range, rusty with disuse, and a modern gas cooker and a sink under the window; being at the side of the house this window had been only partially demolished and the lower panes were still in place. The next door proved to be a store cupboard, but at the end of the corridor he saw a door with neither key nor knob, which struck him as sinister. He heaved at the door with his great frame, felt it strain but not give and stood back for another attempt.

"If this is a cellar, Ernie," he reminded himself, "you be careful or you'll go down the steps with a wallop and be one of these skeletons they'll discover in the Peace Age."

It struck him as peculiar, too, that someone had carefully laid one of those draught excluders that look like snakes in bright red and blue cotton, against the door from the outside. Heaven knew these old houses were nests of draughts, but if there was someone the other side of the door the snake should be inside the room and not outside of it. He looked at the lock, but that was blocked, and when he stooped lower a wave of something that wasn't pure oxygen came at him from under the crack.

"Cripes!" he said. "It's gas. Well, the idea!"

The idea of coming to an empty house in order to commit suicide, he meant, but the next instant he saw his mistake. Because you can't commit suicide from one side of a locked door and put down a draught excluder on the other. He bruised his shoulder in another attempt to break through and thought regretfully of those countries where they entrust the police with firearms. Still, bullets are awkward things to fire through a panel when you've no idea exactly who's on the farther side or how they've arranged themselves.

When it was obvious that he wasn't going to break down the door by brute force he began to hunt for a weapon, and presently he found a coal hatchet and tried smashing down the panels with that. The gas that came out to meet him nearly choked him and he went back to the kitchen, found the appropriate handle and turned off the gas supply. Even so it was pretty bad, but he persevered till he could burst open the door and then his lantern showed him someone lying on the floor in the dark. He'd wanted a body earlier in the evening, but now he'd have given his hope of promotion to feel the stir of life in that limp form. He ducked his head and got hold of the girl and lugged her out into the kitchen, and he shut the door to exclude as much gas as possible and flung up the window. The water supply was cut off as he had anticipated, but there was plenty of water outside. On the sill stood a little square red flower-pot that had once held a plant, and the rain had collected conveniently in that, so he brought it in and began to splash water on the girl's face. It was a pity, he thought, that he didn't know more about first aid.

He went upstairs presently, when it became obvious that the girl wasn't coming round of her own accord, looking for a telephone. But the instrument had been removed some time ago. He remembered that there was a call-box at the corner of Chapel Square, and he ploughed down there, without meeting a soul on the way, and rang up the station. Then he dashed back as though someone might have kidnapped the girl during his absence. But she was still lying on the bare kitchen floor, her face greenish in the glow of his lantern, her fair hair draggled round that ghastly face. He remembered that when people are coming round from gas poisoning they are invariably sick.

This one proved no exception to the rule.

2

Mr. Crook was in his big shabby room in Earl's Court, as fresh as a daisy and as fit as a flea, when the knock fell on his door. Either he had a perfect conscience or none, for he didn't turn a hair when he saw a sergeant of police outside. Instead he opened the door wider.

"Will you walk into my parlour?" he invited.

The parlour was thick with the smoke of the rank black cigars on which Crook cheerfully throve out of office hours. There were papers everywhere, the ceiling had been freshly distempered and the walls likewise. Crook didn't like the distemper which was primrose yellow; his idea of a suitable setting was a nice dark red paper with a pattern on it. He thought the landlord ought to knock something off the rent for making this change without consulting him.

"If any of my regulars come in and see that," he complained, "they'll think I've gone pansy."

The sergeant seated himself gingerly on the chair Crook emptied of documents to receive him, looking as though he expected to find a squeaking roll or a fake banana under the upholstery.

"Beer?" asked Crook.

The sergeant, whose inappropriate name was Peacock, said No, thank you. He was a total abstainer and he didn't smoke. On the other hand, he played hockey for the police.

"Well," said Crook, refusing to be dashed, "I get a lot of queer customers up here, but I must say I've never had a member of the Force before. What's the trouble? Bribery and corruption or—murder?"

"Why should it be either?" demanded the sergeant, who clearly had no sense of humour.

"You'd hardly come to me at this hour for anything less."

The sergeant said, "It looks like murder—attempted murder, that is. And it would have come off, only one of our chaps had his wits about him. . . ."

"And foiled the villain and probably did me out of a job. Are you here to gloat or do I come into this somehow?"

The sergeant took out his notebook and from that extracted a crumpled bit of paper that he laid on the table.

"We found that in the room where the young lady was," he said. "Your telephone number."

Crook snatched it up. "I knew she'd lose it the first time she pulled out her handkerchief. Well, go on, man. Move, can't you? What room was the young lady in and what was your chap doing nosing round?"

The sergeant, who had come to ask questions, not to answer them, was inclined to be stand-offish.

"Can you identify the lady to whom you gave this?" he demanded.

"Look here," said Crook, putting his great leg-of-mutton fists on the table, "you can cut all that. I stand in *loco parentis* to the girl to whom I gave that and if anything's happened to her you can damn well tell me. Any one would think you were a flapper trying to open a bottle of fizz the way you go on," he added, witheringly.

"If you've got any information," began Sergeant Peacock.

"Who am I to do the police's job for them? Not that I expected whoever it is to strike so soon. I suppose something happened."

"You should have come to us," repeated the sergeant.

"Be your age," said Crook, "you can't go to the police about a crime no one's committed. Where is the girl? and how bad is she?" He jammed on his brown bowler, hauled a disreputable mackintosh off a peg and pushed his pudgy arms into the sleeves.

"Lead me to her," he commanded. "By the way, got in touch with her people yet? The in-laws, I mean."

The sergeant, beginning to lose his temper, said, "There's no marks of identification, no bag, nothing. We don't know her name."

"I'll tell you. And while we're on our way you can tell me what happened."

The sergeant didn't like being hustled, but he didn't stand a chance with Crook.

"You get your men cracking for the handbag," the lawyer advised him. "I'll give you a description. I noticed it particularly."

Stella was in no shape to tell any story or give any information when the two men reached the hospital. The doctor said the gas poisoning was pretty bad, but it wasn't the worst. She'd suffered a serious shock, and mustn't be badgered by any one. For himself, he wouldn't be surprised if brain fever set in.

Crook, who had abandoned his normal air of deliberate jollity, stood by, pinching his formidable lower lip between a giant finger and thumb.

"See here, sergeant," he said, "when that girl came to see me this afternoon she hadn't a notion of going to Chapel Row. But according to your chap she was there about seven o'clock. So something happened during the three hours after she left my office."

"Letter perhaps," said the sergeant, but Crook said, "More likely to be a telephone call. Letters hang people, y'know. Who's goin' to trace a telephone call? Look here, I'm goin' along to her place."

"We are going there, naturally," said the sergeant.

"And I'll come with you, like the tin can on the dog's tail. Taxi!"

The sergeant began to point out that he had a police car, but Crook said rudely, "You don't want to advertise your business to the whole neighbourhood, do you? Besides, the landlady won't like it. A police car may have more authority but a taxi has more class."

It was typical of him that on such a night and at such an hour a taxi appeared out of the fog. Laurel House was one of four adjacent houses whose rooms had been "converted," fitted with running water basins, gas fires and rings, and let out as "flatlets." There were three other houses, called Privet, Hawthorn and Honeysuckle. One of the other tenants was letting herself into Laurel House as the taxi drove up, and Crook inserted a skilful and experienced foot to prevent the front door shutting.

"There are times when it don't pay to advertise," he explained and they began the ascent—there was no lift—by the light of Crook's torch. Stella's flatlet was on the top floor and as they turned the corner of the last flight Crook caught his companion's arm.

"Look at that," he said, pointing upwards.

Under the door of No. 22 gleamed unmistakably a yellow bar of light.

"Caught in the act or Crook Always Gets His Man," murmured the lawyer, but the police authority very properly took no notice of that. Nor did he hesitate. Marching forward he banged on the door, then took up a boxing attitude ready to lay out any presumed cut-throat with a hook and a jab or anything that might seem most suitable.

"Charge of the Light Brigade," thought Crook and it was an anti-climax when the door was opened in a perfectly normal manner. But when he saw who it was on the other side, his jubilation returned. For the present inhabiter of the flat was a tall young man in the uniform of a Captain of the Mereshires.

The sergeant began to speak but Simon paid no attention to him. All his thought was for Crook.

"What is it?" he said quickly. "Stella?"

"Why should it be the young lady?" enquired the sergeant, who played centre-half for the police and knew all about tackling and getting in the way.

"It's clearly going to be an evenin' of surprises," murmured Crook. "I take it it wasn't you who phoned?"

"I?"

"Well," said Crook, gently manœuvring his way into the flat, closely followed by the sergeant, "someone rang Miss Reed and made a date at 26 Chapel Row."

Simon stared. Again the sergeant tried to intervene; again no one paid any attention to him.

Then Simon said, "But the place is empty, it's been empty for months. Why on earth should she go there?"

"I'm in the guessing game, too," said Crook. "I suppose there isn't a note anywhere around?"

146

"There wouldn't be," returned Simon. "She didn't know I was coming."

"I thought she might have left one for me," Crook explained.

"Was she expecting you?"

"No, but she was expectin' trouble, and I thought if she was goin' half-way to meet it she might have blazed the trail a bit. I like people who expect a lot, I do really, but she could hardly ask me to guess she was goin' to an empty house."

"I still don't understand," expostulated Simon. "Why did she go?"

"I suppose someone invited her. I see she's got a phone. I wonder now. . . ." He bounced out and banged on the door of the next cell. A young woman in a red jacket and smooth grey slacks opened it.

"I was wonderin' if you'd seen Miss Reed this evening," Crook explained.

"I didn't see her," said the young woman, who was the continuity girl at a film studio and therefore surprised by nothing, "but she came in all right. I heard her. And you're not the first person who wanted her this evening. That phone was ringing solid for over an hour. It rang again when she came in. . . ."

"And she went out? Right away?"

"Not right away. I'd say she stopped to change her clothes. There's something about the slam of a wardrobe door you can't mistake." She laughed easily, one hand on her pretty hip.

"You don't remember the time, I suppose?" suggested Crook, who often achieved miracles because he anticipated them.

"Oh, round about seven, I'd say. I was making one of those delicious dishes out of dried eggs they're so fond of at the Ministry of Food. Better than the real thing. You know. And I generally eat about then. They let us go at six now the winter's set in, and I feed directly I get in."

"Many thanks," said Crook, "very helpful. Any time you're in a bit of trouble just come to me."

"Thanks a million," said the girl, "but I don't have to go looking for it. It comes knocking at my door."

With a face and a figure like that, thought Crook, you could believe her. He came back to No. 22.

"At a guess," he said in his pugnacious Cockney way, "I'd say she

147

thought she was goin' to meet you there. Well, she was dressed handsome enough for me in the afternoon, but it wasn't good enough for whoever she was expectin' to date."

He went across the room and opened the door of the built-in wardrobe.

"I ain't a lady's man," he explained, "but I'd say that was the suit she had on in my office. Well, who's she likely to dress up for but you?" He nodded cheerfully to Simon, then added to the sergeant, "I suppose your chap didn't happen to mention what she was wearing."

The sergeant said coldly that he hadn't.

Simon came back into the picture. "Do you mean that she actually went to Chapel Row?"

"She was seen by a bobby tholing at the pin about seven, which fits in with our lady friend's evidence, and she was found there later in an empty house, in a locked and blocked room, with the gas on. . . . Hold hard! It wasn't me and it wasn't the sergeant. Can't you see what you're up against yet?"

It seemed to take young Captain Oliver some minutes to assimilate the facts.

"You mean, someone tried to murder her? But why?"

"If I knew that I could probably put my hand on the murderer," returned Crook. "That is, I could indicate him to the police and they could put their hand on him. But you're not goin' to ask me at my time of life to believe that any one's goin' to risk swingin' just to prevent you marryin' the only girl in the world."

"The only people who have the key to that house," said Simon very quietly, "are my own family. Even the agent hasn't one. There was no question of letting it in its present state."

"Then that narrows down the field," replied Crook, refusing to be shaken.

"But it's fantastic. There's no sense in it."

"You mean, you can't see any sense in it. But don't make any mistake. This wasn't a practical joke, this wasn't something planned overnight. That house was ready for an emergency that X was expecting would arise,"

Simon said again. "My own folk. But why?"

"Say—she knew too much, just as Tom Grigg knew too much. There are plenty of times where, if ignorance isn't bliss, at least it spells safety. When you start knowing things look out for trouble. Because you've got to know what's in the other chap's mind on top of everything else, and that's what most people don't realize."

"You mean, this attempt on Stella—it was only an attempt or are you trying to tell me . . . ?"

"She's going to be all right. No, you can't see her yet. She's in hospital."

"Which hospital?"

"St. James'. She couldn't be better looked after if she were the Royal Family. She isn't just a person, she's a cog in a murder machine and it don't pay to forget that."

Simon looked round and grabbed his cap. Crook gently took it out of his hand.

"Take it easy, son. They won't let you in to-night. They won't let any one in. Aren't I right, sergeant?"

The sergeant assented dourly. He'd heard a lot about Mr. Crook, though he'd never met him before. But now that he had he couldn't see what all the fuss was about. Rushing around with his tongue out, spilling the beans, taking all the credit. The sergeant sniffed.

"The police'll tell you that one murder often leads to another," Crook went on, "though come to that I dare say I know as much about murder as any criminal, because I know about some even the police have never suspected." He saw the sergeant's mouth begin to open like a clockwork goldfish. "All right," he said hastily, "a lawyer's confidence—you know. The point I'm trying to make is that when a chap commits a murder and gets away with it and then finds he's got to commit another, you can generally count on him doin' exactly the same thing as he did before. A murderer who knew how to vary his crimes might live to get the King's congratulations on his centenary, only they seem to use all their gumption on their first crime."

"Vanity," said the sergeant, "that's what it is. Because we don't drop on 'em right away they go round kidding themselves they can make Aunt Sallies of the police for ever and ever."

Simon interrupted their cheerful repartee. "What clues have you got?" he said. "Has Stella . . . ?"

"Concussion," said Crook quickly. "But don't worry. You've got the best brains in England on your side. Anyway, we don't want to bother her too much."

"Surely there's no reason why I shouldn't see her at least?" Simon protested. "I've got twenty-four hours' leave."

But the sergeant said stolidly that that was out of the question.

"Does he know who I am?" Simon demanded.

Crook explained, but the sergeant didn't unbend. His manner said that in cases of attempted murder husbands and lovers were always the first official suspects. Simon bristled at that, and Crook began to think it might be a case of Three Corpses lay in a Paddington flat, when the telephone began to ring.

It rang and rang with the maddening persistence of its race until the sergeant make a quick move towards it. But Crook was before him.

"I'll take it," he offered, switching the receiver from its hook. "Yes!"

The voice at the other end of the line was clearly startled by this hearty assault.

"I'm afraid I must have got the wrong number," it apologized. "I wanted . . ."

"This is Mountbar 9191."

"Then—I wanted Miss Reed."

"She's not here this evening. Anythin' I can do?"

"I'm afraid—are you expecting her?"

"To tell you the truth there's been an accident. Oh no, nothing serious. She'll be about again in a few days. But she's had a fall—slight concussion."

"And where is she?"

"In hospital. Well, she couldn't look after herself, and . . ."

"Who are you, please?" demanded the voice.

"My name's Crook. You might say I was a friend of the family."

"Then—were you with Miss Reed when it happened? Where did it happen, by the way?"

"Just one of these streets," returned Crook vaguely. "You know how it is. Dark—and she missed her footing or something. And she happened to have my number on her and they contacted me and—here I am."

"How very sad. But how fortunate that they could get in touch so quickly."

"Well, you have to be lucky some of the time," argued Crook.

"And which hospital did you say she was in?"

"I didn't. But she was taken to St. James' by the police. Well, yes, of course they did. If you have an accident and you're by yourself and a policeman picks you up, they take you to the nearest place. And that's one of the things our hospitals are for."

There was a moment's pause. Then the voice said, "I still don't quite understand what you're doing in her flat. I shall come up, of course. . . ."

"I wouldn't," Crook advised. "Why, you don't even know when you'll be allowed to see her or if it 'ud be any good if you were. She may not remember . . ."

"Is she badly hurt?"

"Thanks to the police, who were on the spot—no. But if you're a friend of hers remember that next time you're asked to buy tickets for the Force's Benevolent Concert. By the way, Captain Oliver's here. P'raps you'd like a word with him."

He handed the receiver across.

"Who is it?" murmured Simon.

"I didn't ask," Crook told him. "I thought you might know."

"Hallo!" said Simon. "Good Lord, Aunt Rhoda. Yes, it's a shock to me. I got sudden leave and thought I'd come up. I knew Stella wasn't on duty to-day. Oh I had a key. Yes, she gave it to me. She's out so much, you see. No, I don't think so. They don't seem fussy."

After that he seemed to listen for a long time. Once he said, "Oh, I'm sorry. Well, I don't suppose the question arises now. Yes, when I can."

"These women!" said Crook to the sergeant behind his hand. "Ten minutes she's been on the line, and I daresay she could have crowded everything that she needed to say into one."

At last Simon hung up and turned to the waiting men. Outside the storm raged, as though the wind would lift the slates from the roof and tear the stars out of the sky.

- - -

"That was my aunt," he said. "She rang up at my father's suggestion to tell Stella that my grandmother's got a touch of 'flu and he thought she had better not come down this week-end."

"They believe in Safety First, don't they?" was Crook's comment. "This is only Tuesday."

"She may be a lot worse than Aunt Rhoda would admit," Simon suggested. "As a matter of fact, I shouldn't be a bit surprised if Aunt Rhoda's in for it herself. Her voice didn't sound any too good."

"That could be shock," suggested Crook. "To a lady like your aunt there probably is something a bit shockin' about ringin' up a girl's flat and findin' it infested with males."

"Do you think Stella will be able to tell us anything?" pursued Simon.

"Can't tell. Sometimes in these concussion cases they don't remember when they come round."

"That'll be all to the good," Simon suggested.

"Not from our point of view it won't," disagreed the sergeant.

"What are you doing about it anyhow?" Simon continued with sudden heat.

The sergeant said coldly that they had the matter in hand.

"There's the bag," Crook said, "a nice bag it was. If they could find that . . . It had her initials on the flap."

"That's not to say they'll be on the flap when it's found," said the sergeant, who had a natural gift for looking on the dark side of things. "No need to talk either," he added meaningly, looking at both men.

"That's where I don't agree," said Crook. "If X knows you're on the trail he'll probably try to cover his tracks. So long as he thinks the girl's where your man found her, he'll lie low. If it hadn't been for sheer bad luck—and Timothy Tramp—they would still be lookin' for Tom Grigg. And this is a case where it don't do to despise any one's help," he added as meaningly as the sergeant, "not even the murderer's."

After the sergeant had gone, without overcoming an iota of the obvious suspicion with which he had regarded Crook from the outset, that gentleman remained to fill in the outlines for Simon's benefit.

"I believe it," said Simon, looking whiter than you'd have thought possible, "because it's happened. But it still doesn't make any sense. What could Stella know that I don't. And anyway what do the post cards mean?"

"They were part of a campaign to frighten her out of her wits. I don't claim to have second sight or Scotch blood. or anything like that, but I bet you the next card would have said somethin' about danger to you if she didn't fall out. And if she hadn't fallen out somethin' might have happened. Oh, I don't say you'd have gone the long lone road that all of us must go, but just somethin' unpleasant to give you a hint. And she bein' the sort of girl she is might have stepped down."

"You're leaving me out of the picture, aren't you?" demanded Simon. "Besides, it didn't happen that way."

"Because somethin' else happened."

"What was that?"

"She came to see me. And X knows it. Don't ask me how I know. It's just a habit I have of bein' able to add two and two. X thinks she's told me somethin'—or—well, I'll eat my seven-coupon new boots if it wasn't comin' to my place that did the trick."

Simon looked at him with a gleam of hostility. "What do you know that you're concealing?" he said.

"Nothing," said Crook earnestly. "On my honour, nothing. I may know some more to-morrow, and if so I promise I'll let you in on the ground floor."

CHAPTER SEVENTEEN

You would pluck the heart out of my mystery.
HAMLET.

EARLY THE NEXT MORNING the postman trudged up the steps of Laurel House and dropped a post card through the letter-flap of No. 22. It said: Danger threatens Simon Oliver unless you let him go. Be warned in time. It bore the postmark of the 10.15 outgoing post from Horsfall of the previous day.

153

At about the same hour Crook bounded into his office and enquired about his messenger to Somerset House. But Bill said there wasn't any news yet.

"Oh well," said Crook generously, "I didn't expect him to get the information over the counter. But if I'm wrong I'm back where I was."

But he didn't really believe he was wrong. He didn't see how such an inspiration could be misplaced.

It was afternoon when the man arrived. "Couldn't make it sooner," he said. "Here's the certificate. I say, this'll ruffle the old lady's plumage a bit."

Bill lounged in and glanced at the bit of evidence lying on the table.

"Maybe she knows already," he offered.

"It could be," Crook agreed, "and if she don't she soon will. But there's not much you can tell that dame." He stretched out his hand for the telephone. "I've been three weeks on this case," he said, "and this is the first gleam of light I've had. And I wouldn't be surprised if that led me into a tunnel."

When he got connected with his number he asked for the times of trains running to Bridget St. Mary and was told that, owing to congestion, the local connection had been taken off. He could get to Horsfall that night but no farther.

"Just step across the street and get me a ticket at that office on the corner for Horsfall," he told the messenger, "and send a telegram to the landlord of the Duck and Dragon, saying I'm coming down this evening and can he fix transport."

"Reply paid?" asked the messenger.

"No sense wasting cash," replied Crook sensibly. "I'm going anyhow."

The train left Liverpool Street at 2.58 and was due at Horsfall, with two changes, at 7.2. But thanks to the weather and the addition of a number of carriages for Service men and women, which necessitated the train pulling up twice at every large station, it was an hour and a half late. When Crook got out, however, feeling as though he'd dined on fog, the doughty landlord was waiting for him in a

154

burberry, a relic from the Great War, over his shabby shooting-jacket, and a cap pulled over one eye.

"Joe had to collect a hospital case," he greeted Crook, "but he's promised to come back and pick us up."

He took Crook's shapeless Gladstone bag and together they walked up the steps and stood at the entrance to the station, waiting in a companionable silence. It was a pitchy night; no stars, no lights anywhere. A lion could have walked up to you, reflected Crook, and if you happened to have a cold and couldn't smell him, he'd be on you before you realized he was coming. The enormous silence of the country irked him. It made him understand the immense capacity for evil that existed. No town was ever as dark as this, not even in a fog.

The next morning he went off to the prison to see Mrs. Manners. He had one of his rare moods of self-consciousness, because he not only knew he wouldn't be a welcome visitor but he minded about the old lady's feelings. Generally he didn't bother about that. Asbestos, that's my middle name, he used to say.

He had to wait a little at the prison. The wardress found opportunity to whisper, "She's had a bit of a shock, poor dear. She . . ." But when he saw Mary Anne's face and the two scraps of paper she clutched in her hand, he didn't need to ask any questions. He'd seen these Services telegrams before.

He waited till she had sat down, and then leaned forward and put a huge gentle hand on her arm.

"I'm damn sorry," he said. "When was it?"

"Two days ago I got the telegram," she whispered. "And then his officer wrote. Ever such a nice letter it was." It was one of the two papers she held so tenaciously, as though this was her last link with Ted.

"And how?" probed Crook.

He knew that when people are in trouble they want to talk, even if they don't realize it. He was used to people in trouble of one sort or another and might claim to be an expert.

"On his own airfield. There was an accident—one of our Fortresses crashed with ten men aboard and he went in to try and get the pilot out."

"And he got him?"

"Yes, sir. But that wasn't enough. He went back for another man. . . . He couldn't get them out in time."

"Tough luck," said Crook. "All the same. . . ."

"I thought maybe, being in the police . . ." Her voice trailed away. The animation died out of her face; she was just a broken old woman. Like someone suddenly gone blind, thought Crook, and indeed for her every light must now be extinguished.

"You mean, you hoped," said Crook inexorably. "But you knew in your heart that the Curse always wins."

"The Curse?"

"The heir never inherits," said Crook.

There was a moment's utter silence. Then the old woman whispered, "So you knew—all the time?—that they were married, I mean."

"Not all the time," confessed Crook generously. "In fact I was a bit slow off the mark. But—I had to find some reason why Tom went up to the Manor that night. Tom knew, of course."

She nodded. "Yes. Though I didn't understand that till he came back that night. I don't know who told him, but it wouldn't be Elsie. She wouldn't have told me—her own mother—if she could have helped it. But when it came to the boy being registered, she couldn't hide it then."

"Didn't want the family to know?"

Mrs. Manners gave him a look that made him colour a bit. "You don't have to believe me," she said, "but there isn't a woman in these parts who'd have wanted her daughter to marry the heir. From what she said it wasn't Ted's father's fault the marriage didn't take place any sooner than it did."

"And Ted never knew?"

"She didn't wish him to know. Besides, what sort of a life would he have had up at the House with the old lady and Mr. Reuben, always telling him he was lucky to be born in wedlock, and hinting his father had been ashamed to acknowledge the marriage? And I hoped, like my daughter did, that if we didn't claim anything, Ted might be safe."

Crook might be a Londoner to the marrow of his bones, but he didn't make light of superstition. He knew it's the first and most natural of religions.

"Then, if Ted's mother didn't tell Tom, it must have been Ted's father."

"That's how I worked it out, sir."

Crook eyed her narrowly. "Seems a bit queer, doesn't it, that he should tell Tom and no one else? Unless, of course, he did tell . . ."

"Elsie said he didn't. She said he'd promised not to tell without she agreed. If Mr. Edmund told Tom it's because . . ." she stopped again.

"Suppose," suggested Crook slowly. "Tom went to look for Edmund Oliver to tell him if he didn't leave his girl alone there'd be trouble. And suppose there was a row? Oliver might say, But, you fool, we're married, without thinking he was breaking his word to his wife. We know Tom was out on the moors that day and that he saw the heir. . . ."

"I've thought that," she agreed, "but there's no proving anything now."

"Not that it matters actually," Crook assured her. "We aren't here to show how Edmund Oliver died. The fact remains that Tom knew."

"Yes. Tom knew."

"And thought other people—Lady Cleveland, say—might be interested too? That's why he went to the Manor just after the death and got enough money from them to be shipped abroad."

"I couldn't say, sir."

"Still, it could be?"

"Yes, sir. That's what I've thought."

"And that's why he went back there when he was in a jam."

"I—suppose so."

"And that—ultimately—is why he died?"

But she only said, "I don't know anything about that, sir."

"You soon will," Crook told her grimly.

"It doesn't seem to matter now," she said, and her voice was like a long-drawn sigh.

Crook's big red brows bristled. "You can't throw up the sponge now—now less than ever," he warned her. "What's the good of chaps like Ted being killed for the sake of justice if folk like you and me don't give a damn if justice triumphs or not? That's waste, if you like. It isn't only the people in uniform who's fighting this war or even the ones that Bevin has signed on. We're all in it because the Germans ain't the only chaps who play dirty. There's others not a hundred miles away."

"You don't know that they knew," she said quickly, and he came back at her in derisive tones, "Then why did Tom Grigg die? The hand that bolted that door belonged to someone who knew the truth."

"I still don't know how you found out," she hazarded.

"I think it was the insistence on the cousin that did it," he told her. "Tom told young Simon to look out for his cousin. Well, I met the cousin and any one could see he wasn't dangerous; he didn't even want the place. Then someone started sendin' cards to Miss Reed, and they mentioned the cousin, too. And that got me thinking. You know how it is when you're doing a jig-saw puzzle; you find a bit that looks as if it ought to fit, it's the right size and the right shape, but it don't make the pattern. That's the cunning of the fellow that made the puzzle. If you look round you'll find another bit, same size, same shape, but this one joins up with the rest. Well, I thought, suppose it wasn't this cousin. And then I thought—Suppose there was *another* cousin?"

"Yes," said the old woman. "I see."

"And it wasn't far to look to find the other cousin. After that— well, you see how simple it was. Just one of the Arthur Crook hunches," he added.

"Yes, sir. Still, it doesn't seem to make much difference, does it?"

He looked at her in genuine amazement. "Not make much difference? Why, it makes all the difference in the world. Now I've got a motive to work on. I'll tell you one person who didn't know," he added, "and that's young Simon. He wouldn't have come to see me if he'd wanted to keep that quiet."

"If he'd known he'd have told," said the old woman. "Any one 'ud be glad not to be the heir. I thought I could save Ted. . . ."

"You did save Ted—for thirty years. And thirty good years are more than most of us get."

But she wouldn't be comforted. "A fellow like Ted, a quiet, comfortable sort of chap like that, should have made old bones," she insisted. And it was no use pointing out that younger men get run over or drowned or die of pneumonia or tuberculosis every day of the week; love does a lot for you, but it doesn't teach you logic. Instead he followed up his own line of thought.

"There was something fishy about those cards," he mused. "It didn't strike me till I got down to thinking about them, but none of them said, 'You will never marry Simon,' only: 'You will never marry the heir.' That gives us something else. Whoever wrote those cards knew the truth."

"You mean, was the murderer?"

"I can't prove that and what I can't prove ain't fact. But I could make a guess. Y'know, I can't see the Seventh Earl meekly standin' down and livin' on the dole. Nor any of the others, come to that. Because the estate's entailed. No little nest-egg for Step-mamma or Sister. Any of 'em might have done. You remember what Sherlock Holmes used to say? Eliminate what is impossible and what remains is the truth, however unlikely it may seem. That's what I'm doin' now. Eliminatin'."

He saw she didn't really care what happened now. Her own life wasn't worth anything. Still, Ted dead was still the grandson she had adored. For his sake, she'd got to save herself if she could.

He stood up, picking up his flat checked cap. "I don't want to badger you," he said, "and you've done fine. But there's just one thing. Last time I was here I asked you a question and you wouldn't answer it. I asked you what it was Tom Grigg was looking for in your cottage. Well, I take it it was your daughter's marriage lines. Right? I'll say. Now, just one more word. Did he find 'em?"

Mrs. Manners lifted her fine work-worn hands in a gesture of abandonment.

"Seeing you know so much," she said, "you might as well know it all. Yes, he did find them. It was when I saw they were gone I went up to the church. I was afraid then. I had to stop Tom if I could."

Crook clapped on the appalling cap. "The essence of givin' evidence," he said, like a professor delivering a lecture, "is to know how

159

much to leave out. If you're asked that particular question just stop at Yes. The rest's all right between you and me, but judges get as wooden as the benches the poor dam' public sits on, and they're eiderdown compared with the jury."

But when he left the prison and sprinted for the bus going to Bishops Cleveland, which was due to depart two minutes before his arrival, but characteristically delayed for his benefit, he knew he wasn't going to get any more help from her. He'd got to depend henceforward on the folk up at the Manor, "And," he told himself, "I'd as soon swim on an iceberg in hell."

CHAPTER EIGHTEEN

You should study the peerage. It is the best thing in fiction the English have ever done.

OSCAR WILDE.

IT WAS NEAR LUNCH-TIME when he reached the Park gates and started to tramp up the long path leading to the Manor. They must have been a chummy lot in the old days, he reflected, because it would be the deuce and all to walk down to the local if your family went sour on you. Possibly being so far from the pub accounted for the poor spirits of the Clevelands as a whole.

Miss Oliver was in the front garden, in a disreputable burberry, galoshes and a squashed tweed hat. She carried a stick with which she was poking ferociously at the borders, as if she expected a regiment of spring flowers to leap to attention from their dry bulbs at her command. She had a shabby blue woollen scarf twisted round her mouth, and when she saw Crook she straightened herself defensively and regarded him with suspicious eyes.

For a moment neither of them spoke. Then Crook remembered he was talking to the quality and dragged off his cap.

"How's the cold?" he enquired.

Wherever the cold might not be it was in Miss Oliver's face.

160

"If you are enquiring after my step-mother," she began in freezing tones, but Crook interrupted.

"No, no. I meant yours."

"I haven't a cold—thank you."

"My mistake," said Crook. "Or rather young Simon's."

"My nephew's?" Curiosity overcame her resentment.

"When you rang up last night he said you sounded as though you had a cold."

She stared at him. "But I didn't ring up last night. Why, this telephone was out of commission all yesterday evening. I tried several times and couldn't get through. The engineers have been working on it this morning."

"So that explains it. Your unusual voice, I mean. Simon thought it was a cold. . . ."

"You mean someone was ringing up in my name?" She seemed dumbfounded.

"It's been done before in the annals of crime."

She stiffened again. "May I ask where you and my nephew were when this—person—rang up?"

"In Miss Reed's flat."

"Miss Reed's flat?" The parrot-house, thought Crook, wasn't in it with her.

"Yes. The bell rang and someone said it would be better for Miss Reed not to come down this week-end as Lady Cleveland had 'flu."

"I was unaware that there was any suggestion that Miss Reed should come down this week-end."

Crook made a little gesture as if to say, "Well, I'm common. Naturally, I wouldn't know."

"Is this a practical joke?" Miss Oliver continued, leaving the unfortunate bulbs alone.

"For the girl? Not much. Unless you think attempted murder is a joke."

"Murder? A joke?"

It was like talking to an echo.

"I thought you might know. I thought maybe the police had been around."

"Here?"

161

"Well, Miss Reed's engaged to the heir."

Miss Oliver said abruptly, "Perhaps we had better go up to the house. I think my brother should hear of this."

The Earl was crossing the hall as they entered. He stopped and stared at Crook as if he couldn't quite place him. Miss Oliver said, "Reuben, I think you ought to hear what Mr. Crook has to tell us. It's almost unbelieveable."

"I think," suggested Crook, "Lady Cleveland ought to be in on this."

Cleveland looked furious. "I hardly think that is necessary. I have been head of this family for more than twenty years."

Crook shook his head. "Forty-eight hours would be nearer the truth. That is, since the death in action of the last Earl."

The silence came down like a blind. The room seemed actually darker. Then Cleveland said, "Are you suggesting—another Tichborne claimant?"

Like a conjurer Crook whisked a paper out of his capacious ulster pocket.

"Birth certificate of the Seventh Earl," he said, presenting it to the staggered peer. "Edmund Charles, posthumous son of the late Edmund Oliver, and Elsie, his wife. I can produce a marriage certificate, too, if you'd care for it."

The Earl stood staring at the document. At last, "It's a forgery," he whispered. "It must be."

"You can tell that to Somerset House," Crook advised him.

"But—this is fantastic. These things don't happen."

"You want to read more poetry," Crook advised him. "What price King Cophetua and the Beggar Maid. Anyhow, Somerset House sold me that for three-and-sevenpence over the counter, five and a penny by post. And if you're in doubt, ask Mrs. Manners. She knew."

"That's nonsense," retorted the Earl energetically. "If she'd known—assuming that this incredible story is true—she'd have claimed the estate."

"That's all you know. Why, she spent all her time and thirty pounds of her savings to prevent Ted finding out. If it hadn't been that Tom knew, the story might never have got about. I fancy, you

162

know, that's why Mrs. Manners found her cottage torn to shreds when she got back from the sewing-party."

"I still don't understand. . . ."

"Marriage lines," said Crook simply. "Tom was a simple-minded chap, and it occurred to him that his arguments—with you, say—might carry more weight if they were backed by proof."

"Then why the devil didn't he show them to any one? Because he didn't."

"Oh come," Crook expostulated. "Remember you're talking to a lawyer. What you're tryin' to say is he didn't show them to you. You're not in a position to say he didn't show them to any one else."

"But he didn't see any one," protested Miss Oliver. And stopped. Her hands—those powerful hands with square-tipped fingers—began to shake. "I believe I do see what you're driving at," she whispered. "But it's infamous. No one could suggest such a thing."

"Did you say Ted Manners has been killed?" demanded the Earl, without taking any notice of his half-sister's dismay, and speaking as though the fact had only just soaked into his intelligence.

"Yes," agreed Crook. "Accident on the airfield."

"Then—in all the circumstances, since Mary Anne wasn't anxious for publicity—is there any sense in stirring up skeletons?"

"If he was the heir," added Rhoda, "it means Simon's safe from the Curse. Unless you believe . . ."

"I've told you till my tongue's dry that what I believe don't matter a tinker's curse. It's what we can put over the jury. . . ."

"You mean, it's nothing to you whether truth triumphs or not?"

"It's everything to me," explained Crook, thinking there's something to be said for democracy after all, if this is what the aristocracy are like. "If it don't, I lose my case." You couldn't argue with a man like that, thought Cleveland irritably. It was like wrestling with an eel. He said ponderously, "I don't know whether it is any use assuring you that none of us knew anything of this marriage."

Crook told him cheerfully that it wasn't.

"Do you imagine we should have gone on living here if we had known?"

"I've just warned you—you're talking to a lawyer. The utmost you can say is that you didn't know, and I'm at liberty to believe that or not, as I please."

"I wonder," whispered Rhoda, "if Vicky knew? It was she who persuaded my father to give Tom Grigg money."

"If my father had known about the marriage he would certainly have acknowledged his grandchild," said Reuben stiffly.

"Then we have to assume he didn't know, and that your lady mother framed him with a different yarn."

"Oh, everyone knows the story she told," said Rhoda bitterly, "but at least I always knew it wasn't true. I didn't know till now what the truth probably was."

"In any case," Cleveland persisted, "is there anything to be gained by raking up this story? You know what the press are."

"It's the press I'm counting on," Crook told him. "You do take me for a stooge, don't you. Here have I been three weeks tryin' to unearth some motive why someone besides Mrs. Manners should want Grigg out of the way. It was goin' to be difficult to persuade the great B.P. that any woman would want to conceal the fact that her grandson was an earl—but when the truth comes out—that Grigg had it in his power to turn you all out, which is virtually what it amounts to—why, then we've got a good chance of winnin' our case."

Miss Oliver turned passionately to her half-brother.

"Reuben, you've got to stop this somehow. Can't you see, it spells ruin for everyone."

"Well, not everyone," demurred Crook, who seemed to enjoy being difficult. "It'll be jam for the press. Earl dies incog. Old family curse wins again. Echo of murder mystery. And, of course, if you tack on the story of Stella Reed—Lonely Girl left to die in gas-filled basement—you'll need a tommy-gun to keep the reporters out."

"What basement?" demanded the Earl.

"The basement of 26 Chapel Row."

The Earl stared. "I don't believe it."

"No sense me inventin' a yarn like that," protested Crook.

"You're enjoying all this," Rhoda accused him, furiously.

"Well, I always did like my things twopence coloured," acknowledged Crook. And then before any one could say more the door opened and the Dowager came in. Crook supposed respectfully that she was dressed, though to his irreverent mind fancy-dressed would have described it better. She looked, indeed, like the White Queen minus her crown, but in its place she had assumed a dab of black lace. When she saw Crook she stopped and said ironically, "You didn't tell me you were expecting company, Reuben."

Cleveland seemed somewhat at a loss, so Crook cleared the air by saying breezily, "Oh, I wasn't expected. I was passing and I just dropped in."

"Your journeys take you rather far afield, Mr. Crook," suggested the old lady, and Crook replied in his cheerful way, "You're telling me. But that's my client's fault. They will live at the other end of Nowhere. Takes half a day to get down here and then the train's always late."

"Not always," said Miss Oliver stiffly. She obviously loathed the sight of him. "The morning train keeps time. Of course, if you travel late you must anticipate inconveniences, particularly in a war."

Lady Cleveland said something about the early bird, and Crook said Yes, he'd heard that one, but personally he'd never much cared for worms. And anyhow since his client, in this instance, couldn't come to him he had no choice but to go to his client.

"Oh? You're referring to Mary Anne Manners. How did you find her?"

"She was naturally rather distressed. She'd only just heard of the death of the Earl. . . ."

Even Lady Cleveland was shaken by that. "The Earl?"

Her son broke in. "You had better know the very serious charge Mr. Crook has made. . . ."

His mother's dumpy eyebrows rose. "Charge? Against whom?"

"Perhaps charge is hardly the word. Mr. Crook claims to have proof that Edmund was secretly married to Mary Anne's daughter before the birth of the child. That naturally made him the heir when my father died."

If they'd expected the old lady to be shaken by that they were disappointed.

165

"Really, Mr. Crook? And you say you have chapter and verse? Well, you are a lawyer and doubtless you wouldn't tell such a story unless you could substantiate it. But—tell me—how long have you known and who was your informant?"

Crook began, "Mrs. Manners. . . ." and she nodded composedly, as though that confirmed a suspicion of her own.

"That explains something that has puzzled me from the outset. I wondered why you were so anxious to defend Mrs. Manners, a penniless old lady who kept the village shop, but of course if you knew she was grandmother of an Earl. . . ."

Crook mentally took off his hat to her. She was worth all the rest of them put together. You might detest her, but you couldn't help admiring her guts.

"Did you know anything of this?" Reuben demanded. He was as jumpy as a flea in a gale of wind. You could see him shaking in his shoes at the thought of what the press could do to a story like that.

"My dear son, for a magistrate I find that a most extraordinary question. Naturally, if I had known of the marriage it would have been my duty to inform your father."

"And, of course," suggested Crook, "he couldn't have known? That couldn't have been the reason why he gave Tom Grigg a handsome honorarium to make himself scarce thirty years ago?"

"That was certainly not the reason he gave me," said the old lady, "and when I was a young woman we accepted our husband's word, as we accepted their decisions."

The old war-horse, thought Crook! If her son had half her guts you'd never get him down.

"And that's not all," said Rhoda, "apparently someone tried to murder Stella."

"Oh come!" expostulated the Dowager. "That's absurd. Why on earth should any one consider her a source of danger? I'm afraid her theatrical experience had given her a melodramatic outlook on life."

Crook noticed that she had already passed up the matter of Edmund's marriage.

"You can't treat it like that," persisted Rhoda. "Stella was found in our house in Chapel Row."

"How did she get there?" For the first time the old woman seemed shaken.

"We don't know," said Crook. "She hasn't been able to tell us. A policeman found her and she's now in hospital."

"It's certainly most peculiar and most regrettable," agreed Reuben.

"Perhaps you can offer a suggestion?" murmured Crook.

"I, Mr. Crook? Why should I? I take it the matter is in the hands of the police—to say nothing of yourself."

"I think Reuben and I ought to go up to London," Rhoda added.

Cleveland said something restless about having to go to town fifty-two times a year being quite enough for him, but Rhoda said, "After all, she is engaged to your son. Unless . . ."

"Unless?"

"I suppose there isn't another secret marriage there."

"Why not ask Mr. Crook?" proposed the old lady. "He seems to be better-informed on our family affairs than we are ourselves."

"It might save time if you were to ask your son," countered Crook. And at that moment the telephone rang.

"They're testing it," said Rhoda, but Cleveland went just the same. They heard him talking.

While he was away the old lady asked, "Is this young woman likely to recover, Mr. Crook?"

"For everyone's sake it's to be hoped so. It means a murder trial for someone, if she doesn't. You can persuade juries of a lot but not that a girl can lock herself into a hermetically sealed room, partially sealed from outside, with gas pouring into the room."

"How will you find out who it was?" asked Rhoda, wrinkling her brows.

"We'll hope Miss Reed will be able to tell us."

"But—she may not have seen her assailant. If I were going to murder any one I'd wait behind the door and hit them on the head before they could see me."

"Not had much experience of murder, have you?" asked Crook. "You'd be surprised how much vitality the human creature possesses. One blow on the head may knock a chap out in the films, but in real life you've got to keep at it, and it takes a lot of guts to go on thump-

167

ing a half-conscious person. Besides, whoever it is might have spoken, and she recognized the voice."

"But wouldn't that be very dangerous? I mean, whoever it was might deliberately have imitated someone else's voice."

"You do have ideas," said Crook admiringly. "All the same, a murder remains a capital offence even in the middle of a world war. Remember the Brides in the Bath affair? That was in 1915 when the British armies were bein' shot to hell in France. I know—I was there —but it didn't stop the judiciary spendin' days tryin' Smith. . . ."

Cleveland came in, saying curtly, "That was Simon."

"You haven't cut him off?" asked Rhoda. "I want to ask him about this person who rang up last night pretending to be me."

"He's asking for Mr. Crook," said Reuben.

Crook went like a streak of lightning. You wouldn't have thought so big a man could move so silently. He glanced at his watch as he picked up the receiver. " 'Bout a minute and a half to go," he reflected.

Cleveland bit his thumb resentfully. "What does this chap, Crook, think he stands to get out of this?" he demanded. "Simon hasn't got much money and Mary Anne has even less."

"A man of that stamp is always out for publicity," said the old lady. "In any case, I hardly anticipate that he would be the loser in any action he undertook. Where was Simon ringing up from, Reuben?"

"I didn't ask. I suppose London. I dare say he'd get an extension of leave."

"Did he tell you anything about Stella?"

"He said he'd been trying to get in touch with Crook. He didn't say why. I suppose there wasn't time. They're only allowed six minutes."

"I call it extraordinary to ask for Mr. Crook when his own father was on the premises."

"What a ridiculous observation!" said the Dowager cuttingly. "Simon is employing this person and no doubt wished to give him instructions. And if this—fairy-tale—about Stella has any foundation, you can hardly blame Simon for feeling anxious."

"I wonder if he has any fresh news. Reuben, do you think this will get into the papers? It'll be quite dreadful for you if it does."

"I should imagine a fellow like Crook has a tame reporter in his pocket, and I'm even more certain no story of his will lose in the telling. We may as well make up our minds to the fact that we are going to be in the news. . . ."

The old woman's face set like a jelly in winter. "An enemy hath done this," she announced. "Of course, it's all been carefully engineered to ruin my son."

"But who . . . ?"

That was the luckless Rhoda, of course. Her step-mother turned like a wild-cat.

"I have just told Mr. Crook that it is no business of ours to find out who is responsible. But a man in Reuben's position is bound to have enemies."

They heard the click of the telephone receiver and Crook came storming back.

"What's the news?" demanded Cleveland.

"Good—so far as it goes. She's better—and asking for me. I'll have to go up at once.."

"Where was Simon speaking from?" asked Rhoda quickly. "I suppose she's seen him."

"The police," added the Dowager. "No doubt she has already made a statement."

Crook answered the questions in order. "Simon had to go back on the morning train. He was speaking from his unit. I've promised to keep in touch. No, ma'am, she hasn't spoken to the police yet. Won't make a statement without her legal adviser bein' present—and quite right, too. They're mad enough, some of 'em to try and get her for suicide. When's the next train?"

"Three-ten," said the Earl.

"Haven't they changed it to three-forty?" murmured Rhoda.

"Give me more time to go ahead with my packing, if they have," said Crook. "Well, I'll get crackin'.'"

"Is that all you have to tell us?" demanded the old woman.

Crook touched an imaginary forelock. "I haven't spoken to the

169

young lady yet, and what the soldier said ain't evidence. But I thought Miss Oliver was talkin' of comin' to town."

Rhoda hesitated. "I feel I ought to—for Simon's sake. This must be terrible for him, and one of us ought to be there. In fact, I think we both ought to go."

The Dowager contented herself by saying. "If you do be sure to take your headache tablets. All this travelling upsets you—and of course you're distressed on Simon's account."

Rhoda turned her usual unbecoming crimson, and Crook thought, "How she does like to get under that girl's skin." (To him any unmarried female was a girl, even though an elderly one.) He realized that she fully intended to come and hoped the brand of cigars he preferred would prevent her suggesting sharing his compartment. A lawyer learns early to endure a great deal, but there are unnecessary trials and he felt this would be one of them.

"And you, too, as head of the family, Reuben," continued Rhoda, and her half-brother winced at the ill-timed phrase. But Crook saw that Rhoda at least had already forgotten about the young man in the Air Force Police who until a few days ago had been the rightful Lord Cleveland. "I wouldn't suggest it if Simon were there," she added.

The Dowager most unexpectedly sided with her step-daughter. "It's not often that Rhoda and I see eye to eye with one another," she announced in her grim fashion, "but for once I do agree. I think Reuben should be on the spot."

"The old lady don't trust me," reflected Crook with his twisted grin, and Reuben said, though not graciously because graciousness wasn't a part of his make-up, that if the rest of the family felt so strongly on the subject, naturally he was prepared to meet their wishes.

"You won't mind being left alone with the servants, I take it," he added. "I know Gregory doesn't expect to be back for a couple of days."

"I might quite as well have a horse about the place as Gregory," returned the Dowager with some spirit. "It surprises me when I hear him say Good-morning. I always expect him to neigh."

CHAPTER NINETEEN

The gods—a kindness I with thanks must pay—
Have formed me of a coarser kind of clay.
THE REV. CHAS. CHURCHILL.

1

THE DOOR OPENED with the abruptness of all the doors at the Manor and a grim elderly maid came in. She paid no attention to the company but addressed herself in severe tones to her mistress.

"Now, m'lady, you've no right to be in this cold room. You know what the doctor said yesterday about an even temperature."

"And you know what I said about the doctor," riposted the Dowager.

The maid, looking sourly at Rhoda, said, 'Her ladyship shouldn't be downstairs at all. That was a very nasty turn she had yesterday."

Rhoda said feebly, "I didn't know. . . ." and the maid said in a scornful voice for which Crook would have sacked a Prime Minister, "You could see her ladyship's not herself. Now, m'lady, you come up. . . ."

"No, Forster," said the old woman. "If I die of pneumonia I die of it. It's better at all events than dying of boredom. And we have company."

Forster wouldn't even admit that Crook was worthy of the name. She seemed, on the whole, as aristocratic as the rest of the family. It was obvious that, with the exception of the Dowager and possibly her son, she didn't think them worth a button. Poor Rhoda! thought Crook. She might be the daughter of the late Earl and the old woman no more than her ex-governess, but it was easy to see who was mistress here.

The lunch gong sounded and he got up, saying cheerfully, "Cripes! I shall be late for my joint and two veg, if I don't hurry."

Lady Cleveland astonished them all by suggesting, "Mr. Crook had better stay and take pot-luck with us, had he not, Reuben? And then perhaps you could give him a lift, since you are all going to town."

Reuben said unenthusiastically, "Certainly," and asked where the lawyer was staying.

Crook said, "Bridget St. Mary. The Duck and Dragon," and Rhoda blundered in half a field behind the hunt as usual, observing that perhaps Mr. Crook (with a marked glance at her step-mother) was afraid of catching influenza. Crook, however, laughed and said he should worry and he only caught the things he wanted to. Things— and people—were always after him. Jerry had been after him for four blinking years during the last war, and seeing how many there were of him and only one Arthur Crook you'd have thought he couldn't miss, but he had. And the same ever since. Plenty of chaps had tried to put his light out, with bits of gas tubing and guns and poisoned cigars and blunt instruments (anonymous) but they were still trying. Heaven, he added, fitting himself comfortably between his chair-back and the edge of the table, didn't seem to be in any hurry for him. . . .

That got them started on the soup, that was a compound of yesterday's potato and brussels sprouts water, thickened with what was left of the potatoes and garnished with the outside leaves of the sprouts. During the next course, which was stewed rabbit (Crook had noticed that the Earl asked a blessing on the lunch and by the time they got to this stage he thought he could understand why), Rhoda said she did wish everything had happened a day earlier and then she wouldn't have had to desert her W.V.S., who simply counted on her on a Friday.

"Rhoda," said the old lady, "goes out before the rest of us have begun to think about breakfast, and returns after dark."

Rhoda said, "These volunteers are the backbone of the country's war effort," and the old lady, "Tell that to the Army—and the Marines."

During the rice pudding made with powdered milk, and served with some bottled plums that had clearly fallen off the tree and been discarded by the wasps, the Earl brought the conversation round once again to the amazing story of the missing heir.

"If any one calls remember you are not at home," he said impressively. "It'll only be the press and we have no statement to make."

"It's going to be very unpleasant for Simon," murmured Rhoda clucking like a distressed hen.

"I hardly see how my son is affected," put in Reuben sharply. "If you had said it might be unpleasant for me. . . ."

"There's no reason why it should be unpleasant for any one," rasped the Dowager, scraping a plum-stone in a way that would have commended her to the Ministry of Food. "No one can prove that we had any knowledge of this marriage, and Mr. Crook will tell you that if they suggest any such thing, that will be libel."

"Or slander if it ain't in writin'," agreed Crook, counting his stones. "This year, next year, sometime . . . Could I trouble you for another stone? Like the villagers in these parts, I'm superstitious."

You have to be up bright and early in the morning to catch the old girl, he told himself; she knew her onions all right. Who was going to prove she'd ever heard of the marriage before to-day? Possibly only two people had ever been in a position to do so—her husband, who was dead, and Tom Grigg, who was dead, too. It seemed quite improbable that she would confide in her lumpish son. At the time of Grigg's first departure the secret wouldn't be worth a great deal. True, the widow was with child, but there was no telling whether it would be a girl or a boy. Well, it had been worth the gamble, and as it turned out it was probably the best investment Cleveland ever made. Crook didn't blame the late Earl, telling himself he'd as soon be in the grip of an octopus as of the Dowager.

Water was served with the lunch, and coffee, made presumably from acorns, after it. The Earl explained, "We don't drink, except on major occasions, during the war. For patriotic reasons."

"More money for war savings," put in Rhoda.

"Call it thrift if you like," returned Crook in his jolly outspoken way, "but don't kid yourself it's patriotism. Well, just see it straight. All this money you put into certificates will have to be repaid with interest one of these days, whereas anything you buy in a bottle is one-fifth the goods and four-fifths purchase tax, which goes back to the Government. The best patriots at the present time are the chaps who're drinking themselves into expensive graves."

173

"That," observed the Dowager, "must be a great consolation to them. I hope they see it like that."

"Like hell you do," thought Crook, and pushed back his chair.

Rhoda got up quickly and went into the hall to telephone to her club to reserve a room. Cleveland took no such precaution. He wouldn't have belonged to a club that couldn't produce a room for an Earl without notice, even if it meant putting some upstart commoner in the bath. He didn't take any luggage; he said he always kept a spare set of everything in town in what was irreverently known as the headquarters of the Gas Company. Rhoda wasn't more than five minutes either, but came bundling down with the sort of suit-case you'd expect. They set off with Cleveland at the wheel and his passengers sitting together at the back of the car. The Earl stole the road ruthlessly, the farmers' carts and little trade Austins getting respectfully out of the way as the Bentley drove through them. Crook supposed he got his petrol through his cousin who had to make concessions if he wanted any peace at all. Not for the first time he reflected that there's a lot to be said for being middle class, independent, careless of appearances and free from relations. They made a detour through Bridget St. Mary to allow Crook to pick up his fat Gladstone bag, settle his bill and hearten his guts, as he put it, with about a quart of beer. Arrived at the station Reuben said pointedly to his sister, "I know you don't care about travelling in a smoker," thus making it clear that he had no intention of making the tedious journey to town in her company. Rhoda, equally anxious to avoid travelling with Crook, agreed, "No. But I'm sure Mr. Crook does." Crook said, "I go third, y'know, I don't hold any railway shares."

Cleveland looked as if he hadn't believed anything so outrageously ill-bred could be permitted within arm's-length of the peerage. It was pretty well known that all the Cleveland money that wasn't in the estate was in railway stock, and he wouldn't have credited the truth that Crook didn't know this. People as exalted as the Seventh Lord Cleveland never can believe that other people aren't consumed with curiosity to know everything about them.

So it happened that during the first half of the journey they travelled in separate compartments. They had two changes and Crook toyed with the idea of dressing up his bag in his ulster and cap and going to the guard's van, to see whether any one tried to put a bullet through the cap or pitch the whole caboodle out of the door, but he never had the compartment to himself at all, which was protection enough. The second change was at Cheston Junction where they had ten minutes to wait. Rhoda said she must telephone her club and make sure they had kept the room; they were so stupid now that the regular porters had gone, and the old ones who'd been retired years ago on a pension had been brought back into service. Crook said he'd do a spot of telephoning, too, and Cleveland, who couldn't do nothing because that was the way he was made, went to the post office and sent off a telegram. The bar was open by this time so Crook strengthened himself with a little more beer, and then the train came in with men in uniform standing in all the corridors and civilians standing in all the carriages. Crook took one glance and went to reserve a good place in the guard's van, where he was presently joined by the other two members of his party. Cleveland said in a cold voice that there was very little advantage in travelling first-class if the company either provided insufficient accommodation or permitted holders of third-class tickets to fill the seats.

A little bullet-headed man in reach-me-downs said, "You ought to complain to the War Office about letting soldiers travel by rail. They could march, couldn't they? And seeing that's what they go into the Army for, a bit more foot-slogging one way or the other wouldn't hurt them."

Cleveland said coldly he didn't want any insolence, my man, and the other said we could do with a bit of Hitler right now.

Rhoda said, "If only the people travelled who must travel," and Crook replied in cheerful tones, "That's what they all say, lady."

Just as the train was starting some more people pushed their way into the van, and the guard said that when they reached Liverpool Street the porters wouldn't know which was luggage and which was passengers. One of the new-comers, a Canadian who, like Crook, had obviously visited the bar en route, caught Crook's eye and said, "Nice load of pork they're taking this trip, aren't they, chum?" and Crook said a nice pork chop was what he could do with right now. The guard volunteered the information that no one could cook a pork chop the way his missus did, and Crook said talking of pork chops made him think of apples and he took two out of his pocket. He offered one to Miss Oliver but she said, "No, thank you," in a voice that was a shudder. So Crook gave one to the Canadian and kept the other for himself. The Canadian ate his with the skin on, but Crook, of course (thus the disgusted Miss Oliver) had to pretend to be refined and peel his with a pocket-knife that he'd probably used to cut the cat's claws in the first place and what with the crowd and the jostling the knife slipped and he cut his finger, and she turned pale, because she hated the sight of blood. Crook unconcernedly mopped up the mess with his handkerchief, and then asked if any one had any iodine. Miss Oliver reluctantly agreed that she had and opened her large hideous leather hand-bag and began to rootle in its inside and Crook had the temerity to say Can I help? and rigid with offence she handed him the little tube and he daubed the stinging stuff on the cut and handed it back with a sort of bow which made him bump into the Canadian who said something amusingly vulgar, which made Crook laugh, and the guard, but froze the Clevelands. The Canadian who had been in the wine trade until he joined up, began to talk shop and Crook and he exchanged the sort of stories that never get into the papers until the train reached Liverpool Street almost dead on time.

"Good going," said Crook appreciatively, trying to disentangle himself from the luggage.

Rhoda mistakenly tried to effect some running repairs with a powder puff before alighting and someone (she said it was the Canadian who was clearly not sober) barged into her and upset her bag, and she flopped down at once, convinced that an attempt was being made to rob her of her little leather note-case which contained all her money. Crook and the Canadian, but not Cleveland, grovelled to help her, and she snatched the note-case out of the Canadian's hand without so much as a Thank You; someone, probably Cleveland, stood on Crook's hand. Someone else trod on the little pocket mirror which cracked from side to side, and Rhoda almost cried and said, "Oh dear. Seven years' bad luck. I wouldn't have had that happen for anything."

Crook said, "Cheer up! You don't believe in superstitions. Besides, I'm working off my last seven years and look at me."

Miss Oliver looked but was not, apparently, cheered. Cleveland's voice could be heard saying, "No need to shove," and the gent in the reach-me-down suit, replied, "Not for you, p'raps, guv'nor, but some chaps have to earn their living."

Cleveland emerged, much to his annoyance, with his hat over one eye (deliberately pushed, he said in tones of icy fury) and a button hanging off his coat. Rhoda caught his arm and said she was afraid she was going to faint and had he seen the Canadian deliberately assault her. The Canadian overheard and said something unrepeatable and Crook hastily covered up by saying, "The bar's open. How about a drop of ladies' wine?" But Rhoda, shuddering away from him, said she'd have a nice cup of tea at her club. Cleveland dissociated himself from the pair of them at the earliest possible moment by waiting till his sister's face was once again hidden in her bag, reassuring herself that she had lost nothing, and commandeering the only standing taxi in sight. Miss Oliver said forlornly, looking at Crook with such loathing that he began to feel sorry for her, "He might have given me a lift," so he had to play the part at being a gentleman and let her have the only other taxi that came up. She didn't offer to take him anywhere, and though he wasn't a coward he didn't ask, but meekly stood in a queue of people waiting for more taxis to materialize. The train had reached Liverpool Street just after seven, and at twenty-five past it occurred to Mr. Crook that a tube might save time, so he left the taxi queue and joined the queue to the box-office, and when he got his ticket he stood in a crowd on the platform and was presently jammed into a westbound train, which he left at Marble Arch Station. Here he joined yet another queue for a bus that deposited him near St. James' Hospital, and as he neared the dark mass of the building a clock began to chime eight. It was a very dark night, but the lights of a small car were visible in the little parking ground reserved for visiting doctors. It was the only car there and he made for it with confidence. As he drew near the invisible driver leaned across and opened.

" 'Evening, Crook," said Bill Parsons. "I'm like the eggar hawk moth that scents its mate three miles away by means of its antennae. I knew it was you as soon as you turned the corner."

"All Sir Garnet?" asked Crook, putting one foot on the running-board, but not attempting to enter the car.

"Hope so," said Bill. "You should have seen the pride of Putney disguised as a plain-clothes man. She's a bit of an iceberg, that matron. Still, she didn't actually ask me for my credentials."

"I suppose you had 'em all fixed in case she did?"

"What do you think?" drawled Bill. "Oh, she swallowed it all right. Police orders, I told her. No one was to be allowed near the girl without instructions from the police or Mr. Crook. They'd get the instructions in due course. She asked how soon and I said she wouldn't have to wait long."

"The sooner the better," agreed Crook briskly. "Right, Bill. You might as well take us back. I'll just get the young lady."

He didn't look remotely like a visiting doctor, a lawyer or even a plain-clothes man as he marched up to the porter in the hospital and asked for the matron. He'd only been there once before, on the day that he identified the unconscious girl, but they recognized him at once. Crook didn't feel flattered. There couldn't be two like him anywhere. He had to wait some time before the matron appeared. He didn't fidget. Patience was one of his attributes. Probably she was telling the girl to get ready; he didn't know she was having supper and didn't intend to be disturbed if the whole police force was waiting on the doorstep. There'd been enough trouble about that girl as it was. Afterwards, even her critics had to admit she couldn't know she was playing the ace for the murderer.

Presently she came in quite untroubled and, as Crook observed, about as human as the Queen of Hearts in a pack of cards. "I'm sorry to keep you, Mr. Crook," she said. "It's a little late. . . ."

"Not if she wraps up warm," said Crook cheerily. "I've got a car outside."

"She . . . ?"

"Miss Reed." Must have had a couple with her dinner, he decided, charitably. She couldn't assume he was a bishop in disguise, and if he wasn't that, what other interest could he have in the patients?

This time the matron seemed a little taken aback. "Miss Reed? Oh, I'm afraid there's some mistake. Miss Reed left the hospital under police orders more than an hour ago."

178

2

When she left her companions at Liverpool Street Miss Oliver drove straight to her club which was near Hyde Park Corner and asked if there were any messages. The shell-backed old porter on duty said they'd be on the board and there weren't any, anyway. "All right," said Rhoda, "I didn't expect any." She never did, but she always asked or else it looked as though you knew no one cared whether you were in London or not. It seemed to her this evening that the hall of the Countrywoman's Own looked like an aquarium with a few old faded plants swaying to and fro in deep green water; being patriotic, as most women are, they kept the lights down to a minimum and, since the most of the members dressed alike and since they were much of an age, it wasn't easy to distinguish them apart. Rhoda looked round but couldn't see any one she knew and decided to have a bath. She told the porter as much and asked him to take any messages there might be—that was in case Reuben or Simon rang up.

As usual, they had allotted her a room without a private phone, but there was a call-box on the landing, and call-box calls were only 'wopence while calls from private rooms were threepence so it was a gain in some ways, when you got your bill. She rang up Reuben's club but they told her he wasn't expected, and she put the receiver down feeling rather annoyed, because there was twopence wasted straight away. They might forget your requests at the club, but they never forgot to charge you for your calls and keep a note of the numbers in case you queried the account.

Coming out of the telephone box she made for the bathroom—none of the rooms had private baths—but now that rationing had made food in town so difficult, all the resident members made for the dining-room early, and it wasn't likely any of them would risk a bath immediately after a meal, not even the sort of meals women get in clubs during a war. As she liked to tell her step-mother, everything about the place might want repainting (including the members, Lady Cleveland would interpose viciously) but the water was always hot. She watched it run in, steaming and pale green, because the

179

baths were all painted pale green. "Easier for the sluts of house-maids," said Lady Cleveland. "You can't see dirt so easily on a green bath." Then she spread her towels (at least they didn't expect you to provide those) on the hot rail and locked the door. She supposed Crook had gone straight to the hospital; probably he expected her to suggest accompanying him, which would have given him an additional opportunity of making her feel small. She would ring up the hospital presently, and ask when she could go round, and suggest the morning. She might have told Mr. Crook that hospitals don't care about his sort of visitor in the evening, but of course Crook wouldn't take any notice of a thing like that.

Another member, passing the door of the room a few minutes later, saw the bar of light and wondered who was being·mad enough to take a bath immediately after a meal. Dangerous, she thought. Those modern girls. (She was 82 and anyone under 60 was a gel.) Thought they knew better than their mothers. One of these days one of them would be taken with cramp and drown and then she'd know better. At least, one hoped she would. Anyway, it would serve her right.

She may have hoped, even, that the rash occupant of the bath-room would meet her deserts, but about an hour afterwards Rhoda again approached the porter and enquired if there had been a message. Reuben hadn't rung up—but then he never did—and she thought she'd try and get Simon. She could explain that she hadn't telephoned him the previous night—and anyway it was a good excuse. And she could be sympathetic about Stella. But her luck was out. She was told Simon wasn't available—and that was another wasted call. She decided that Reuben was probably at some picture house. Films were his secret vice; she had once said she believed he only went up to town once a week in order to go to the pictures.

3

The Earl abandoned his taxi at Piccadilly Circus and bought a cheap seat at the London Picturedrome. He didn't as yet want to go to his club where he would be recognized and pinned down by the usual ageing bores. But the picture turned out to be not very entertaining so he didn't stay to the end. At about ten o'clock he dropped into his club demanding accommodation, and was told that Rhoda had left a message. Grudgingly he rang her up, to find, as he had anticipated, that she had nothing special to say.

"Don't go to the hospital," she warned him. "I got through and whoever was on the other end of the phone says that Stella has left. I suppose Mr. Crook, in that insufferably conceited way of his, has taken it on himself to remove her."

"I told you there was no necessity for us to make this tiresome journey and there were a great many things to do with the estate that need my attention," he replied in disgruntled tones, and rang off. Later he was seen in the smoking-room, explaining to a somnolent audience what was wrong with British films.

CHAPTER TWENTY

Let us have a quiet hour;
Let us hob and nob with Death.
TENNYSON.

1

THE GIRL, Stella Reed, had been smuggled out of the hospital by a private door to prevent her being mobbed by reporters. That, at all events, was the official explanation. True, it was late and the blackout had been proclaimed two hours before, but newspapermen are like vultures—they can tell a corpse miles away—and matron was taking no chances. Her instructions were to send the girl back to her flat, accompanied if possible, since Mr. Crook and the police were on their way, and although it was most inconvenient, she had spared a nurse and had summoned up a taxi, and the pair had driven off. Matron weighed up the inconvenience of sparing a nurse when staff was short with the even greater inconvenience of being desperately short of beds. Besides, there'd been too much publicity about this young woman. The sooner she was off the premises the better.

The nurse selected was a middle-aged woman, wildly curious about the whole affair, thrilled at having been chosen, and hoping against hope that the police and the extraordinary Mr. Crook would arrive before she had to leave her patient. She tried to get her to talk in the taxi, but the girl was singularly unresponsive. When they reached Laurel House the nurse said, "All these stairs? Think you can cope, dear? Well, well, good for the figure."

Stella went up like a doll—no animation at all. The room she entered struck her as cheerless, bearing that air of desolation that afflicts all unfamiliar places when the occupant has been some time away. Besides, this had never spelt home to her, being at best a perching-place until she could begin her real life with Simon. The nurse exclaimed suitably at this and that, put up the black-out and lighted the gas fire. She said encouragingly, "How about a nice cup of tea?" but Stella, longing to be rid of her and not knowing that once again an angel had appeared in strange guise, said, "No, not yet." She added that she'd wait until Mr. Crook and the others came, and meanwhile she would just rest quietly. She felt so tired it was as though life was ebbing out of her body. The nurse, unable to think of any good excuse for remaining, said rather primly, "All right, if that's what you prefer," thinking it's funny people don't seem able to show more gratitude when you've only their good at heart, and went clumping down the stairs, and Stella collapsed into a chair and wondered if there would be trouble with the authorities if she tried to get in touch with Simon.

She decided, however, that it would probably be wisest to do nothing without permission, and anyway she didn't want to be a nuisance and he'd been half-crazy over the affair as it was, so she lay back and wondered what questions the police would ask, whether they would be angry because she could tell them so little. She had been back some time when the bell rang and an authoritative hand rapped on the panel.

"That will be Mr. Crook," she decided, certain that Crook would never let the police force beat him to it, and she got up and went into the travesty of a hall. With a hand that shook she opened the door, and Murder walked in.

2

She was so surprised at the sight that she fell back involuntarily.

"Oh," she faltered, "I—I didn't know you were in town. I was expecting Mr. Crook."

"Simon telephoned," said Murder, who was more friendly than ever before, though still not gracious because graciousness, like charm, is an inborn quality. "I came at once. I was naturally anxious."

"That," whispered Stella, "was very kind." But she wished either that Murder would go away or that Simon would suddenly materialize. As for Crook, she would have preferred a glimpse of him to a vision of angels.

"I understood from the hospital," said Murder, taking a small uncomfortable chair and contriving to look uncomfortable in it, "that you had come back here, and I thought, as Simon had had to return to his unit, I would see whether there was anything Simon's family could do to help you. I'm afraid you have had a very severe shock. Though naturally," added Murder in more forbidding tones, "we have no details at present."

"I'm afraid I can't add very many," said Stella.

"You have seen the police?"

"Not yet. They're coming and Mr. Crook—at least, I hope Mr. Crook is coming. Have you—have you seen Simon?"

"He telephoned. Naturally he is greatly distressed. It is largely on his account . . ."

"Yes," said Stella. Of course it would be on Simon's account. Seeing how they all regarded her, it was ridiculous to expect any of them to make a special journey for her benefit. But her sense of loneliness increased.

"What actually took you to the house?" The careful voice put the question with no sign of emotion.

."He telephoned—Mr. Oliver, I mean."

"Mr. Oliver?"

"Your cousin—Gregory. He said Simon was going there and wanted me to meet him."

"But surely it must have seemed to you a palpable trap. Simon would hardly have been going to an empty house."

"He said it wasn't empty—and there was a caretaker. Yes, I suppose it does sound crazy now. I felt rather uncertain at the time, particularly as he said he couldn't be sure it was Simon's voice speaking."

Murder looked puzzled, which wasn't surprising. "In any case, it could hardly have been my cousin—not from the Manor, that is. He has been away for some days. He left on Monday."

"This was Tuesday," agreed Stella, and Murder's eyes narrowed. Either the girl was very clever or she was abnormally stupid. It was impossible to tell whether she suspected anything and, if so, what. "Oh, I've thought and thought, and I see now it couldn't have been Mr. Oliver unless, in some way, he was in it."

"But what had he to gain?"

"I don't see what any one had to gain. But there was that odd remark Tom Grigg made about the cousin being dangerous. That must have meant something."

Murder let that pass. "And when you reached the house, what happened?"

"I rang—and someone let me in."

"Who?"

"I couldn't be sure. I'd expected a woman, and so it was rather a shock."

"You mean, it was a man?"

"That's what makes me wonder if it could have been Mr. Oliver. Only—oh, nothing makes sense. That's where Mr. Crook will come in."

"You mean . . . ?"

"I mean, he can make sense of anything. You know, I still don't understand what happened. There was a voice and a hand on my wrist. . . ."

"And that's all you remember?"

"That's all I remember at present. But when Mr. Crook comes he may help me."

"Yes," said Murder in sombre tones. In the cunning brain thought wriggled like a worm. Discover everything she knows, cover yourself

184

at every turn. This is your chance. The police will be here in a few minutes. They mustn't find you.

"Do you think," asked Stella, "they would mind if I rang up Simon?"

"Simon's on his way. He won't be here for about an hour, but he's coming. Try to keep your mind clear till the police come and then do all you can to forget what happened."

"I don't feel as though I'd ever forget. I don't feel I'll ever go to a strange house without wondering who's really on the other side of the door—or go to the letter-box without expecting to find another post card there."

"Post card?"

"Yes. There have been four. When Mr. Crook comes I must show him. I mustn't forget. There are so many things I mustn't forget. And I have to be on guard all the time. Do you think I'll ever trust people again?" She laughed suddenly. "It's new to me, trusting people. Simon got me into the habit, but I think I was wiser before. Well, this has been a lesson."

"You must keep calm," said Murder authoritatively. "Otherwise you'll become confused. You won't know what you're saying. You may say what isn't true, and then there'll be trouble. You've brooded too much on this. You'll contradict yourself and that'll make things harder."

Stella nodded. "I know," she agreed feverishly. "It's as though a wheel were going round and round in my brain, faster and faster. It makes such a noise I can't think."

"That's reaction," Murder assured her. "What about a cup of tea?"

"Oh no, thank you," said Stella quickly. She was intimidated by the vague way in which her visitor looked round, not at all in the manner of one accustomed to making cups of tea for distressed young women. There is little solace in tea if you have to get up and fill the kettle and set the tray. Besides, above all things now she wanted to be alone, and she wondered how she could convey this to her visitor without seeming churlish.

"You look feverish," said Murder in what was intended for a solicitous tone. "How about an aspirin?"

"Oh yes—no, it doesn't matter. I don't believe I've got any."

But her companion was ready for anything and fished a little bottle of white tablets from a coat pocket.

"These are not aspirin but they're similar. I always carry them with me and I find them very useful. Ladies in trains sometimes feel rather faint and there are times when I'm glad of them myself. You should take two—or even three and then lie down for a little. You are not sure when the police will come?"

"I don't know. Not too soon, I hope. I should like to feel rather less muddled before they arrive."

"Then suppose you take these and lie down on your couch and try to sleep for a little. You needn't be afraid they won't wake you. The police don't belong to the Silent Service.

Stella tried to join in the laugh that accompanied the words, but it wasn't much of a success. The room wasn't actually swimming, but it was beginning to rock a bit. Perhaps if she agreed to take the tablets her visitor would leave her. Meekly she accepted a glass, held out her hand. You wouldn't think death could be so small, so innocent-looking, lying so quietly in the palm of your open hand.

Murder received the glass back, washed it—because everybody knows about fingerprints, stood by while the girl rather self-consciously lay down on the divan and pulled a rug over her and then asked, ears astrain for the approaching police, "Would you like me to wait till they come? I could get some dinner later.'

"Oh no, thank you. Please don't wait. I know I shall be all right now. I—I do appreciate what you've done."

You'd almost think, now she'd nearly died, that Simon's family wanted her in their circle. At the back of her mind was the thought, There's something wrong. I've made a mistake. Mr. Crook would know what it was. Perhaps if I'm alone I shall remember. So, "Please don't let me keep your any longer. You've been very kind," she pleaded.

Nothing suited Murder's book better. "What about the light? Shall I turn it off? The gas fire's on, so you won't be in the dark."

She said doubtfully, "Oh yes, please." After all, the fire gave a heartening glow, and if she found she didn't like the semi-darkness she could always turn the light on again. But she couldn't—she couldn't argue. She wondered if she were going to get hysterical, she who had known Life's pitiless face most of her years and was still mistrustful of kindness.

"Then I'll leave you. Perhaps you'll sleep."

"I think so. I feel as though I could sleep for ever."

Murder smiled. That, did she but know it, was just what she was going to do. Sleep for ever and ever.

As the hand of the departing guest unlatched the door something tinkled very gently to the ground, so gently you'd have to be waiting for the sound to hear it. But Stella was already feeling drowsy, and Murder wanted to be gone. So whatever it was that had fallen remained where it had dropped.

3

Crook nipped out of the hospital a deal quicker than he had gone in, and into the car where the patient Bill was waiting.

"Station," he said tersely. "Police station. Those damned fools. If we had any intelligence test in this country we'd soon solve the problem of over-population. D'you know what they've done, Bill? They've let her out. D'you get me?"

"You mean Stella Reed? Whose authority?"

"The murderer's. Can you believe they'd be such fools? Get a message that the police would like to see the girl at her own flat this evening if the doctor thinks she's fit to be moved—and they let her go. *They let her go!* Upon my Sam, I'm not surprised at the murders that are committed; I'm astounded there aren't thousands more with this damned democratic Government letting lunatics run around un-attended the way they do."

Bill shaved a cyclist who was going home without a light and murmured pacifically, "Well, you couldn't lock 'em all up. Who'd fill up the ranks of the Civil Service?"

"And if anything happened to that girl and I tell that *image* she's an accessory after the fact, as she will be, she'll try and run me in for insultin' behaviour."

"They are like that," agreed Bill, who never allowed even immi-nent murder to shake him. "Here we are."

Crook hurtled out of the car which shook like a cockleshell with the violence of his exit and bounded into the Police Station. The man on duty thought he was a bit merry and wondered how these chaps know where to find the stuff.

"Where's Sergeant Peacock?" Crook demanded. "All right, all right. Who is on duty then? Get a move on or there'll be another murder committed for which no policeman will swing."

A door on the left opened sharply and a cool voice murmured, "Crook or I'm a Dutchman," and Crook saw a tallish ordinary-looking man in ordinary-looking clothes, carrying a black bowler hat.

"The Lord looks after His own," ejaculated Crook. "Field or I'm another. I was never so pleased to see you before."

"If you get much more pleased you'll explode," said Field, who was a pretty distinguished member of the C.I.D. and was in the neighbourhood after a gang who had just stolen several thousand clothing coupons and were believed to have their headquarters in a very respectable private service-men's club. "What is it?"

"Murder I wouldn't wonder. Come on. I've got the car. We're going to Laurel House and I'll tell you all about it on the way."

It said a good deal for Crook's reputation that Field didn't stop for argument. He bundled into the back of the absurd car and Crook sat sideways in the front seat and told his story, while Bill rushed them across London. Only once Field stopped the narrative to peer out and say, "Which way's he taking us?" Crook said briefly, "The shortest. We've got a night's work ahead." Field said reflectively, "For there is great news to be heard and fine things to be seen, before we come to Paradise by way of Kensal Green."

Crook, however, would have trusted Bill to get him through the Gates of Hell to the Delectable Mountains if Bill thought that was the quickest way, and in a remarkably short time they stopped in front of the dark narrow house. It was Bill who opened the door of No. 22 without the convention of a latch-key and Field thought what a loss he must be to a number of high-class gangs and what a death-blow it had proved to many an ambitious young officer's hopes when a police-bullet struck him in the heel several years back, causing him to go a bit lame and inevitably putting an end to that side of a conspicuously versatile career.

The flat was in darkness except for the faint flicker of a gas-fire that was noiselessly expiring as the shillingsworth of gas in the meter burnt itself out. Crook stamped across the room to renew the supply, Field flashed on his official torch and Bill lugged one, heavy enough to brain a man, from the pocket of his coat. As the gas flared up again Crook straightened himself and came to stand by Field's side. The girl, Stella Reed, lay on the bed in a deep sleep. She was very pale and so thin the bones of temple and jaw seemed as though they might break through the skin.

The detective bent over her. "This is a nasty business," he said. "The girl's at her last lap. Get a doctor."

It was characteristic of Bill that he knew the number of a local man without even having to consult a telephone directory. While they awaited his arrival Crook began to prowl round the flat. His little torch picked out every inch of the carpet and the cheap linoleum surround. Near the door he stooped with a mutter and picked something up.

It was a button off a coat.

Field was across the room in a flash. "What's that? H'm. Who does it belong to?"

"The last time I saw it—or it's twin brother—it was on Cleveland's coat. I noticed it was hanging loose."

"And he didn't?"

"I suppose not. I wonder if he's found out by now that he's lost it."

"Even so he may not know where. It was all Lombard Street to a china orange against its being found here."

"Remember what Scott Egerton used to say?" Crook reminded him. "That Providence has a way of sleeving the winning ace and playin' it on the side of virtue. And so she does, Field, so she does."

Field looked a bit dubious. "I wouldn't care to bet on that. D'you suggest it was Virtue made the murderer drop his button on the scene of the crime?"

"You've been goin' to too many pictures," Crook reproved him. "No, what I meant was by havin' me as Mrs. Manners' defence. Well," and absently he slipped the button into his pocket, "we can't always prevent murder bein' done, and I suppose, speakin' professionally I'd be in a jam if we could; chaps like me are goin' to line up

189

for the dole in the Kingdom of Heaven—but if we can put our finger on the chap we shall have done our best and an angel can do no more."

There was a little commotion as someone stumbled on the dark stairs, said Damnation! and came on again. Crook opened the door to the doctor.

"Bill and I won't stop," he said, "seeing the police have taken over. Besides, we've got work of our own to do."

"You're still Mrs. Manners' defence," observed Field rather abruptly.

"Teach your grandmother!" retorted Crook. "How d'you think I've made my pile? By letting my clients swing? Rather not. I'm like the patriot—My country right or wrong—and by the time I'm through they're always right. Bill and me have got to find the chap responsible for this."

"We're always glad of your co-operation," acknowledged Field humbly.

Crook winked. "Well, who else d'you think's going to be any good to you? Believe me, one of these fine days you're going to say Thank You to your old friend, The Criminals' Hope and The Judges' Despair, for solvin' one more desperate crime and bringin' one more killer to justice."

He nodded to Bill and they went out. They had driven off when it occurred to Field that Crook had taken the incriminating button with him.

CHAPTER TWENTY-ONE

Murder may pass unpunished for a time,
But tardy Justice will o'ertake the crime.
DRYDEN.

CLEVELAND WAS BREAKFASTING with his usual gloomy thoroughness and wondering whether his indomitable old mother would respect an Englishman's privilege to be the first person to open the *Times*, when he was called to the telephone. Crook was at the other end.

"Glad to have got you," said Crook. "I tried two or three times last night."

"I was out last night till late," said Cleveland at once. "They didn't give me a message."

"They couldn't," said Crook. "I didn't leave a name."

"Any special reason?" asked Cleveland.

"I didn't want to give you a chance of fobbing me off," returned Crook bluntly. "Look here, there's been a serious development. It affects Miss Reed."

"I understand she left the hospital yesterday evening."

"So you rang them up?"

"Certainly not. I telephoned to my sister—at her Club—in accordance with her wishes—when I came in. She had been in touch with the authorities and told me that she intends to visit Miss Reed this morning."

"She'll be a bit late," said Crook slowly. "Miss Reed won't be there."

"Won't be where?"

"Wherever Miss Oliver thinks of finding her."

"At her flat, I understand."

"Look here," said Crook, "something happened last night—I told you that before. Last night before I got there, the murderer arrived and . . ."

Cleveland interrupted sharply, "I thought you said the police had put a guard round her."

Crook sounded more impatient than he usually permitted himself to be. "If people didn't now and again creep under the official guard there wouldn't be any crime," he pointed out.

"And—what happened to Miss Reed?"

"I told you—she was unfortunately left alone for a short time—and the murderer beat us by a short head. Luckily, we have some evidence as to identity. But we need help."

"If I—or my sister . . ."

"We believe both of you might be able to lend a hand. Can you come here to 205 Bloomsbury Court by ten o'clock? I'm just going to ring her and pop the same question. Miss Reed having no family of her own we have to fall back on the next best thing."

191

"Very poor taste," thought Cleveland with the famous family sniff, and he said aloud, "That is rather stretching a point, but naturally, for my son's sake, we shall be glad to help in any way we can. By the way, does he know anything of this latest development?"

"He's on his way. I'm afraid he blames us. That's natural. But you'll probably see him at my place, unless the train's derailed en route."

He rang off before Cleveland could voice any of the objections that instantly occurred to him, and the Earl went back to his breakfast. He wondered what he ought to expect in the course of the next hour or so and what, if anything, he could do to prepare himself for it. In about ten minutes he was again called to the phone. This time it was Rhoda, stammering with excitement.

"Reuben, Mr. Crook's just rung me up. He said he'd been on to you. He told me about Stella, too. How that man dares to call himself a detective. . . ."

"He doesn't," said Cleveland. "He's a lawyer."

"This will break Simon's heart," declared Simon's aunt dramatically.

"It won't do the police any good," was Cleveland's unemotional rejoinder.

"The police! That's all you ever think about. Can't you see this from a personal point of view?"

"I can see it's a very shocking thing to have happened," acknowledged Cleveland, "but we were all agreed that this marriage would be a disaster for my son."

"It would be more of a disaster if Simon were to do something rash," cried Rhoda in such passionate tones that a fellow-member passing the little glass-fronted cubicle in which she sat, lifted her white eyebrows and thought that these young women didn't know the meaning of self-control.

"You are forgetting that Simon is my son and, as such, is not likely to be unmindful of his responsibilities," was Cleveland's cold reply.

Rhoda, however, refused to be impressed. "If you mean the Estate, he has never pretended to be particularly interested. . . ."

"I mean that the country is at war, and that he holds the king's commission."

"That sounds very high falutin', but it isn't going to help him if anything's happened to Stella. The police must have been mad, of course, though they'll get out of it, because they're like Royalty, they can't do wrong. But I shall always hold them responsible."

"It might be as well to withhold judgment until we know all the facts," suggested Cleveland. Even Bill Parsons had nothing on him when it came to keeping his head in a crisis.

"That's why I rang up. I suppose he's asked you to come, too."

"As the head of the family. . . ." Cleveland frowned. He was old-fashioned. He didn't believe in women coming to funerals or readings of a will or any place that might be a breeding-ground for emotion. And Rhoda in her present mood would accentuate the extreme uneasiness which even a peer of the realm is bound to feel in such ticklish circumstances.

"Anyway, I rang up to know when you were going to start. I thought I'd come with you. I couldn't possibly go alone."

"Do you think you are really wise . . . ?"

"My dear Reuben, I have been invited as much as you. And though it's true Simon is your son, he is the next-best thing to a son to me. It may also be true that I can't do much to help him, but . . ."

"I shall leave the club at twenty minutes to ten," said the Earl, coldly.

"I'll pick you up," said Rhoda. "But twenty minutes to ten is running things rather fine, isn't it?"

"A taxi," began the Earl, and Rhoda said naïvely, "Oh! I thought of going by tube."

The Earl shuddered; you could detect that shudder even over the wire. It was bad enough to contemplate Rhoda's overwrought presence in any case, but to have it plus the publicity of a packed tube train was intolerable.

"Very well," said he more coldly than before. "If you are determined to come, I shall be leaving at twenty minutes to ten."

If you'd met Rhoda anywhere in London you'd have known she was a member of the Countrywomen's Own. She had that indefinable air. In novels, shabby tweeds are distinguished and inalienably well-cut, but in life even well-cut tweeds get baggy and look remarkably like something from the Sixty Shilling Tailors, and Rhoda had never been able to afford Hanover Square anyway. Her half-brother surveyed her stonily, hoped she wasn't going to cry in the taxi and winced when she greeted him in a voice pitched on a note calculated to attract attention all the way to Piccadilly. In the taxi she was restless, talked a lot, supposing this and that, wondering what really had happened. You read such awful things in the papers, she kept on saying. Not in the *Times*, corrected Lord Cleveland.

"Do you suppose Simon will—see—her?" she queried.

Cleveland wished heartily that Crook had chambers in Piccadilly Circus; the journey seemed endless. As she stepped out of the taxi Rhoda tripped and would have fallen if he hadn't caught her. Her hat was knocked over her eye; she had powdered unevenly, and a tail of hair came down beneath her unfashionable hat. He steadied her, thinking it's a good thing it's early and people can't think she's intoxicated, and then he took her severely by the arm and led her into the building where Crook's offices were situated.

A tall man with a handsome ruined face and a distinctive limp led them in. He didn't seem remotely interested in their identity or in the matter in hand. He merely said, "Crook's expecting you," and opening another door ushered them all in. Crook was sitting at a big scarred writing table, covered with papers, and there were two men with him, wearing plain clothes. Crook introduced them— Chief-Inspector Field, Superintendent Dalton of the Belgravia Police Station.

"This is a bad business," said Cleveland, shrugging himself out of his overcoat. "You didn't make yourself very clear over the telephone, but I gather there's been a further incident."

Crook unable to withhold a certain amount of admiration for a man in the Earl's position who could adopt this cool attitude, said, "Sorry I sounded muddled. As a matter of fact, the murderer got in ahead of us last night."

"And—is she dead?" Rhoda twisted a ring on her big square hands. "I don't know what Simon will do. He'll be demented."

"What precisely happened?" enquired Cleveland, intent on keeping emotion out of the situation.

"Well, of course, anything I can say is only a matter of surmise," acknowledged Crook, "but I read it something like this. Someone—call him X—got wind of our proposed visit and telephoned the hospital with a fake message, saying that the police would prefer to interview Miss Reed at her flat, if she was fit to be moved. The matron said she was. That told X the first thing he wanted to know. Miss Reed went back with an escort who returned to the hospital, practically, I gather, at Miss Reed's request, and X took a chance and went straight round. I say took a chance because she might have kept the nurse there, but if she had X had only to pretend he'd come to the wrong flat—the nurse would certainly have opened the door—and got away without leaving a name. The luck held, though, and the girl was alone."

Cleveland interrupted to say, "Have you any idea of the identity of the visitor?"

"It's safe to assume it was either someone she recognized or else it was someone who was able to persuade her he represented the police. There's no question of a forced entry. X was admitted by the room's occupant, and since there's no sign of any struggle we can assume the girl didn't realize her danger. At some time during the conversation X persuaded the girl to take either some tablets or some kind of draught—probably some kind of tablets."

"I don't see how you can tell that," whispered Rhoda resentfully.

"Things being the way they are, it's not likely the girl would com-mit suicide, and we've medical evidence to show that it was some form of sleeping-mixture that was responsible for her condition when we arrived. Because though we can't have missed the murderer by many minutes, we were too late to get any statement from her. She was—beyond all that."

His voice dropped. Cleveland was staring straight ahead. Rhoda whispered, "How terrible you must feel! I mean, if you'd guarded every avenue she wouldn't have left the hospital, would she?"

"And yet," pointed out Crook sharply, "if this hadn't happened we might never have been able to lay our hands on the murderer of Tom Grigg."

"Tom Grigg!" Rhoda's voice dismissed Tom and all his works.

"Don't get me wrong," Crook warned her. "My job is to find out who killed Tom. All the rest is so much parsley round the dish."

"Have you any more—surmises?" enquired Cleveland. Oh, he might have integrity—you wouldn't know—but he'd never have charm, because charm's inborn.

"It's difficult to blame X," said Crook. "He was in a spot all right. He thought he'd got rid of the girl once and for all in the basement of an empty house, and here she is again, and how does he know what she remembers or what authority will make of her evidence? He's got to put out her light before the police come on the scenes. Well, when we searched the flat we found one glass that had just been used—it had been washed but not properly dried—and all the other glasses were as dry as the prophet's bones. There was a cloth hanging in the kitchen that had just been used—a bit crumpled and so forth—but naturally we shall have to wait for the doctor's report to know exactly what it was Miss Reed took."

Cleveland said, his big hands rigid in his lap, "She was rather indiscreet, wasn't she, considering the circumstances?"

"That's what makes the police and me decide it was someone she knew," agreed Crook.

Rhoda leaned forward earnestly. "And have you no clues?"

"Funnily enough," said Crook, "we have." He put his big hand into his pocket and brought it out the next second, a big clenched first, holding something worth more than its weight in gold. "We found this," he said. "Funny how murderers do so well for a time and then suddenly make a bloomer any tyro would be ashamed of. X wasn't a fool by any means, but he blundered all right, the way they always do." He opened his hand, palm upwards, and they all saw a round brown button lying there.

Cleveland looked at it, folded his mouth like a rat-trap, glanced at Field, and said, "Does that help? It's a pretty ordinary sort of button. I have something very like it on my own coat."

"But," stammered Rhoda, "that's just it. Don't you see . . . I mean . . ."

"You mean that you saw a button identical to this one on your brother's coat only yesterday?"

Rhoda recovered herself quickly. "As Reuben says, hundreds of people have buttons like that."

"One of them had worked a bit loose, hadn't it?" pursued Crook inexorably.

"Suppose it had?" flashed Rhoda. "What then?"

"I only mean that a button that's worked loose might easily—fall off."

"Are you trying to tell us you found that button in Stella's room?" demanded Rhoda.

The Earl said nothing. He was thinking hard.

"We did. The Yard will bear me out in that."

"It still doesn't mean anything. There are thousands of buttons like that."

"Bill," said Crook pleasantly, "you've got his lordship's coat on that chair, haven't you?"

"Do you want it?" asked the expressionless Bill.

"Pass it over."

Bill handed it across.

"I just wanted to know how many buttons there are on it now," explained Crook.

They all leaned forward, all except Cleveland, as he turned the coat over.

"Three," Crook agreed. "One of them seems to have been very recently sewn on, though. And—it's not quite the same as the rest."

You had to hand it to Cleveland that he knew how to cover up. "When I got back to my club last night," he said, "I realized that one of my buttons was missing. I gave the coat to the hall porter and asked him to get someone to sew one on for me. That, I presume, is the best match he could find."

"Too bad!" murmured Crook. "I mean, it was a good plot up to a point and there was a lot of thought in it, but it just didn't make the grade."

He thrust his hand into the pocket of the coat, raised his thick red brows, and brought out a little bottle of small white tablets.

"Well," he observed grimly, "that wasn't very clever of you." He put it down on the table. Rhoda stared incredulously.

"Do you mean that—those—are they poison?"

"I'd say that's what Miss Reed was given last night. I told you it was clever—up to a point."

Cleveland spoke roughly. "Not very clever of you," he said. "I've never set eyes on that bottle before."

"I fancy I may be able to prove that," said Crook. He nodded to Bill, and Bill opened the door behind him and said, "Come in, Mr. Weston."

A little man with a crumpled leather face marched into the room.

"Mr. Weston," said Crook, "you recognize this coat?"

"Yes, sir. It belongs to His Lordship."

"And you recognize this button?"

"It's one I sewed on last night. His Lordship explained that he'd lost one travelling and asked me to replace it. And then he said I might as well press the coat at the same time. It had got a bit damp and of course travelling at close quarters does crush a coat, and his lordship was always careful of his clothes."

"And to press it you'd have to empty the pockets?"

"Of course, sir."

"But naturally you'd put anything back that you found there?"

"There wasn't anything. His lordship never carries things in his pockets. He says it spoils the shape of the coat, and he's quite right."

"Still, a little bottle like this . . ."

"There wasn't anything like that, sir. I'll take my oath."

"Curiouser and curiouser," said Crook. "Why on earth should Lord Cleveland break his rules and put a bottle in his pocket—a highly incriminating bottle, mark you—just to call on me?"

"I've told you," said Cleveland, raising his voice with irritation, "I know nothing of that bottle. I never saw it before."

"Still, you admit to seeing me take it out of your pocket just now."

"Don't answer him, Reuben," said Rhoda quickly. "It's a trick. You saw him bring his hand out of your pocket with a bottle inside it, but you didn't see what was inside his hand before he put it in."

"You do think a lot, don't you?" murmured Crook admiringly. "Well, if I won't go all the way with you, but not believin' in any miracles but my own, I agree that if your brother didn't put it in his pocket someone else did."

"Your colleague," cried Rhoda, pointing at Bill. "He had the opportunity."

"You're talking nonsense, Rhoda," said Cleveland. "What point would there be in that? Besides, they couldn't have put the button in Miss Reed's flat."

"Mr. Crook might," said Rhoda. "He said himself he noticed it was hanging loose."

"But why should he?" enquired Cleveland. "He didn't know there was going to be another attempt on Miss Reed's life."

"Besides," continued Crook, "me and Bill were at the hospital when it all happened. We've got an alibi all right."

"So have I," flashed Rhoda. "I was having a bath at the club. You can check up the times with the porter if you like."

"Well!" ejaculated Crook, looking as delicate as was possible for a man of his build.

But Field, taking a part in the conversation for the first time, leaned forward to say, "Miss Oliver, how do you happen to know what time the attack took place?"

CHAPTER TWENTY-TWO

"The shroud is done," Death muttered, "toe to chin."
He snapped the ends and tucked the needles in.
JOHN MASEFIELD.

IT'S THE LITTLE THINGS that hang men, the unguarded word, the dropped match, the unexpected passer-by. History—criminal history —is full of these minute, essential details. Not that Crook would agree. Criminals, he says, hang themselves, usually by an excess of caution. Later he acknowledged he'd never have got Miss Oliver for the murder of Tom Grigg if she hadn't handed him the ace of trumps.

"I knew all along you were guilty," he told her. "I knew it couldn't be any one else, but what the soldier said ain't evidence, and I'm not out to make myself a laughing-stock to a British jury, that can be

199

trusted to laugh in the wrong place anyhow. But on the facts it was clear from the start that you were the only person, bar your nephew, who could have seen Tom that night."

"How do you make that out?" flashed Rhoda.

"Simple matter of timing," Crook replied. "Ask any chap in the theatre why one actor goes over and another don't and he'll tell you timing's half the battle. Not too slow or the audience gets bored, not too fast or they get left behind. Now, just look at the facts. Simon Oliver says that at 6.30 Tom Grigg was talkin' to him and a few minutes later, say 6.40, they parted by the Manor gates. He went indoors, got his message, strapped his box, which he'd hardly begun to unpack anyway, collected his young lady and set out for the high road. It takes, say, twenty-five minutes to reach the Park gates on foot, so Grigg couldn't at best be there till a little after seven. Just after seven —he'd heard the clock strike, remember—you come sailing through the gates almost slap into the car, because you've got no lights. You hadn't seen Tom Grigg coming along, had you?"

"I've told you I hadn't," said Rhoda. "Or perhaps you don't believe that, either."

"I believe that all right, because I happen to know it's true. Grigg couldn't have got to the gates more than a minute before the car even if he'd been a human greyhound, and that's a straight road. The lights of the car must have picked him up if he'd been there. And even if he'd been running young Simon would have passed him afterwards and he didn't."

"So what?" demanded Rhoda, unconscious of the slang term.

"Ergo—he hadn't been through the gates. And if he'd been on the path they'd have seen him or you'd have met him head on. You did cycle back? Didn't spring a puncture or anything?"

"Certainly not," snapped Rhoda.

"And not havin' a light didn't bother you?"

"Any reasonable person can get accustomed to moving in the dark. I never carry a torch myself in any weather."

"And I dare say you had a spare battery up at the House."

"Spare batteries are a sheer waste of money. They need to be used at once or they deteriorate. I bought one next day in the village."

"They open early, these village shops," suggested Crook.

Rhoda stared. "I don't know what you mean by that. I bought mine about eleven o'clock—but perhaps that is early for London."

"Just what I thought," agreed Crook. "Well, then you came pedallin' along in the dark. It takes a quarter of an hour, say, from the gates."

"Less," snapped Miss Oliver. "To an experienced cyclist definitely less."

"Funny that," commented Crook. "I mean, seeing you left your nephew right after seven, and didn't get in till about seven-forty."

"I . . ." Miss Oliver looked momentarily at a loss. "If you're going to take the word of a servant as to the precise moment I arrived on a particular night, I'm afraid you may have some difficulty with the jury."

"Point of fact, my witness isn't a servant. It's your cousin, Gregory Oliver, and he remembers that night pretty well, because it was the night of the Home Guard exercise, and your nephew having just gone off unexpectedly, and things being a bit at sixes and sevens, he remembers your coming in late and not having time to change out of your W.V.S. uniform. Well, what the jury will want to know is—what were you doing between seven and seven-forty? You've admitted already it wouldn't take you all that time to cycle back to the house."

"And where," demanded Rhoda, "are you suggesting I was?"

"I'd say you were havin' a little tête-à-tête with Tom Grigg. He didn't come up to the Manor for nothing, and he was a fairly desperate man. He'd asked for you specially, you know, and your nephew had made him a present of the fact that you were out. But that meant you must be comin' back some time, so I think he waited for you."

"And how was it that neither my brother nor Miss Reed, who was incidentally picked up by my brother in his car, or my cousin saw us, singly or together?"

"I don't think either of you was anxious to be seen. There's a little—gazebo the Reverend called it—nice and handy for the Manor gates. I think you were in there. On a dark night no one would know, and your business wasn't the kind that you'd go shouting for everyone to hear. I think Tom told you about the marriage, and I

201

think, too, he showed you the late Mrs. Oliver's marriage lines, and he asked just what they were worth to you."

Rhoda made a gesture of contempt. "What sense would there be in that? I had no money. The whole village knows it. Why, I've less than old Mary Anne."

Her bitterness was very great; Field stared at the floor; Cleveland was like an image; Crook was like a machine that goes steadily round and round at even pressure, though the skies fall.

"That's why you had to find some other way of shutting his mouth," he agreed. "No, don't say anything yet. I'll tell you how it happened. You asked him where he was staying, and he told you and you said, Go back for to-night and I'll come to-morrow. I dare say you promised him money if he'd wait till morning. By that time the family was safely indoors and you don't have visitors after dark at the Manor, so there wasn't much fear of any one seeing him go home. You went back, a bit late, and didn't have time to change your clothes, and your step-mother had a bit of fun at your expense, but I don't think you took much notice—that night. Other, more important things to think of, see? The next day you got up pretty early—Lady Cleveland told us you were out before the rest of the house had started thinking about breakfast—and you went down in the dark—not even a light on your machine, not so much as a torch in your hand—down to the church. Of course it would be dark inside so early in the day, so you'd want a candle. I knew, when I thought about the candle, that Mary Anne wasn't the only visitor to that church in the hours of darkness, and she wouldn't want to strike a match anyway, because she had a torch. She always took a torch with her. You never carry a torch, but you do smoke, so you'd have matches."

Miss Oliver had been listening with a deathly intentness, but now she threw back her head with a harsh masculine laugh.

"And are you suggesting that Tom didn't hear me coming? Or that he just stayed in the vestry and waited for me to lock the door on him?"

"Was he in the vestry?" asked Crook. "Oh well, perhaps the brazier was out by then. Did you re-light it or did he?"

"It wasn't out," said Miss Oliver. "It . . ."

Cleveland suddenly put up his hand and would have spoken but Crook silenced him.

"No," he agreed, "it wasn't out. I didn't think it would be. That place would freeze a man to death in such weather if he hadn't some sort of heating. But he couldn't have slept in the vestry with the door shut and the brazier burning or he'd have suffocated during the night. So he must have had the door open, so of course he'd hear you come in. Besides, you had to be sure about the brazier. That was important."

"Do you suggest," enquired Cleveland, getting in a word in spite of them all, "that he meekly allowed my sister—or any one else—to shut and bolt the door, knowing it meant certain death?"

"There wasn't any sign of a struggle," said Crook, "and if there had been Tom would have won it. He was a merchant seaman, remember. He couldn't be that and a weakling. No, he must have agreed to that door being shut. If he hadn't he could have kicked up such a hullabaloo that anyone in the village would have heard him."

"Then why . . . ?" Cleveland began again, and again Crook took the words out of his mouth.

"That's what I had to decide. I think Miss Oliver must have assured him it was for his own sake. He knew the police had tracked him as far as King's Fossett. Mrs. Manners had told him that. And you knew at the Manor that the police were after him, because they'd been to call. I think, Miss Oliver, you told him they were on the warpath, were hunting everywhere and in due course would reach the church. He'd be taken like a rat in a trap, for there wasn't any secret way out. But suppose the vestry door was locked and the curtain drawn, if the key was turned and the bolts shot, no one would imagine he was on the further side of the door, because a man like Tom Grigg can do a lot of things, but he can't lock himself into a room and leave the key on the other side. And if there's a table standing against the curtain and an alms-dish on the table—well, even a policeman might be excused for not guessing there was any one the other side. I don't see how Tom could have done anything but agree if you'd told him a story like that. No one ever goes inside that church, practically speaking, and even Guppy lives at Bishops Cleveland, so they wouldn't notice any rearrangement of the furniture.

203

And you'd get away quietly. I wonder how long he waited before he realized he'd been fooled, that he wasn't ever going to get out. There's something about a policeman's tread that you can't mistake, if you've ever heard it, and he knew what it sounded like all right. He must have wondered and wondered, and then maybe he thought they weren't going to try the church after all. So he waited and waited—for the door to be unlocked. The air must have got a bit thick. And after a time it must have dawned on him what had really happened. That he was shut up there for the rest of his life. He battered on the door—you remember his hands."

Miss Oliver said, "I never saw him after he was dead."

"You didn't, did you? Well, that's what happened. But battering and shouting wouldn't help, even if you were heard, because they'd only think it was the ghost, and no one would go there by chance. The Reverend put it at once a month and any one who'd taken a look round would believe him."

Cleveland spoke again. One of the most notable things about the conversation was the complete silence of Simon Oliver, who had quietly appeared. It seemed to contribute almost as much to what was going on as Crook's speech. It was the more notable because as a rule he was like his lost cousin, young and gay and warm-hearted. Even Crook felt the atmosphere slowly icing over, not with Rhoda's fear or Cleveland's shame. Of them all, young Simon was the most dangerous. He was glad to see that Bill was standing unobtrusively close, and whatever you might say about Bill he never lost his head in a crisis.

Cleveland said, "But surely—wouldn't he have suspected a trap?" To which Crook replied heartily, "No, and what's more, you wouldn't either. That's one of the queer things about human nature. We all know murders happen; we read about 'em in the paper, see 'em on the screen. But in real life we never expect them to happen to us. And so we're not on our guard. I ought to know," he added, with the air of making a handsome confession, "I've had the thugs after me often enough, and yet I can never really believe they'll get me. Psychologists 'ull tell you that's vanity, and I dare say it is, but if so it just shows what a lot of good vanity does you." His dauntless grin proclaimed him a man of unconquerable conceit.

Rhoda spoke again. She said, "It's a good story, but you still can't prove any of it." And Crook agreed at once, "Too right. And if you'd been content to leave it at that I might have had to buy off the jury when my client came up for trial. But you didn't leave it at that. They never do—specially amateurs. You looked round in case you were in danger, and of course you saw your lion—lioness rather— right in the path."

"If you could talk plain English," suggested Rhoda, "it might save time for all of us. My brother is a very busy man. . . ."

If Crook thought that this scene was better than anything you'd get on the films he had the decency not to say so. Besides, even he was aware of an electric humming in the atmosphere, and he shot a warning glance at Bill. He didn't want another murder done right under his eyes, and there was something about young Simon's face that wasn't reassuring.

"I get you," he said, more quickly than usual. "What I mean is you saw Miss Reed, and you realized she might sell you down the river without even meaning to."

"I said plain English," Rhoda reminded him, not batting an eyelid.

"You didn't see the body, did you? Grigg's, I mean?"

"I've told you I didn't."

Crook made a movement with his hands which meant, "It's in the bag." "Then how is it, Miss Oliver, that you could tell Miss Reed that you supposed your step-mother had always seen him as he was now—gross and common—because he was good-looking enough when you last saw him, wasn't he? Nothing gross then. Well, Miss Oliver?"

"I didn't—say that to Miss Reed, I mean."

"She swore you did."

"She was confused. She had a very powerful imagination. I recognized that from the beginning."

"She was prepared to take her oath on it."

"I'm afraid it's too late for that now."

"Too late?" Crook looked staggered.

"She's dead, isn't she?"

The great red brows rose like a hedge. "Who told you that?"

"But—you telephoned. You said . . ."

"I said there'd been another attempt, but . . . All right, captain."
He nodded hastily to Simon. "Call it a day."

Simon went forward without any change of that stony expression
that frightened Crook more than he'd have acknowledged. He
opened the door through which he had come and Rhoda fell back
a pace. Even the Earl was shaken. For there, on the threshold, her
hand automatically seeking Simon's as though it was he and not
Crook who'd saved her, stood Stella Reed. White-faced, shaking,
blue circles round the eyes, but Stella, alive and breathing, ready to
give testimony.

For an instant no one moved. Then Rhoda whirled round, made
a wild snatch at the little innocent-looking bottle that stood on the
table, and before any one could speak had wrenched off the cap and
shaken half-a-dozen tablets into her palm. Only as she lifted her
hand to her mouth did Cleveland suddenly remember his official
standing and exclaim, "Stop her, you fools. Can't you see . . . ?"

"Too late," said Crook. "Anyhow, it was better this way. She
hadn't a hope—and she knows it."

Rhoda had moved backwards, so that she stood against the wall,
her big square hands flat out, as though she could find some support
on the smooth surface.

"You're right," she said. "It's too late. And this is the best way.
Well, you can have the truth for what it's worth. I did kill Tom.
I had to. He knew about Edmund's marriage—but I swear I never
knew until that night and Reuben didn't know until you told him."

"If I had known," interpolated Cleveland in a voice of steel, "do
you imagine I should have retained the title?"

Crook thought it best not to answer that one.

"He wanted money and I hadn't got it. But if I had what would
have been the use of giving it to him? He'd have gone on draining
us for ever—and no one could guess that Ted Manners would be
killed in an accident within a month. No, it was Cleveland I had to
think of, and this was the only way. I had to save the place—for
Simon."

Simon looked as though he were going to say something, but Bill
caught him by the elbow. Like Crook, murder (among other things)

was his bread and butter, but he didn't want one committed in this office. Simon shut his mouth again and Crook said, "I don't say I blame you, but—you might have left Miss Reed out of it."

"No," said Rhoda fiercely. "She knew too much."

"I didn't know anything," said Stella in a low voice.

"You knew about the marriage. I don't know who told you—Mrs. Manners perhaps—but it was your secret weapon and I couldn't afford to let you use it. Oh, you can shake your head now, but you knew it. You told me so that night in your room. Even families like the Clevelands have secret marriages sometimes, you said, and you'd stop at nothing to get Simon. But you didn't realize that I'd stop at nothing to save Cleveland—and him."

"But I didn't mean that," protested Stella. "I didn't know anything. I couldn't have given evidence. All I meant was that if you tried to stop me marrying Simon in the parish church, you couldn't separate us, because a secret marriage is valid. I meant . . ."

Rhoda's face wasn't pleasant to see.

"I don't believe you," she whispered.

"And I couldn't have given any evidence against you about the house in Chapel Row either, because I didn't know. I thought it was a man's voice, it was so deep. . . . Even last night I didn't guess."

"That's so much red tape," said Cleveland contemptuously.

Field took a hand in the conversation. "I don't think Miss Oliver should say anything more without benefit of legal advice," he said. "I have a warrant. . . ." He put his hand in his pocket.

"This, thank God, is never coming to trial. Those tablets she took —how long do they take to act?"

"Don't worry your head about those," said Crook. "Half-a-dozen aspirins never hurt any one yet."

"Aspirins?" Brother and sister echoed the word simultaneously.

"That's all they were. Well, if they'd been what you thought how do you imagine Stella would have been here to-night? I'd promised Captain Oliver to look after her, and I haven't made my little pile by forgettin' things like that. I sort of guessed there might be trouble this end when I saw how anxious Miss Oliver was that both of you should come back to town with me, so when the lady's bag happened to fall open and spill the linin' on the floor of the guard's van I just changed the bottles, see? The original one, which is red-hot death if you take enough of it, is safe with the police. Oh, it wasn't anything. Any two-a-penny conjurer could have done it."

"I don't believe you," declared Rhoda, but now she shook in a way horrible to watch. "You didn't know they were there."

"I heard your lady mother—step-mother—say something about headache tablets and that gave me my cue. I couldn't be quite sure till I'd peeped inside your bag, of course, so I cut my finger and asked for a dab of iodine. That gave me my chance. After that, it was plain sailin'. Your little bottle didn't have any label either."

CHAPTER TWENTY-THREE

The wheel has come full circle.
KING LEAR.

THE EARL, preparing to take his departure, after Rhoda and her escort had gone, said coolly, "It was an abominable affair. Oh, I'm not speaking of what she did to Grigg. I'm not her judge. But you might have expected family feeling to have compelled her to draw the line somewhere."

"Stella and I aren't married yet," Simon pointed out. "She presumably hadn't any family feeling. . . ." And to begin with, he thought, she probably was thinking of Cleveland.

His father observed him glacially. "I was not thinking of Miss Reed," he said.

"Well, of course he wasn't," remarked Crook when the Earl also had taken himself off, "he was thinkin' of Reuben, Seventh Earl Cleveland, dragged into a sensational affair, one successful murder and two narrow escapes, possibly suspected—as your aunt certainly intended him to be, assuming suspicion had to fall on one member of the family. That's why she chose Tuesday for her attempt on you," he nodded towards Stella. "Everyone knows that cheap seats in the pictures are his particular vice, and it wasn't likely he'd be able to produce an alibi for the occasion; that's why she insisted on his coming up yesterday, because she meant to have a final desperate attempt on your young lady and she meant her precious half-brother to suffer for it. And mind you, if he had swung, I believe she'd have been glad. Men like your father don't guess the risks they run."

"One does feel for him," observed Simon.

"It's obvious," said Crook, "you have the real family feeling." Personally, he'd have felt for a poisonous snake before he'd have experienced any sympathy for the Earl.

"There's still one thing I don't understand," acknowledged the young man, "and that is how Aunt Rhoda managed to be in the bath and in Stella's flat at one and the same time."

"She didn't," said Crook, "but in this decent country gentle-women don't have an audience when they're in the bath. All she had to do was go into the bathroom and run the water and then come out, leaving the light on and locking the door from the outside. The sort of members they have at the Countrywomen's Own wouldn't dream of doin' a bit of key-hole work, even if they weren't too stiff to get down to it, and any one passin' would see the light under the door and draw obvious conclusions. Even if they thought she was ex-ceedin' her quota and tried the door just in case some one had left the light burnin' they wouldn't get in, and bein' nice women they'd just say 'Sorry' to the empty room and go scamperin' back to their own. I've seen the hall of that club. Like the Abode of Shadows, and I defy any one to recognize one lady member from another if she went creepin' through it after black-out. Her only fear was bein' seen leavin' the bathroom, and even then if she ducked her head she'd only have to say somethin' about the room bein' occupied. No, it was a good scheme, but it's like the poet says, 'How hard it is for women to keep counsel.' A woman who knew how to keep her mouth shut could get anywhere she set her mind, but Providence, not wantin' to load the dice too much, sees to it that she don't."

They were all silent for a minute, thinking of Rhoda. Then Stella asked, "Did it make a lot of difference, do you think, my coming to see you that afternoon?"

"Well, hell!" Crook looked hurt. "It made all the difference. Naturally. If it hadn't been for that, they—meanin' the police—

209

wouldn't have known who you were when they lugged you out of that gas chamber. It was another classic case of a scrap of paper—but I suppose," he added pityingly, "that doesn't mean anything to you. You're too young."

"You forget I've got a cousin who fought in the last war," put in Simon. "Anyway, Stella would have been missed . . ."

"By you. Not—to their eternal shame—by any one else. You'd have come up to her flat and you'd have found the post cards and you would have thought, as you were meant to think, that she'd ducked back into the dark because she was afraid of her own past. You might have gone looking for her for months, but—how long would it have been before you'd thought of searching Chapel Row?"

"That's true." Simon looked absurdly pale for a young man in uniform. "That's what she was counting on, I suppose."

"You must admit she had the most infernal luck. First of all, she hides a man who wants to stay hidden in a place where you couldn't expect him to be found for weeks—and I come along, doing my tourist stunt, and spoil that little trick. Then she hides another body—more or less—in an empty blitzed house, and some nosey parker of a constable, mad keen on his stripes, comes along and takes the next trick. It was enough to take the heart out of any one, but —she persevered."

"I suppose she rang up pretending to be Gregory?"

"That was something else she couldn't foresee—that the bad weather would bring the telephone wires down, so that no one could have rung up from the Manor."

"And when she telephoned Stella's flat that night—she wasn't speaking from the Manor at all?"

"I could have told you that from the start," retorted Crook, good-humouredly. "Why, she was ten minutes on the line, and our democratic government don't allow you to have a trunk call of more than six."

Simon frowned. "What was the idea of ringing up Stella anyway, since she was so sure she wouldn't be there?"

"The idea that undoes most murderers—a need for reassurance that there hasn't been any hitch. She knew Stella couldn't be there— but she had to be absolutely sure. She wanted the satisfaction of hearing that bell ring and ring, with no one to answer it. She must almost have fallen off her perch when she heard my voice on the other end. I will say she covered up pretty quickly. Still, she made slips like all these amateurs do. When I went down to the Manor thirty-six hours later she underlined everything by telling me the lines had been down that night, and she knew it because she'd been tryin' to get through. And then your grandma's maid came in and said the old lady had had a nasty turn the night before, but of course Miss Oliver wouldn't know that. Why wouldn't she know, if she'd been on the premises?"

He looked at them triumphantly, but Stella only said in a low smothered voice, "I know she's a murderer, I know she'd have killed me if she could, but all the same I can't help thinking how awful it must have been when she heard you telling her what happened and found out that—that . . ."

"She'd missed the bus," contributed Crook helpfully.

"Yes. She must have known she'd lost. Though as a matter of fact, I couldn't have given any evidence against her. I didn't know about the secret marriage, and I thought it was a man, not a woman, in the empty house. Of course, she has that very deep voice. I'd forgotten that."

"Well, you couldn't be expected to remember everything," said Crook soothingly.

"I know what she felt like. It's indescribable to know you're in a trap and you can't get out. You go round banging at doors and . . ."

"Take it easy," said Crook. "That's what Tom Grigg did."

"That's what I knew," whispered Stella, "that night in Chapel Row."

"Don't waste too much pity on her," Crook counselled. "She'd have done for you if she could, without a conscience pang. She'd have done for your father, too, Simon, if the luck had gone her way. And of course she must have telephoned the hospital while we were waiting for our last connection. That was pretty clever of her," he added, "I put Bill on to watch the front, but I never dreamed of her spiriting you away."

"But when she saw me she must have realized I didn't know any-thing," protested Stella. "I mean, I let her in."

"When you're as desperate as that, you don't take chances. You were goin' to tell me your story and she couldn't guess what I'd make of that. Besides, she still thought you knew about the secret marriage."

Simon said abruptly. "I suppose she was mad, really. Will they . . . ?"

"That's not our job," Crook assured him. "You asked me to get Mary Anne out of jug and I'll say I've done it."

"And Stella? Will they drag her in the witness-box?"

"Stella?" Crook looked amazed. "Why, she don't know anything —about Tom Grigg's death. That's all we're concerned with. Besides, Miss Oliver won't hold out. Things have gone too far. Even I'd think twice before I'd take on a case like hers. And if you'll take a bit of advice from me," he added in a fatherly tone to Simon, "you'll take your young lady to church as soon as may be and have her out of the way before the balloon goes up."

Simon turned to Stella; he held her arm as though he'd break it. "If you can still endure the thought of marrying into my family," he said, "I'd say that's the best idea Crook's had to date."

"There's gratitude for you," sighed the lawyer. "I save your old nurse, I save your young woman, I even save your father. . . . Bill, stick your head out of the window, and see if you can see a taxi, will you? I might as well be talking to a blank wall as these two."

"There's a taxi drawing up now," said Bill, "and a chap getting out. If you hurry . . ."

Simon said, "I suppose we do seem damned ungrateful, but I swear if ever I'm in a jam again, I'll make a beeline for you." He held out his hand.

"Forgotten there's a war on, haven't you?" suggested Crook, unemotionally, nearly breaking the young man's wrist. "If you lose that taxi you probably won't get another till the day after to-morrow. Who is it, Bill?"

As the door closed behind the young couple Bill said, "Looks to me like Benson. You know. The chap who phoned for an appointment."

"Fellow the police think is involved in that smash and grab in the Camden Road?"

"That's it. Benson rather thinks he was involved in it himself."

Crook laughed cheerfully. "Send him in. By the time he's been talking to me for ten minutes he'll be asking where the Camden Road is—and I shan't be able to tell him."

>>> If you've enjoyed this book and would like to discover more great vintage crime and thriller titles, as well as the most exciting crime and thriller authors writing today, visit: >>>

The Murder Room
Where Criminal Minds Meet

themurderroom.com

www.ingramcontent.com/pod-product-compliance
Ingram Content Group UK Ltd.
Pitfield, Milton Keynes, MK11 3LW, UK
UKHW040435280225
455666UK00003B/83